"Why, Scott?

"Why are you suddenly so eager for my help when you've turned it down every other time?"

He sat down beside her and resisted the urge to take her hand in his. That, unfortunately, wasn't the proper approach with Ariel. "This is science, not personal."

"Not personal." She looked at him skeptically. "That means no funny stuff like back in the pantry?"

"You thought that was *funny?* I'm insulted."

"Promise me, Scott."

"Okay, okay. I promise I won't touch you in the pantry."

"You won't touch me anywhere. You have to give your word."

"You have it," Scott said slowly. "Unless—"

"No exceptions, Scott."

"Unless," he insisted, "you want me to."

Dear Reader,

Welcome to Silhouette **Special Edition** . . . welcome to romance. Each month, Silhouette **Special Edition** publishes six novels with you in mind—stories of love and life, tales that you can identify with—romance with that little ''something special'' added in.

We've got a celebration going here this month! We're introducing a brand-new cover design for Silhouette **Special Edition**. We hope you like our new look, as well as our six wonderful books this month. We're pleased to present you with Nora Roberts's exciting new series— THE DONOVAN LEGACY. *Captivated* is the first tale, and it's full of magical love galore! The next books, *Entranced* and *Charmed,* will be heading your way in October and November. Don't miss these enchanting tales!

And rounding out this month are books from other exciting authors: Judi Edwards, Marie Ferrarella, Billie Green, Phyllis Halldorson and Betsy Johnson.

In each Silhouette **Special Edition** novel, we're dedicated to bringing you the romances that you dream about— stories that will delight as well as bring a tear to the eye. And that's what Silhouette **Special Edition** is all about— special books by special authors for special readers!

I hope you enjoy this book and all of the stories to come.

Sincerely,

Tara Gavin
Senior Editor
Silhouette Books

JUDI EDWARDS

NOBODY'S BRIDE

Silhouette®

SPECIAL EDITION

Published by Silhouette Books New York

America's Publisher of Contemporary Romance

To my children, Scott, Chris, Brett and Bethany

SILHOUETTE BOOKS
300 East 42nd St., New York, N.Y. 10017

NOBODY'S BRIDE

Copyright © 1992 by Judi Edwards

All rights reserved. Except for use in any review, the reproduction or utilization of this work in whole or in part in any form by any electronic, mechanical or other means, now known or hereafter invented, including xerography, photocopying and recording, or in any information storage or retrieval system, is forbidden without the permission of the publisher, Silhouette Books, 300 E. 42nd St., New York, N.Y. 10017

ISBN: 0-373-09765-4

First Silhouette Books printing September 1992

All the characters in this book have no existence outside the imagination of the author and have no relation whatsoever to anyone bearing the same name or names. They are not even distantly inspired by any individual known or unknown to the author, and all incidents are pure invention.

®: Trademark used under license and registered in the United States Patent and Trademark Office and in other countries.

Printed in the U.S.A.

Books by Judi Edwards

Silhouette Special Edition

The Perfect Ten #470
Step from a Dream #658
Nobody's Bride #756

JUDI EDWARDS

was born and raised in Chicago. She spent many years teaching elementary school in remote areas of Canada, and she now lives with four children and her spouse of twenty years in Tucson, Arizona. She prefers writing romances to the software manuals she also writes—the endings are happier, even if they aren't as good for curing insomnia.

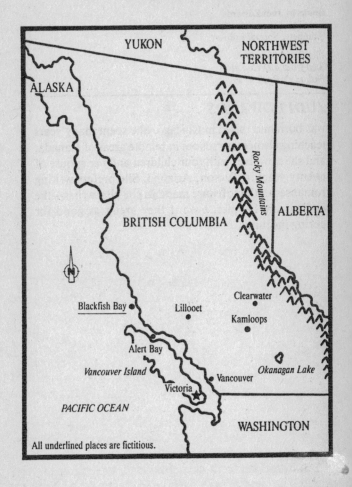

All underlined places are fictitious.

Chapter One

"MacKenzie, you're what—thirty-three, thirty-four years old?"

"Thirty-five," Scott MacKenzie croaked, though he knew the other man couldn't hear him. He poured tepid tea into a metal cup that he pulled from a packing box. He was pleased that he could force his hands to shake only a little. Another example of the intellect ruling the body.

"A man with your ability," said the voice on the radiophone, "should be running the department by now, instead of arguing his way into a posting on some godforsaken island."

Scott raised the mug in two hands. "I'll drink to that. But you're the one who schemed and maneuvered to put me here, old pal."

Static crackled from the radiophone, blotting out several words. "... and as your supervisor, I expect a preliminary report on the orca population by then. Over."

The radiophone was silent for several seconds. Scott sipped the barely palatable tea, hoping he'd be able to keep it down.

"You aren't even listening, are you, MacKenzie? Over."

Scott shuffled across the small office and sat heavily on a swivel chair that squeaked a protest. After taking a deep breath, he picked up the microphone and pressed the transmit button.

"I'm listening, Phil." He and Phil Majesky had been friends for a decade. Their careers in the Oceans and Fisheries Ministry had run parallel, with Phil being Scott's subordinate until recently. The collapse of both of their marriages two years ago had deepened the bond between them—or so Scott had thought. His friend's betrayal was a raw wound.

"Static makes it hard to hear you, Phil. Over."

"How much," Phil said more loudly, "have you gotten done so far?"

"Not much. The Blackfish Bay outpost was shut down for a year, remember. I've been cleaning the office and my cabin so it'll be ready when my daughter arrives next week."

"Aren't you finished with that yet?"

Scott ran his fingers across his cheeks, rough with three days' growth of beard. He caught his sallow reflection in the glass covering a photo of Deb riding his shoulders at the Vancouver Aquarium. Even without a mirror he could see that he looked like hell.

"The place was a mess," Scott said. "Squirrels had camped here over the winter."

"Still," Phil said, "it's not like you to spend half a week on trivia. You aren't going to sulk because you lost your argument with the minister, are you? The pod of orcas up there is one of the largest on the coast, and we need you to gather hard data on their numbers and habits."

Scott stared at the microphone, marveling at Phil's apparent sincerity. They both knew this posting was makework invented to sever Scott from his power and influence in the West Coast division of the department.

He made a disgusted sound, then picked up the microphone. "I've been ill, if you must know. Sorry, but I forgot to fill out the proper forms requesting a fever."

"Ill?" Phil's voice lost its briskness.

"Stomach flu, food poisoning, something like that. I'm nearly over it now."

As if on cue Scott's stomach rumbled, but this time from emptiness, he assumed. He hadn't gotten to the general store before he became ill. His only food was what that weird little man, Angus, had given him yesterday—warm beer and stale graham crackers.

"Why didn't you radio for a floatplane to take you to a doctor? Over."

"Because it wasn't serious." That was stretching things— Scott hadn't been this sick in years—but he didn't want pity, especially from this man.

"If it had been serious, MacKenzie, would you actually have swallowed that independent streak of yours and admitted that you needed someone's help?"

"I'm not stupid, Phil."

The radiophone was silent. Scott could picture his supervisor pulling at the end of his immaculate black mustache. By Phil's standards, stubbornly pushing politically unpopular environmental standards *was* stupid when you worked for politicians. As a result, Phil was now supervisor on the British Columbia coast while Scott languished in the Fisheries Ministry equivalent of Siberia.

The radiophone crackled. "I'll let you in on a secret, MacKenzie."

"Me and every fisherman on the coast listening to his radio," Scott muttered without pressing the transmit button. His stomach growled again, and in an attempt to assuage his hunger, he walked over to the filing cabinet, pulled out a warm bottle of beer and opened it. He sniffed to see how the smell would affect his stomach.

"You're a top-notch marine biologist," said Phil.

"Gee, thanks," Scott said, without bothering to return to the microphone. The beer didn't smell all that bad, considering.

"I've even heard you mentioned as a candidate for deputy minister."

"And that's why you seized the chance to ship me up here," Scott said to the beer bottle. The sound of a plane drew him to the window, where he viewed without pleasure the picturesque bay that would be home for the next eight to ten months.

"But you won't make it," Phil said, "while you have the reputation as someone who likes fish more than people. Over."

"That's a lie," Scott said mildly as he caught sight of a yellow floatplane descending toward the bay. "Only some people compared with some fish."

"You aren't listening again, are you?" Phil paused, then exhaled loudly. "Persistence is one of your strongest traits, Scott, except when it crosses the line into mule-headed stubbornness. That's what got you into this mess. Stubbornness."

"I wasn't stubborn," Scott said to the window. "I was right."

Phil's next words tumbled over Scott's, since he hadn't used the microphone. "You'd do your career a lot of good if you learned to be more flexible."

The sincerity in the other man's voice broke through Scott's dull anger. Though he felt like a softhearted sucker, Scott returned to the desk. "I'm listening, Phil," he said into the microphone. "I'll keep in mind what you've said. Over."

"Good luck, MacKenzie. Over."

Scott sighed and stared at the microphone. "Yeah," he whispered, "good luck."

He'd survive Blackfish Bay, but how would Deb adjust to such an isolated place? She'd miss her cousins. She'd miss shopping malls, the flowered wallpaper in her bedroom and drives in the country. She'd miss television most of all and would probably drive him crazy from boredom. Well, tutoring her on things she'd miss learning at a one-room school would help fill the evenings.

Scott grasped the transmit button and spoke firmly. "Thanks, Phil. We'll manage just fine without any help. Over and out."

The floatplane drew closer, its sound roaring off the cliff at the eastern side of the bay as it came in for a landing. Scott picked up the beer and a graham cracker, then shuffled outside to greet the new arrival.

Blackfish Bay was more spectacular than Ariel Johnson remembered.

It looked different from the air, of course, with all trace of humanity lost in the green upholstery covering the jumble of rugged hills. When winter grayness descended, she'd see little of the scenery except occasional glimpses of mainland fjords through the narrow mouth of the fingerlike bay. She savored the grandeur while she could.

After the bush pilot unloaded her belongings and took off, Ariel stood at the end of the dock and absorbed the stillness that flooded her ears. A cool breeze ruffled her long brown hair and filled her lungs with the smell of salt and ocean. Seaweed waved to her from rocks at the bottom of the clear water.

Speaking of waving... Ariel glanced around at the scattered dwellings fringing the water, surprised that the arrival of the plane hadn't drawn anyone. Not that there were many people to draw; only eleven people lived around the bay. The students at Blackfish Bay School came on the school boat from logging camps on other parts of Mowitch Island.

No one was visible. Even the unfamiliar old boat tied to the dock seemed empty. That meant she'd have to carry her sizable pile of suitcases and boxes to the teacherage by herself. Not for the first time, she wondered at the wisdom of bringing an exercise bicycle.

Ariel's face brightened. The purpose of an exercise bicycle was to get exercise, right? Well, it would start doing her good right now. She grasped the awkward box and started up the dock.

The tide was low, and the ramp from the dock to the bank was steep. Ariel was puffing by the time she plunked down the box at the top. The school was a quarter of a mile away, and she had at least three more trips to make. Ariel wiped her hands on her white skirt and bent to pick up the box again.

When she straightened, she suddenly saw a man skulking in the shadows by the abandoned fisheries buildings.

Ariel shrieked. The box fell with a muffled metallic clang. For several seconds she stood there, covering her heart with her hand.

The man didn't look threatening, she decided—not threatening enough to justify her shriek, at least. He was unkempt, though, and his face was dissipated, as if he drank. The beer bottle in his hand confirmed that hunch.

On the other hand, his open shirt gave no hint of a beer belly, and his solid build belied his dissipated face. Was he one of those drifters who washed ashore on remote places, stayed awhile and then disappeared on a high tide?

She'd find out sooner or later. In a place the size of Blackfish Bay, probably sooner. Ariel picked up the box and headed toward the cabins.

A thought brightened her steps. Perhaps the stranger would help carry her things.

"Hello," she said cheerfully. "I'm Ariel Johnson, the schoolteacher."

"Scott MacKenzie. Fisheries." He swayed slightly and leaned against the white clapboard cabin.

It disturbed Ariel that such a virile man needed a building as a crutch. Scott MacKenzie's shoulders were broad and his frame muscular, yet he couldn't even stand upright. What a shame.

He didn't offer to help with the box. He just looked vaguely in her direction.

Ariel took a deep breath, then shifted to get a better grip on the box. "Are they reopening the outpost?"

"Yes." The man looked as if he was going to say more, but suddenly his face sagged and turned green. "Excuse me." He put his hand to his mouth and lurched inside the cabin.

Ariel hurried away, unaccountably shaken. She didn't slow until she was out of the band of trees and into the sunlight of the playground. Her heart still beat a quick rhythm.

The sight of her beloved school failed to calm her. She didn't want to have an alcoholic as her closest neighbor. She put down the box for a moment, a thoughtful expression shadowing her features. A different explanation for Scott MacKenzie's effect on her popped into her mind. He was six feet tall with an appealing body that projected not just strength but power, too.

No, Ariel thought, sex appeal wasn't it. A single woman had to be careful, that's all, and alcohol implied weak self-control.

Maybe she could help Mr. MacKenzie with his drinking problem. Action was always a better approach than fear. She smiled, picked up the box and began whistling as she approached the school with its attached teacherage.

The teacherage had a closed-in smell, and a layer of dust covered everything. Aside from that, it felt like home. Ariel spent a few minutes opening windows and checking things. She then tried to decide whether the exercise bicycle would fit better in her bedroom or in the spare room she used as an office and library. Eventually she went out into the crisp ocean air for a second load.

When she entered the shadowy woods, though, Ariel slowed. What if Mr. MacKenzie was there again?

Nonsense. What if he was? She forced her pace back to normal. She and he were neighbors now. The fisheries cabins were on the path to the dock that was her lifeline to the world. Her friends, groceries, mail and transportation all were accessible only via the dock. She'd pass Scott MacKenzie dozens of times during the coming school year.

As she rounded the small buildings, she saw him sitting on the porch steps. As if waiting, he rose and walked toward her with a strange smile on his face. Ariel had to either walk around him or stop to talk. Good manners, of course, dictated that she talk.

"Hello again, Mr. MacKenzie."

"Hello." He didn't hold the beer bottle anymore and he looked somewhat more alert, but the smell of alcohol lingered. "I'm afraid I didn't catch your name."

She wasn't surprised, in his condition. "Ariel Johnson." Good manners dictated that she offer to shake hands, so she did. His grip was surprisingly firm.

"Glad to meet you, Mrs. Johnson."

"Miss," she corrected. "I'm not married."

Scott nodded, continuing to shake her hand.

He was holding her hand too long, so she pulled it away and spoke briskly. "I'm the schoolteacher."

Scott nodded, then ran a hand through his light brown hair, as if realizing that it was a mess. Up close she could see that his chin and cheekbones seemed strong, as did the hazel eyes that studied her closely. What a waste.

"I'm glad to meet you, Miss Johnson. My daughter will be going to your school."

Ariel smiled. He suddenly seemed much less threatening. "Can I meet her? What grade is she in?"

"Deb's starting grade two. She's staying with my sister in Victoria while I straighten up the cabins."

"I'm sure they need it. No one has used them since I started teaching here last Christmas. Maybe longer." Ariel laughed lightly, then stopped when she noticed his expression deepen as he looked at her intently. She tried to ignore the awkwardness that flashed through her. "Uh, after I get my things put away I'll come down and help you scrub."

"Thanks," Scott said, "but I don't need help."

"Of course you do."

"No, really. I'll manage."

"Oh. I see." Ariel clasped her hands in front of her and glanced from side to side, avoiding looking at his face. She was overly aware of his gaze still flickering over her with more intensity than was strictly polite. The awareness spread till it bathed her in a radiant sheen in which her skin seemed to vibrate. Finally she met his stare. "Is something wrong?"

"Wrong?" He seemed oblivious to the implications of the word.

"You're staring at me."

Scott blinked. "I'm sorry." He put a hand on the back of his neck and turned toward the cool forest as if searching there for words. "There's a smudge on your cheek, that's all."

Ariel dismissed the thought of a smudge with a laugh. She hadn't come to a place like Blackfish Bay to be concerned about dirt on her cheek.

But then Scott stepped toward her, close enough that politeness vanished. Another step, and they became a man and a woman, alone. Ariel swallowed and started to back away, but then she made the mistake of looking into his eyes.

Scott's head was turned at an angle, and the corner of his mouth curved upward. His widened eyes made him appear as if he was observing rather than directing his own actions. An innocent sense of wonder glowed in his eyes. It was the kind of look Ariel saw only in her youngest students, before they learned to stifle the expression if not the emotion.

Startled but unafraid, she opened her mouth to speak.

Before words could form, however, Scott reached toward her cheek. Ariel's mouth froze, half-open. As if waiting for her to speak, he paused with his hand raised. For a heartbeat he stood like that, reminding her of an awestruck child reaching a hand toward a rainbow.

Scott's heart beat painfully inside his chest. What was happening to him? He was pretty sure he was dreaming, that Ariel was nothing more than a sprite who would vanish when he tried to touch her. Or maybe his hand would go right through her and he'd feel nothing.

Maybe Phil had been right about calling a doctor. Maybe he was dead and seeing an angel—an alluring angel with high, aristocratic cheekbones, flashing brown eyes and a divinely full figure.

When Ariel said nothing, he took a deep breath and closed the gap between them. She was going to let him do it, going to let him touch her. He paused when rough fingertips brushed smooth skin. She was real?

The moment seemed unreal to Ariel. Why was she letting him do this? As he moved his fingers back and forth, sensation rippled like the wake of a boat across her cheek. The sensations dimmed as they fanned out, yet her skin didn't return to its normal state. Against Ariel's will, her cheek became the center of her world.

Then Scott lowered his hand.

Ariel stepped backward blindly onto the uneven forest floor. His touch had lasted only seconds, yet it was longer than that before she found her voice. "Mr. MacKenzie, really!"

Scott's expression didn't change. She didn't know what emotion went with the expression, but it was fervent, as if she were the only thing he was aware of at the moment.

"The smudge is gone," was all he said.

This man had nerve, Ariel thought. Any smudge that would disappear under that...that *caress* was only an excuse. Her initial uneasiness returned stronger than before, flooding her neck with warmth. Without taking her gaze off him, she stumbled farther back, into a warm shaft of sunlight. She folded her arms across her chest. "Is there anything else you find wrong with me?"

Ariel immediately wished she hadn't said it. She'd practically invited him to inspect her from head to toe, which he did with that same profound gaze. Her fingernails pressed into the flesh above her elbows.

"Not a thing," Scott said. "Everything else is exactly in place."

Ariel swallowed. This man was dangerous.

Without another word she turned toward the dock, forcing herself to walk rather than run.

When Ariel got to the dock she looked back. At least he hadn't followed her. She took a deep breath to still her pounding heart, yet it still pumped adrenaline that told her to escape.

She decided to circle through the woods to the teacherage. It was a hilly route through dense rain forest, but it was preferable to seeing Scott MacKenzie again so soon.

Why had she let him touch her?

After hauling her belongings into the woods, Ariel paused. As she stared in the direction of the white cabins, she lightly touched her cheek.

Scott leaned forward so the top of his head rested against the washroom mirror. He shook his head. "Dumb, MacKenzie, dumb. Deb's teacher, of all people."

He straightened, looked at himself in the mirror and ran his hand across the bristles on his jaw. Something told him he hadn't made a good first impression.

On top of his appearance, he'd touched her. Only her cheek, true, but it still had been rude. His only excuse—and it sounded pitiful, even to him—was that he hadn't been able to help himself. She had looked so appealing, so heavenly, like a sprite sent to dispel illness and loneliness....

The name, that was it. Ariel. Her name had made him think of magic. But she wasn't a sprite. She was a woman— a woman who undoubtedly wouldn't appreciate the ethereal impression she'd made at a moment when he was ill and hadn't eaten in days. Scott touched his forehead to the cool mirror and shook his head once more. It would never happen again; that was certain.

He remembered the look in her eyes. She'd been startled at first, then he'd glimpsed a readiness, almost an eagerness. Or maybe he'd just imagined that part. There had been no imagining, however, that after she pulled away, her expression had congealed into narrow-eyed wariness. No, more than wariness. Fear.

And this was Deb's teacher. Scott muttered under his breath, "Dumb, MacKenzie."

He began lathering his face with shaving cream. How to make amends?

The razor in his hand trembled as he began shaving. Cutting his throat, even accidentally, wasn't the answer. He'd best take it slow, both with shaving and with Ariel Johnson.

The razor tugged at his brittle beard as he drew it across his cheek. Today he'd go to the general store if the motion of the boat didn't unsettle his stomach. While he bought food he'd pick up some token of apology. Flowers sprang to mind, but from what he'd heard of the place, he doubted the general store carried flowers. Well, he'd find something. Tomorrow morning first thing he'd deliver his peace offering.

He paused with razor in hand as an image sprang into his mind with the vividness that sometimes accompanied fevered dreams. Ariel, standing in a shaft of sunlight, her clothes aglow. Ariel, her hair long and deliciously thick, highlighted to a sensuous incandescence. Ariel, her pale complexion giving her face an irresistible glow of vulnerability.

Ridiculous. Scott growled at his own reflection. This whole thing was illogical.

He blinked away the image, then continued shaving. Man, he really had been ill.

When the timer finally rang, Ariel groaned and collapsed against the handlebars of the exercise bicycle. Twenty minutes had seemed like twenty hours.

She smiled, though, as she wiped the sweat from her eyes. She'd done it. Twenty nonstop minutes on her first try. Not bad, considering that she had more determination than muscle tone.

As Ariel sat and huffed, she recalled one of her prime goals for this year—losing ten pounds. She wasn't fat, but her frame would never be considered petite and extra pounds accentuated that fact. Last year, after accepting that love and marriage had passed her by, she'd let herself go.

Ariel forced herself upright on the cycle as her mind wandered to the singular incident by the fisheries cabin. A smile crept onto her face. Maybe she should try for fifteen pounds?

She shook her head briskly. No. At her age she had to start doing things like exercising for her own sake rather than for a man. Ever since childhood she'd done things for other people rather than for herself. Probably it had started because helping out had been the main way she'd gotten approval from her reserved parents. It had gotten to be such a habit that she scarcely knew what she herself wanted.

She would always be like that to some extent—look at the way she was a mother hen to her students—but last year's realization that love wasn't part of her fate had been the first tiny step toward independence. She'd lose weight for herself, not for a man.

When Ariel climbed off the bike, her legs nearly gave out. She rubbed her stiff thighs as she hobbled into the bedroom and grabbed a towel from an open box. After flopping onto a chair, she wiped her face and neck. As good as sitting felt, though, she knew she had to stretch or she wouldn't be able to walk.

Ariel rose, then placed one leg on the bed and bent far forward. As she switched to the other leg, she caught sight of herself in the mirror on the back of the closet door. Perspiration darkened her shiny purple spandex leotard.

Switch legs, stretch. The new leotard fit like a second skin, but the friend in Victoria who'd recommended it was right. It was comfortable.

Ariel stood with feet together and touched her toes. Of course, she wouldn't be caught dead wearing this in public. She'd feel practically naked.

After one last stretch, Ariel slipped the leotard down to her waist. A bath would feel terrific, soaking while she read one of the books she'd lugged so laboriously from the dock this afternoon.

Just then she heard a sound. She froze, her ears straining and her heart beginning to pound. Just when she'd convinced herself she was hearing things, an unmistakable sound jerked her upright.

Outside her bedroom window. Grass rustling as someone walked through it.

Someone was watching her.

For what seemed to her like an eternity, Ariel stood rigid, pinned by the light as effectively as a butterfly pinned to a display board. Then she clutched a towel in front of herself and backed from the window, banging her elbow painfully against the door frame.

Apparently knowing he was discovered, the Peeping Tom stopped muffling his footsteps. He bumped against the house, then blundered away.

Ariel flipped off the lights and crept to the window. The night showed none of its secrets. Scott MacKenzie had disappeared.

Ariel clenched her jaw as she searched the darkness. It had to be Scott, after the way he'd looked at her and touched her this afternoon. Of the few people at the bay, no one else knew she was back. No one else would do such a thing.

She hurried to the living room to lock the door. Last year she hadn't bothered with locked doors or closed drapes, but now she'd have to be more careful. A hot wash of emotion poured down her spine.

She wished she could utter words vile enough to describe Scott MacKenzie. Instead, she grabbed a pillow from the couch and, with a shriek of frustrated anger, hurled it at the door.

Chapter Two

Scott filled his lungs with a deep, invigorating breath. The path to the school paralleled the tidal flats at the head of the bay, yet the tangy mud-flat aroma soothed rather than assaulted his nostrils. He must be well.

The morning sun cleared the fog from Scott's mind. He was himself again, refreshed after sleeping sixteen hours last night.

The closer he got to the school, though, the sillier he felt. Bringing Ariel Johnson a gift wasn't logical. Scott shifted the box to his other arm as he paused to press down one end of a teeter-totter. It needed oil.

He was making too much of yesterday's incident. His dreams had been haunted by the memory of touching Ariel's cheek, but in morning's light the whole thing seemed juvenile. Yet Scott amazed himself by whistling as he drew close enough to see a quilt hanging on the living-room wall of the teacherage.

He mounted the wooden porch steps and knocked. He rested the box on the porch railing. The box was too big, but it was the smallest he'd yet unpacked.

The general store had run more to fifty-pound sacks of potatoes than to knickknacks suitable as peace offerings, so he'd had to settle for something more expressive than he'd intended. Not that he was complaining, though. He'd thought of Ariel Johnson as soon as he glimpsed the light gleaming off the glass flower.

With a creak, the teacherage door swung partway ajar. Ariel guarded the opening with her body.

"Hello," Scott said.

Ariel moved her head in the smallest of nods.

Scott scarcely noticed her rigid posture. His eyes focused instead on her hair, which billowed to her bosom in a rich brown cascade that was the width of her shoulders. This was the kind of hair that should exist only in movies, not real life, the kind of hair that fed fantasy. Scott jerked back from a vivid image of the fresh smell and soft, tickly luxury of burying his face in those sandy highlights and dark undertones.

Ariel pulled the collar ends of her blouse together and returned his stare without flinching. Also, he realized abruptly, without friendliness.

The realization made Scott remember why he was here. He held up the box with an awkwardness that would have astonished his Victoria co-workers. His former assistant had bragged that Scott could handle the minister of Oceans and Fisheries, the prime minister of Canada and, just possibly, the queen herself.

But Ariel just stared at him. The queen, he was sure, would have been more polite.

He had to say something. "Here," he said in a brilliant display of the verbal pyrotechnics that had made him a legend within his profession. "For you." He held out the box.

Ariel's gaze flicked over the box. When she looked up at him, her eyes glinted with a sardonic, barely suppressed laugh. He felt like a teenager appearing for a first date with his fly open.

"Margarine?" she said.

"What?" Scott glanced down at the box, which had once held two dozen cartons of margarine. "No, of course not."

As he opened the box, Ariel's chuckle grated at his ears. She was laughing *at* him. In this woman's case, good looks and cuddly hair were misleading. She acted more like a great white shark than a friendly porpoise.

"Here," he said. He grasped a wire stem and held up a rose of spun glass. Sunlight shone through delicate green leaves and made the red petals glow with fire.

"What's this for?"

"For you." Scott held the flower toward her.

She made no move to take it. "Why? I don't understand."

"Well . . ." That was a harder question than it should be. "It's my way of apologizing for yesterday."

Ariel wiped her hand on the cleaning rag she held and took the flower, carefully avoiding contact with his fingers. She put the flower to her face as if inhaling its glassy fragrance. For a moment she posed like that, her eyes lowered.

Ariel looked him full in the face. "I'm surprised. I never dreamed someone like you would have the conscience or the nerve to apologize."

Scott revised his estimate of how obnoxious he'd been.

She burst into a smile, and the flower seemed to shine brighter. "You're a strange man, Mr. MacKenzie, but I accept your apology. But *please* don't ever do it again." She extended her hand.

"Of course not." Scott wondered briefly why she reacted so strongly to what had been, after all, only a touch on the cheek. They shook hands.

"Well . . ." Ariel withdrew her hand. She took a half step back, no longer guarding the entrance.

"You're looking nice today, Ariel."

"Thank you."

"Even nicer than yesterday."

Again Ariel tugged her collar together. One corner of her smile wilted. "Thank you for the flower," she said somewhat dismissively. "It's beautiful."

"Not nearly as beautiful as you are," Scott said.

Now where had those words come from? He didn't sound like someone trying to apologize to his daughter's teacher. He sounded instead like a male interested in a female. Scott began to retreat from the thought—his life was too much of a shambles right now for entanglement—but he stopped himself.

Why not? They were both single. The evenings would be long and empty come the winter rains. There needn't be emotional involvement, just two friends tending to mutual physical needs. Those were the best relationships, anyway.

"Mr. MacKenzie," Ariel began.

"Call me Scott."

"Mr. MacKenzie," she said with noticeable emphasis, "I don't want your compliments."

Scott ran a hand across the back of his neck. "Sorry if I'm coming on too strong. And I hope I didn't come by too early. When I met you at the cabins yesterday, you made such an impression on me that I couldn't wait to see you again."

"You couldn't *wait* to *see* me." All trace of her smile had disappeared. "Is that supposed to be adequate excuse for acting uncivilized?"

Scott glanced at his wrist. "Nine-thirty is uncivilized?"

"You know very well what I mean."

Scott ran his fingers along the stubble of his jaw—he hadn't shaved since yesterday afternoon, he realized—then removed his cap. "Actually, no." He cleared his throat and spoke in his most polite, civilized voice. "May I come in and discuss it?"

"I don't think that would be prudent."

"Ariel," he began. He took a step toward her but stopped when she jerked back as if afraid. The glass flower slipped from her fingers and fell to the floor with a tiny musical crash.

She glanced at the broken flower with a look of regret but made no move to pick it up. "Look, Mr. MacKenzie, I'm sorry you have problems—"

"How do you know about my problems?"

"—And I guess I have no hard feelings. But please, leave me alone. Understand?"

"I'm not sure I understand anything."

Ariel nodded as if he'd agreed with her. "All you need to understand is that there can never be anything between us. I don't want to know a man like you."

Her polite smile was probably meant to take the sting from her words, but it only confused Scott further. "Well . . . could you at least tell me why not?"

She opened her mouth but then lowered her eyes and shook her head. "Goodbye, Mr. MacKenzie."

And she shut the door.

For a full minute Scott stared at the closed door. Finally he turned and, as he descended the steps, he ran a hand through his hair. What had he gotten his daughter into?

He wanted to pound on Ariel's door until she opened and talked sense, but he suspected that was hopeless. Tossing the empty box to the ground, Scott kicked it so hard that his toe pierced the cardboard.

Ariel's anger and frustration flared again as she stopped at the top of the bank. Despite his promises last June, Angus hadn't fixed the rickety ramp that led from the shore to his float house.

She took a deep breath to control her annoyance. Her encounters with Scott MacKenzie were more to blame for her anger than Angus's laziness.

She gazed down at Angus's float house while she summoned her courage to walk the ramp. Like most of the residents of Blackfish Bay, the school maintenance man lived on a house resting on a raft of cedar logs. Float houses had once been common on the north coast because of the rough terrain and because they were easily moved when a logging company migrated to a new island. Angus's shack, for example, had been a dynamite shed for logging-road construction. Ariel sometimes wondered if leftover sticks hid in the dust under the old man's bed.

A narrow ramp anchored to the bank led down to the raft that held Angus's junk, next to the house raft. The railing on one side of the ramp had rotted away, and the other railing wobbled like one of her pupil's teeth just before it came out.

Well, staring at the ramp wasn't getting her any groceries. With a sigh, Ariel spread her arms like a tightrope walker and edged down the ramp, slick from the misty rain.

She took a deep breath when she reached the relative safety of the raft holding Angus's shack. Glancing back at the shore, she saw no hint of human habitation, no white clapboard cabins peeking at her through the evergreens.

Ariel walked to the front of the shack and knocked. She heard the squeak of bedsprings, but no one came to the door.

"Angus, let me in."

After a long pause a reedy male voice pushed through an open window. "I'm sorry. Now leave me be."

"It's me, Ariel."

"I said I'm sorry. Go away."

"Sorry for what?"

"You know, the garbage barrel. It won't happen again."

Ariel groaned inwardly. Not another mess like the one she'd found this morning in the cloakroom. She hadn't been out back where Angus burned the school's garbage, but now she knew to avoid the area until he cleaned it up. "It's okay, I guess. Let me in."

A curtain of indeterminate color jiggled slightly, but the door didn't open.

"Angus," Ariel said in the I'm-trying-to-be-patient voice she used with naughty students, "you've regressed over the summer."

In a crowded city Angus might be either a scared, homeless derelict, or in an institution. At Blackfish Bay he managed an independent, if reclusive, life. Angus did the best he could, which was more than Ariel could say for some people she could think of—such as someone who turned to alcohol as a crutch.

The door swung open. A gnomelike old man just taller than Ariel's shoulder peered out at her.

"May I come in, Angus? It's starting to drizzle again."

"I suppose so." Angus sat on the edge of a messy bed and gestured toward a chair piled with clothes. He was even bald in a sloppy way, with odd gray curls frizzing this way and that.

Ariel moved the pile of clothes from the chair to one end of the bed. She sat and folded her hands in her lap. "Did you have a good summer?"

"Save that one for your students, lass." Then, with typical directness, he asked, "Tell me, are you still determined to be a spinster like you decided last year?"

Ariel winced at the blunt question. She supposed she had it coming, though, for choosing a confidant such as Angus.

One night last winter, when she'd been reexamining her life, the school's generator had broken down. Though Angus would have preferred being left alone, Ariel had handed him tools in the cold, shifting lantern-shadows of the generator shed. She had started making small talk and ended up pouring out her life story.

In his own way the old man had been a good listener. He understood, for example, the urge that had landed her here. To him, running to seclusion was completely natural and not a bit cowardly. It was a bond between them, in fact.

"I haven't *decided* to be a spinster. I'm just facing the facts."

"You're being smart, lass."

The idea of Angus approving of her was unnerving. Ariel had always dreamed about finding a man. And even now, at age thirty-four, she couldn't quite understand why it hadn't happened.

Ariel's innate optimism tended to bring her bouncing back after each disappointment, but each bounce added new scrapes and scars. It had taken many months and many tears to become reconciled to the harsh truth.

Ariel spoke earnestly, defending her hard-won self-knowledge against the hermit's approval. "You know how toddlers at the beach try to fill a sand bucket with their hands? When the hands get to the bucket, there's no sand left. Well, time slipped through my fingers, and I've ended up with an empty bucket."

Angus nodded. Though he didn't say anything, Ariel knew that he of all people would understand.

"I've been proposed to three times," she said. "Do you know why I didn't accept?"

"Uncommonly good sense—for a female."

"They wanted me to take care of them, not love them. I always thought that somewhere out there was a man who was meant for me. I'd look into his eyes and I'd *know.* Without question."

For several seconds Ariel was quiet. Then she laughed and spoke in a soft voice. "I've fallen in love at first sight so many times.... I never told you about the last time, did I? The time that made me decide to chuck everything and move to the middle of nowhere?"

Angus shook his head.

"It was love at first sight, et cetera, et cetera. At least on my part. A very chaste love, I might add, because as far as the guy was concerned, I was just a buddy."

Ariel cleared her throat. "Anyway, for two years I made a fool of myself trying to pretend a romance. Then Grant met Chantelle, looked into her eyes and knew she was the one for him. He married her without even realizing how I felt." Her laugh was barely more than a whisper. "They're expecting a child this winter, and I'm glad for them both. But when they married, I moved here and started to reassess my life.

"Either God was cruel," Ariel whispered, "and gave *my* man to someone else, or I was getting to be such a desperate old maid that I . . ."

"Come on, lass, I hate when women cry."

"I wasn't going to cry." Ariel blinked several times, then continued. "I'm thirty-four. By now, my man is already married, has two-point-eight children and is looking, at most, for an affair on the sly. To heck with that. I refuse to make a fool of myself over a man again."

Angus rubbed his chin. "You've got everything backward, lass. Affairs are fine. It's marriage that's not so hot."

Ariel smiled at him. "Statistically the chances of someone my age marrying for the first time are minuscule. But I'm like you, Angus."

"Yes, lass, I've noticed."

Ariel shook her head. "I mean that I originally came here to escape, but I'm doing the best I can with what life has given me. I have children who need me. The whole island is my family."

"Family." Angus gave a dismissing shake of his head. Then, in a softer voice, he said, "I was engaged once."

"*You* were engaged?" Then, wondering if the old hermit was finally ready to confide the sorrowful events that had spurred his withdrawal from the world, she lowered her voice to a sympathetic murmur. "What happened?"

"I came to my senses two weeks before the wedding and skipped town."

Ariel stared at him.

"Smartest thing I ever did, lass."

"But . . . but look where it got you."

"Same place you are, lass."

After a few seconds Ariel shook her head again. "I brought you something, though I'm not sure why I bothered." She took a large book from her purse and tossed it onto the bed beside him.

"You shouldn't go doing things like this, you hear?" Angus took the book and squinted at it. "What is it?"

"It's a repair manual for the engine in your boat. I figure that's the only book you might actually read."

Angus said nothing as he leafed through the book, but his lips parted in one of his rare, gap-toothed grins. "I gave the new fish guy a housewarming present."

"Mr. MacKenzie?"

"Something like that, yeah. A good Scottish name."

Ariel blinked. "A *present?*"

"Yep." The gap in Angus's teeth was again framed by a grin.

"You actually went to someone's house and gave a present?"

Angus nodded. "I gave him food and all the beer I had. Three full bottles."

"Why?" There had to be a reason. Angus, give a present?

"Water."

"Water?" Ariel knew that despite annual rainfall of over six feet, potable water was precious because the islands were too small to store much year-round runoff. But what did that have to do with a housewarming present? "I don't understand."

"Never you mind, lass." He tapped the side of his head. "Old Angus knows what he's doing."

Ariel shrugged and didn't press him. She'd learned that, when pleased with his cleverness, he eventually confided in her. "Speaking of food," she said, "my cupboards are bare. Can you take me to the store?"

Angus looked at his hands, which still held the book. "That's one of the things the school board pays me for, I suppose." Ariel suspected this was as close as he would come to thanking her.

Suddenly the float lurched as it did when someone hopped across from the junkyard. A familiar baritone voice called out, "Angus!"

The old man stepped outside with a spryness that seemed at odds with his age and personality. "It's my friend, the fishy man. Come on outside and meet him, Ariel."

"We've met." Reluctantly she followed Angus outside.

Scott MacKenzie rounded the corner of the house like a charging bull moose. Despite the thin rain, his hair stuck out at odd angles. A leafy twig poked from the collar of his plaid shirt. "You've taken all my water, you old—"

Scott noticed Ariel and bit off the rest of his sentence. He nodded to her, stood straighter and lowered his voice. "After tramping through the woods for a few hours, Angus, I've discovered that you're connected to the fisheries water supply."

Angus edged back so that Ariel was between him and Scott. "All that water was just sitting there," Angus whined, "with a concrete dam on the creek and everything, with nobody using it."

"I'm using it now," Scott insisted. "In fact, I was using it for a shower when I discovered that there wasn't enough for two households."

"Oh," Angus said. "I see."

The old man suddenly darted into the house and closed the door. Ariel heard the sharp click of the lock.

The drizzle felt colder as she turned from the closed door to face Scott. Alone. Her mouth went dry.

Scott spoke to her for the first time. "Is he a friend of yours?"

"Yes," she said defiantly.

"That figures."

Ariel pretended she didn't notice his tone of voice. "You shouldn't blame Angus. Water is too precious to waste until you happen to show up."

Scott shrugged off her words. "I'll give you two days to make other arrangements," he called through the window, "then I'm disconnecting your pipe."

Ariel heard the creak of springs as the old man sat on the bed. He didn't answer.

"I hope you're in the shower when I do." Scott looked at Ariel. "Does he take showers?"

"He's not a slob, if that's what you mean."

Scott pursed his lips and darted his gaze from the dingy curtain to the junk-float.

"Okay, he's a slob," Ariel said as she felt her neck grow warm, "but he bathes."

Scott hooked his thumbs in the waistband of his jeans and leaned against the side of the shack. He looked at her with one eyebrow slightly raised, saying nothing, just staring.

Ariel glanced down to see if her blouse was unbuttoned. She had to force herself not to touch her hair to see if it had come loose from its ponytail. "What is it? Why are you looking at me like that?"

"I'm trying to figure you out."

Ariel crossed her arms and turned away from him. After several minutes of uncomfortable waiting, she stepped to the door. "Angus," she hissed, "what about my ride to the store?"

"Is the fishy man still there?"

Scott looked at her, a sardonic smile on his face.

"Yes," she said, "the *fishy* man is still here."

The cabin grew as quiet and watchful as the woods when a wolf was present.

Well, a wolf was present. With a sigh Ariel faced Scott. She hoped he wouldn't make a scene when she squeezed past him.

But he spoke before she took a step. "Do you need groceries?"

"I can wait till tomorrow."

"No need," Scott said. "I appreciate your predicament. I'll take you."

"That isn't necessary."

"But eating is." When he stepped toward her, she braced herself, but he merely came to her side. "Let's declare a truce until we return from the store. After that you can go back to hating me."

Ariel glared at him. He made her sound like a petulant child.

"If you insist," Scott said, "I'll even let you sit outside in the rain so you don't have to share the wheelhouse with me."

Ariel raised her chin and began walking toward the ramp. "In that case, Mr. MacKenzie, you have a deal."

Chapter Three

The twenty-minute trip passed quickly even in the sturdy but old fisheries vessel.

Despite the sarcasm in Scott's suggestion, Ariel did sit outside. The rain was just a mist, no heavier than when she sprayed the leaves of her houseplants. She wished she had a thicker sweater, though, because the ocean breeze was cool. Ariel kept her head high, averted from Scott's shadowy form, as she watched their slow progress.

The general store, like the houses at Blackfish Bay, was on floats. By the time Ariel emerged with her groceries, the rain was falling in discrete drops rather than just a mist, but it hadn't driven Scott inside. He was sitting on the deck of his boat, laughing with an ease that tugged at her harsh assessment of him. When she reached the boat, she saw a flash of sleek fur as a creature darted over the side of the boat without a splash.

"That was a mink," Scott said. "It likes stale graham crackers."

Ariel rested her food on the gunwale. "It likes fresh groceries, too, so be careful where you stow your supplies. The women at the logging camps swear that the store owners trained it to ransack grocery boxes so they have to run back and buy more."

"From your tone of voice I take it you don't believe that story."

"No. You should see their dogs. They aren't that good at training animals."

Ariel unwound the bow line from the cleat on the dock. Scott laughed as he put her groceries in the wheelhouse. "I suppose it's all right to tame mink." He held out his hand to help Ariel aboard. "The main problem is that it can make them easy prey for a predator."

Ariel looked into his eyes as she took his hand, then wished she hadn't. He had the hypnotic stare of a predator.

Or maybe, she admitted, the eyes of a virile male who somehow managed to rouse nighttime thoughts in his prey. Darn. Until that stare, she'd been planning to sit in the wheelhouse. She censored her musings, then took a seat at the stern.

Scott looked up at the sky, then at her. "What do you think you're doing?"

"I like the smell of the ocean," she replied without looking at him.

"Crazy lady," he muttered. When he stepped into the cabin, he closed the door more forcefully than was necessary.

Watching the scenery was less enjoyable on the return trip. Ariel was cold, especially when rain trickled from her hair down her neck. She was beginning to feel stubborn and silly.

They were halfway home when the engine died to a low mutter. Wondering what was the problem, Ariel stood and stepped toward the wheelhouse.

From inside, Scott glanced at her and gestured out the window, away from the island. Then he opened the throttle wide and turned the craft away from land.

Ariel glanced in the direction he'd pointed but saw nothing except a deserted island across a wide channel. She ran to the homeward side of the boat and, with one foot poised on the gunwale, stared at the receding forest of Mowitch Island. Unease swelled her throat. She was at the mercy of this perplexing, intimidating man.

After a few minutes the rain ceased and the boat moved into a patch of sunlight that warmed Ariel's back but did nothing to warm her spirits. In another minute the rumbling of the engine died to an idle purr, though they hadn't gone far enough to cross the channel. Why were they stopping?

Ariel rose to her feet just as Scott emerged from the wheelhouse. His face was intense and focused, the face of a man who'd temporarily forgotten everything but the present. Ariel shivered and buried her hands in the warmth of her armpits.

Scott stared out to starboard. "Did you see them?"

"Take me home, Mr. MacKenzie."

"In a bit." He didn't even glance at her.

"Now."

Scott continued to scan the sea, but his jaw moved as if he was clenching and unclenching his teeth. He put his hand on his hip and turned, a frown darkening his features. "Why are you always so difficult? I'll take you home in a few minutes."

Faced with the tangible power in Scott's expression, Ariel's determination deflated. Her mouth went dry. "I . . . I'm too cold for side trips."

Scott's mouth slowly relaxed into a hint of a smile. "I wonder why you're cold. Would it have anything to do with being afraid to share the wheelhouse with me?"

Ariel drew herself straight, even though that position made her colder. Returning resolution warmed her from within as she glared at him.

"No," he said with a laugh, "of course not. How foolish of me to suggest it."

He didn't look dangerous when he smiled like that, Ariel reluctantly acknowledged. Appealing, perhaps, but not dangerous.

On second thought, maybe more dangerous. She mustn't forget that despite his handsome face he was an alcoholic and a Peeping Tom.

"Use my sweater." He pulled off his heavy Cowichan Indian sweater and held it as if to slip it onto her arms.

Ariel instinctively took a step toward the proffered warmth, then halted a few feet from him. Instead of letting him put it on her, she reached for the sweater, extending her arm to its full length. Scott held the sweater in place, refusing to close the gap to her fingers. He made her come to him.

Ariel leaned forward to bridge the last few inches. When she snatched it gingerly, Scott chuckled. The sweater was too warm for her to ignore that it was fresh from embracing Scott's body.

Ariel was rolling up the long sleeves when the ocean exploded. Her heart jumped.

Steam hissed in a sudden rush of massive power. Spray fogged her vision.

The deck rolled crazily under her legs.

"Oh, my God, what..."

Water boiled and cascaded.

Scott chuckled again. "That," he said, so close to her ear that she felt the warmth of his breath, "was a whale. Don't worry, it was only coming up to breathe."

Ariel's throat felt clogged. Scott wasn't afraid, she told herself, so she shouldn't be, either. With a conscious effort, she relaxed her muscles....

Only to jolt to rigid attention when she realized Scott was holding her. She didn't remember retreating into his arms. Yet there she was, several feet from where she'd stood moments before. One of his hands kneaded her shoulders through thick wool. The other rested at her waist.

Ariel stepped away.

A patch of deceptively flat water marked the spot where the whale had dived, no more than fifty feet from the boat. She kept her eyes glued to the spot so she wouldn't see the smug look on Scott's face. "What kind of whale?"

"An orca."

"A killer whale? Is that why you took me out here?"

"Yes."

Orca. Killer whale. Blackfish. By any name, the predator that had just surfaced ruled the seas. Even sharks and other whales feared the orca. Yet with people, Ariel knew, they sometimes showed the same playful friendliness as their smaller cousin, the porpoise.

The adventurous spirit that drew her to isolated places stirred in Ariel, yet she held her feelings close inside her. "I grew up on the coast, Mr. MacKenzie, and I've seen whales before. If you were trying to impress me, you didn't succeed."

Scott chuckled. "Don't flatter yourself. I was sent up here to study the orcas, even though I'm not the best man for the job."

"That I believe."

He ignored her sarcasm. "I don't have any particular research in mind, unfortunately. I was told, in effect, 'go watch whales or something and stay out of our hair for a year.'"

"I believe that, too."

"It's been twelve years since I worked with orcas," he explained. "When I saw the spouts, I figured I'd take a look."

Ariel scanned the slate gray water. She spotted six tall fins emerging from the water in perfect unison. Six puffs of vapor ballooned skyward, so distant that the sound was only a whisper above the soft breath of the wind. No creature approached them now, however. Only the one orca had been brave—or curious—enough to come closer.

The sound of paper drew Ariel's attention. She glanced at Scott, who was flipping through a small guidebook.

"Hmm. The orca who surfaced was a member of the local pod that lives in this strait year-round." He scanned the sea with a frown chiseled into his face. "I suppose I'm going to get to know these fellows pretty well."

Against her better judgment, Ariel was curious. "How do you know about the whale?"

"Her dorsal fin matches a description in the department's records. Orcas are identified by the fins because that's the most visible part."

"You got a look at her fin?"

"Didn't you?"

Ariel shook her head. "I thought the world was exploding."

"And I hadn't even kissed you yet."

Ariel glanced sharply at him. Darn. Just when she'd begun to forget, he had to trigger her anxiety again.

"Yes, I saw the orca's fin." A half smile softened Scott's face. "That's what sets us scientists apart, I guess. Our powers of observation."

Ariel hugged her elbows. Coming from him, the word *observation* had ominous overtones.

"We're trained to observe what other people miss," Scott continued. "That dorsal fin had three waves on the trailing edge. And you," he continued without changing his tone of voice, "have petite ears, recently washed your hair with a strawberry-smelling shampoo that leaves your hair astonishingly full and soft and have a milky complexion that other women would kill for."

Ariel swallowed. "Don't."

"Don't what?"

"Just don't."

Scott's breath gusted loudly. "Now that's really clear. No matter what I do, I can't win in the face of a statement like that, can I?"

Ariel shrugged and buried her hands in the rough wool of the sweater. She stared at the orcas as they swam in a slow, casual arc around the boat.

Silence stretched uncomfortably. Scott made several notations in his book. Three more orcas appeared, making a total of nine spouts that plumed in unison every few minutes. The silence screamed at Ariel, drowning her joy in viewing the magnificent creatures.

Almost out of habit, she made the first move to break the silence. "Does the orca have a name?"

"B-7."

"What kind of name is that?"

"It's a scientific name. It's in the 'B' pod, the seventh member identified. Simple. Elegant."

"And boring. I don't like it."

"Somehow that doesn't surprise me."

After a moment's pause, Ariel said, "Wavy."

Scott's thick eyebrows drew together until they nearly touched. "Wavy?"

"Yes. It's descriptive and much easier to remember than B-7. She isn't a vitamin, you know."

"I'll try to remember that."

"See that you do."

Scott put one foot on the engine compartment and rested his elbow on his knee as he leaned forward. He pointed. "It seems B-7 is coming back."

Ariel studied the direction in which Scott pointed. A sturdy black fin rose above a sleek black body. Though she wouldn't admit it to Scott, she would never have noticed the ripples on the fin if he hadn't mentioned them.

Ariel shaded her eyes. There seemed to be a smaller fin, partly hidden behind Wavy's, flopping from side to side. When Wavy spouted, a smaller plume of vapor merged with that of the bigger whale. "I think she has company."

Scott said nothing, but he disappeared into the wheelhouse and returned with a pair of binoculars. After a moment he lowered the binoculars. "My first piece of new data. Wavy is now a momma."

"A baby whale?" The sizable part of Ariel's heart that softened at the mere mention of the word *baby* began melting. "So young it's still with its mother," she breathed.

"It'll stay at its mother's side until it's two years old."

Ariel strained forward for a better look. "I didn't know whales took such good care of their young."

"B-7 will be a good momma. The baby will remain in its mother's pod for the rest of its life. Orcas are extremely social creatures."

Wavy stopped fifty yards from the boat, but the baby continued closer. "Isn't it scared? Will Wavy get worried about her baby and charge us?"

"Orcas don't know the meaning of fear. There's nothing for them to be afraid of in their world." Scott's voice gained enthusiasm. "Orcas are intelligent, maybe the smartest of all the whales. As best as we can tell, they're smarter than most of the primates, too. I wouldn't put it past B-7 to have brought the calf close so it could get a look at humans."

Perhaps they were the first humans the baby had ever seen. Ariel liked that idea.

The calf stopped ten feet from the boat. A sheen of water made its rubbery black skin shimmer in the sunlight. The prominent dorsal fin slapped the water as it flopped to the left.

Ariel knelt at the side of the boat. "Can it see us?"

"In air they see about as well as a cat does during daytime. Their hearing is incredibly good."

She waved. In response, the calf edged closer. It pulled its head and snout from the water, giving Ariel a view of the white underside of its jaw. This baby could never be rocked in her arms, of course; it was larger even than Scott. Yet aside from a case of halitosis, it was as cute as a kitten.

The whale calf looked calmly at Ariel. Ariel looked excitedly at the calf. She had the sinking feeling that she'd just fallen in love.

"B-18," Scott said.

"Flopsy," Ariel corrected.

Scott groaned.

"Is it a boy or a girl?"

"Too soon to tell," Scott said. "If the dorsal fin grows to six feet, it's a male. Three feet, and it's a female."

The calf let out a rapid series of high squeaks, drawing a gush of laughter from Ariel. She leaned toward the whale and answered with a string of baby talk. "I think it's a girl," she said to Scott. "What do you think?"

"As I said, I think it's too soon to tell."

Scott's serious expression was so at odds with the lighthearted delight Ariel was feeling that she warily stood up. "What's wrong?"

"Nothing, I suppose." Scott glanced from her to the calf and back again. "I'm a scientist, though, and I find it hard to accept irrational divinations of a whale's gender."

"Are you accusing me of being irrational?"

"I'm not accusing you of anything. But Flopsy is a ridiculous name for a whale."

"It's better than B-18!"

Her sharp tone of voice must have startled Flopsy, for the calf let out a squawk and swam rapidly back to its mother. "Now look what you made me do."

"I didn't make you act emotionally rather than rationally. You did that all by yourself."

Ariel took a deep breath and met his gaze levelly. After a dazed moment, however, something made her eyes lower till she was looking at the faded white paint of the deck. She didn't know if that something was her habitual tendency to avoid confrontation, or the blush of femininity that Scott managed to stir.

Ariel ran her finger along the rough braids of a coiled rope hanging from the wheelhouse wall. "Did you mean what you said about taking me home?"

"Of course."

"May we go now?"

Scott looked toward the disappearing pod of whales. He closed the notebook and tucked it under his arm. "On one condition."

Ariel shook her head. "No conditions."

"On the condition that you ride in the wheelhouse where it's warm."

Glad to have the chance to atone for her earlier cowardice in lowering her gaze, Ariel hardened her voice. "Very well. *If* you agree to stay away from me in the future."

Scott shifted his weight onto one leg and seemed to consider her offer. "Let me get this straight. You'll let yourself be warm if I give in."

Ariel shrugged. She didn't care how silly he made it sound, as long as he agreed.

He ran his fingers through his hair as he watched her intently. Ariel had the feeling she was being observed in the same spirit he would observe the orcas. Her motivations and intelligence were being analyzed and weighed—and, she suspected, found wanting.

Then Scott sighed, and his scientific detachment was gone. "You're one crazy lady, you know that? But you have nerve." A spark flared in his eyes before being dowsed by a resigned nod.

Regret tugged at Ariel when the flame died. She slapped the feeling down and held her head higher.

"All right." Scott's face was expressionless as he opened the wheelhouse door and motioned her inside. "I won't try to see you again."

When she hesitated, he crossed his heart. "I promise, okay? Now get inside."

"Frère Jacques, frère Jacques..."

Untuned piano music mingled with untuned voices in an enthusiastic, noisy ripple. Ariel and several of the children had good voices, but they were drowned out by the majority.

"Dormez-vous? Dormez-vous?"

Ariel glanced over her shoulder. Though she was a good pianist, she didn't enjoy playing for this class. Damien Prescott and Vinnie Dascholtz, disdainful of singing, took advantage of her turned back. When she played jazz or classical, those two acted even worse.

Sonnez les matins, sonnez les matins..."

Ariel smiled at Parmijeet, the new girl who spoke no English, let alone French. Parmijeet ducked her head shyly and began moving her lips without sound.

"Din, dan, don. Din, dan, don."

During the last line the young voices dwindled, leaving Ariel's clear alto to finish the final words alone. Something was wrong. She turned to glare at Damien and Vinnie.

The students, however, had stopped singing because visitors had entered the classroom. Twenty heads were turned toward the door, where Scott MacKenzie held a young girl's hand. Straight black hair framed an apprehensive-looking face.

"I'm sorry to interrupt your fine singing, class," Scott said. He nodded to Ariel. His shoulders seemed even broader in an impeccably neat white dress shirt. "I came to enroll my daughter."

Ariel looked at him briefly, then turned her attention to the class without answering him. "It's almost time for the bell, children. Return to your seats and get your homework together. Cheryl, remember to erase the boards. Eva, quit flirting with Damien and help Cheryl."

Twenty pairs of young feet shuffled or clumped from the rug area to the desks. The children's gazes kept straying to Scott's daughter, who turned her cheek against her father's shirt. Ariel empathized with the girl. She felt the same way facing Scott as the girl did facing the class.

Ariel returned to her desk, grateful for the reassurance of its oaken barrier. She hadn't seen Scott since the day of the whales, nearly a week ago. Now, on her own turf, she found his presence only marginally less nerve-racking.

Scott approached the desk. "Miss Johnson, this is my daughter, Deborah."

"Everyone calls me Deb," the girl said. "Deborah is my mother's name."

There was something about the way Deb said *mother*— not with anger really, and not bewilderment or longing, either, but with some complicated mixture of emotions. Ariel's heart softened.

She held out her hand. Deb shook it solemnly. "I'm Miss Johnson. Your father mentioned that you're in grade two."

"Yes, ma'am."

"Grade two is one of our largest grades this year, and you'll be glad to know that most are girls."

A nervous smile flicked across Deb's lips and then disappeared. She said nothing.

Ariel guided the girl with a hand on her young shoulder. "Have a seat until I dismiss the other children. Then we'll get you registered."

Ariel divided her attention between Scott, Deb and the class. Though it seemed important for Scott to see her firmly in control, in the first week her control was tentative. These children were far from mean, yet they were capable of appalling behavior in the name of fun. Luckily Scott's presence threw them into shy good behavior as they gathered books and lunch kits.

She was aware of Scott's gaze on her. The awareness made her awkward. When she went to press the button that rang the dismissal bell, she accidentally knocked a pile of children's papers onto the floor. She rang the bell, then leaned over to pick up the papers.

A shadow darkened the papers. Ariel tensed, hoping she wouldn't have to deal with Scott in such close quarters. He didn't seem to have been drinking and surely he'd behave well with his daughter present. Nonetheless, this man roused a deep wariness in her.

"May I help you, Miss Johnson?" Deb was already on her knees, gathering papers.

"Thank you." Ariel let the girl get the papers.

By the time she straightened up, most of the children were already outside. The sounds of their games were a comforting reassurance that she wasn't alone with Scott.

"So," she said, "you really do have a daughter."

Scott's eyebrows drew together. "Of course I have a daughter."

"When you didn't bring her the first day, I thought that—"

Scott interrupted, as if he didn't want to hear what she had thought. "She stayed with my sister while I got everything ready." He looked around the classroom, then settled on Ariel with a broad smile. "So, they actually allow you to teach children."

"They let me out of the mental institution early for good behavior." Ariel had to remind herself not to return his smile. She reached into a drawer for a registration form. "Fill this out, please." She couldn't resist adding in a bantering voice, "You do know how to read, don't you?"

"My daddy's a good reader," Deb said as she put the papers on Ariel's desk. "He taught me to read before I even started school."

"You go outside and play with the other children," Scott said.

Deb nodded obediently, but took only one step before pausing to gaze through the window at the loud groups of children. Her face had the same expression as when all the children had turned to stare at her.

"Would you rather look at our class library?" Ariel pointed to the shelves across the room.

"Yes, thank you." Within seconds Deb was devouring a thick book as if her life depended on utter concentration on the task.

Ariel watched the top of Scott's head as he bent to read the registration form. A few strands of gray caught the light. Time and youth passed for everyone, not just her. But at least Scott had a daughter. She had no one.

Shoving the thought away, Ariel laced her fingers together and rested her chin on them. She had to remind herself to regain her bantering tone. "Seen any good vitamins lately?"

"Vitamins?" Scott looked up at her briefly, his brows drawing together. "I saw the orcas yesterday. I'm still trying to come up with a research plan, if you must know."

"Deborah," Ariel said, to see Scott's reaction to his wife's name, "seems like a smart girl."

Scott looked up, his expression wary. "Thank you."

"Maybe she could think of some research that wouldn't be too hard for you."

Scott chuckled. "She prefers being called Deb. Since she does, you won't have to tax your brain to think up a nickname like Mopsy or Cutesy-Wutesy."

"If you say so, Daddy-Waddy."

Scott grimaced as he handed her the form, but amusement danced in his eyes.

"Will your wife be joining you soon?"

The amusement in Scott's eyes crusted over, though it didn't disappear. "I'm divorced." He leaned forward, his elbow on her desk. "And just to set the record straight, I have no intention of getting married again. I have no objection to women friends, though, provided they are reasonably sane and meet minimal standards of attractiveness."

His gaze flicked over Ariel, making her feel undressed. She narrowed her eyes, trying to repel his unwanted inspection.

He noticed her stare and smiled. "One out of two isn't bad."

"If you don't find me attractive, then why stare at me?

Scott's answering laughter was rich and warm and seemingly straightforward. So he considered her attractive—which didn't surprise Ariel too much—but not emotionally stable. She was intrigued and saddened. When he wasn't drinking or acting all macho and intimidating, Scott was good company.

She suppressed her feelings of empathy. When he *was* drinking or being . . . well, masculine, he was unnerving.

After filing Scott's registration form, she stood and headed briskly toward the door. She opened it, keeping one hand on the doorknob. "Thank you for registering your daughter, Mr. MacKenzie."

As he walked to the door, Ariel found she had to look away. Though he wasn't doing anything menacing, his walk was so deliberate and so masculine that her mouth went dry. He stopped when he was close to the door.

For a long moment he stood there, getting on Ariel's nerves. She glanced at his face, then turned her gaze to the clutter threatening to spill from Tammy Fearson's desk.

Ariel cleared her throat and spoke softly. "I suppose I should thank you for keeping your word. About staying away from the teacherage at night, I mean."

Scott chuckled softly. "I always keep my word."

Ariel hugged her elbows. Her gaze fell on the girl, curled into an impossible position on the rug as she read. "Deb, would you like to borrow that book?"

"Yes, ma'am." Deb slowly stood, still reading.

Ariel turned back to Scott. "Goodbye, Mr. MacKenzie."

This time there was no mistaking the amusement—or the promise—in his eyes. "I'll be seeing you."

And then he and Deb left.

Scott's words reverberated through Ariel's mind as she marked papers and planned work for the coming week. She found herself staring into space for minutes on end. *I'll be seeing you.* Probably a veiled threat, but...

Ariel snapped her daybook shut. No buts. The problem was annoying, yet straightforward. She'd make sure that he couldn't spy on her. That meant closing her curtains, of course, but there might be more that she could do. She decided to look over the back of the building, hoping for an inspiration.

On her way out, she picked up a couple of empty boxes from texts the school board had sent. There was no telling when Angus would take out the garbage.

Inspiration was missing from the narrow band of overgrown grass between the building and the forest. A floodlight was a possibility, but it would leave numerous places to hide in the trees.

Ariel put the boxes in the burning barrel. As she replaced the lid, she stared into her bedroom window, trying to grab an inspiration that had almost but not quite surfaced. She bent her head in thought as she walked to the front of the school building.

Suddenly she froze in midstep as the idea that had been floating around her crystallized. Her heart started racing before she clamped fiercely on her hopes.

Angus had said something about the garbage barrel. Could the Peeping Tom have been him?

If she were right, of course, she had some apologizing to do...but that wasn't likely. Ariel laughed aloud. In fact, the thought was almost too ridiculous to entertain. The old man wouldn't have the nerve, even if he had the interest.

Still, if Angus had gotten the courage to give Scott a housewarming present, then almost anything was possible. Scott might be innocent. She'd ask Angus the next time she saw him.

Ariel glanced back before she turned the corner. She laughed again. The air smelled fresher than it had moments before, but that was undoubtedly only because she was away from the garbage barrel.

Chapter Four

Ariel rang the school bell.

Most of the children darted from the room immediately. The rest lingered over a drawing or a piece of homework. Ariel brushed chalk dust off her hands and watched as Deb MacKenzie wandered along the bookshelf by the windows, her attention more on the children playing outside than on choosing a book.

Deb, with her thin, elfin face and expression halfway between bewilderment and uncanny wisdom, hadn't made a good adjustment during her first week and a half at Blackfish Bay School. She had no friends or playmates. The other children didn't treat Deb badly, but they ignored her and that could hurt just as much.

Deb was brilliant, though. She was already reading with the fifth-graders without difficulty. There were no sixth-graders this year, and placing a second-grader with the king-of-the-mountain seventh-graders would worsen her social problems.

Scott would undoubtedly like to know what special provisions she was making for his daughter's abilities. Ariel owed him that much. More, as it turned out.

Much more.

Ariel sat behind her desk and took out the note she'd written to Scott. As she turned the envelope over and over in her hands, she tuned out the chatter of the children still in the room and let her mind wander to yesterday afternoon.

After school she had finally spotted Angus. He'd started to run away when she asked him about the garbage barrel, but she was faster. Under duress, he crumbled and admitted that he'd seen her in her bedroom that night.

Scott was innocent.

It was an accident, Angus insisted. He hadn't known she'd returned or he wouldn't have been fitting a new lid for the barrel at that time of night. He was afraid she'd hate him for it, though, and so he'd been avoiding her ever since.

"I'll never do it again," Angus had said. "You don't hate me, do you?"

"No," she had said. And she didn't. Instead, his admission had made her heart soar. Scott was cleared of the worst charge against him. She hadn't realized till that moment how important it was for her to regain her optimism—an optimism that had been sorely eroded by time.

Now all she had to do was apologize to Scott.

"Teacher," said a grade-one boy holding a metal cookie tin. He wiped his runny nose on the back of his sleeve. "This is for you. I forgot to give it to you last week, and my mom wants the tin back."

"Why, thank you, Ronald." The present reminded her of the flower Scott had given her, the pieces of which still sat in a bag on her shelf. Determined to be more appreciative of this gift, Ariel smiled. "What is it?"

"It's from my mom, for cooking when my dad broke his arm."

Ariel opened the tin.

"It's salmon steaks," Ronald said.

Ariel quickly stuffed the lid back on as a stench engulfed her. The other children screeched and bolted for the door.

"Mom said you should put it in the fridge right away," Ronald added virtuously.

"Uh, tell your mom thanks." Ariel held her breath as she put the tin on the bookcase near an open window. She leaned outside for a quick breath.

When she turned around the boy was watching her curiously. He wiped at his nose again, making Ariel wish she, too, had a cold. "Is there anything else, Ronald?"

"You're supposed to put it in the fridge."

"A few minutes won't matter, Ronald. Believe me."

The boy sniffled and looked around at the empty classroom. "Where'd everybody go? Hey, guys, wait for me!"

Hoping the smell would fade by tomorrow, Ariel joined the children outside. Most of them pointed at Ronald with noses held.

He waved, reveling in the attention. Ronald would survive this incident, partly because he was thick-skinned and partly because eight of the children were his cousins. The Prescott family stuck together. They wouldn't let Ronald forget this incident, but neither would they let anyone push the youngest Prescott too hard.

One child remained on a swing, barely rocking back and forth, watching the others. Deb MacKenzie.

Ariel walked to the side of the school and sat on the swing next to Deb. The girl gave a quick smile that touched only her lips, as if she didn't dare do more until she gauged the other person's reaction.

When Ariel smiled, Deb grinned, making her face much cuter than did her usual serious expression. Poor Deb had gotten few of her father's good looks.

Ariel thrust aside the reminder of Scott and forced a chuckle. "It's a good thing Ronald doesn't mind this attention."

"I don't get it," Deb said. "His father's a fisherman. How could he not know the fish would rot?"

"He probably didn't think about it."

Deb shook her head, as if she still didn't understand.

"Ronald has five brothers and sisters, all of whom are at least twenty years old. On top of that, he's the youngest of all the cousins on the island."

Deb chewed her lip, thinking. "You mean he's made a life out of letting other people do his thinking?"

"Something like that."

"That's dumb."

"Ronald isn't dumb. Just helpless." Ariel glanced at the group of children. "Deb, why don't you go join them?"

Deb glanced at the loud group, then set her swing moving. "I guess I don't want to right now."

Ariel didn't believe that. Unlike the others, Deb walked home. If she didn't want to be with the children, she'd have left.

Ariel sighed. Though it was frustrating, she knew she couldn't solve the girl's problem. No teacher could order children to like someone.

Just then the school boat's horn echoed off the hills. The children's noise sharpened to the note of panic that always accompanied the coming of the boat. They dashed off so as not to be last. Ronald brought up the rear.

Her eyes avid, Deb watched the children till they disappeared.

Ariel couldn't leave the girl like this. "I have something I need to dump in the bay," she said with a wry glance at the smelly classroom. "Can I walk you home?"

Deb immediately hopped off the swing. "Sure, Miss Johnson."

As soon as they rose, ravens flapped to the crossbar of the swing set and looked for scraps of after-school snacks. Ariel gratefully put the canister of rotten fish into the plastic bag that Deb offered. Despite the double layer of plastic and metal, the ravens got wind of the fish and abandoned the swings. With raucous croaks and arguments, they hopped and glided behind Ariel and Deb toward the white cabins by the bay.

Ariel's heart began beating more loudly. She wasn't looking forward to apologizing. It felt as if she'd be giving away some vague sense of security by admitting that she, and not he, was in the wrong. She wouldn't apologize if politeness and decency didn't demand it. Even so, she was tempted to ignore the whole thing.

"How do you like Blackfish Bay, Deb?"

"It's all right, I guess."

"You don't sound very enthusiastic."

"I like Victoria better. I have cousins there."

"I haven't lived in Victoria for years, but I was born and raised there."

"Really?" Deb gave Ariel the biggest smile she'd yet seen from the girl. "We lived near Oak Bay. Where did you live, Miss Johnson?"

They chatted about their hometown until they arrived at the fisheries cabins. Deb ran up the steps to the tiny porch of the apartment cabin. She turned to Ariel with a shy smile and the barest hint of a curtsy. "Thank you, Miss Johnson."

Ariel ran her palm along the thigh of her skirt. "I'd like to speak to your father." *Liar,* she scolded herself.

"He's out in the *Simoom Queen.* That's his boat, you know."

"When will he be back?"

"Sometime before dinner." Deb reached into her T-shirt for a key on a string, then rubbed the metal between her fingers. "I'm not supposed to let anyone in when Daddy's away, but . . ."

"That's okay." Ariel held up the plastic bag. "I have to dump this before I'm mugged by ravens."

"May I come with you?" Deb's face was an eloquent picture of loneliness.

"Of course. I'm surprised you'd want to, though."

"The smell doesn't bother me," Deb said, though she wrinkled her nose. "Some of Daddy's specimens smell like that. I'll dump the fish if you'll let me. Please?"

"How can I say no to such a polite request?" As they proceeded toward the dock, Ariel ran her hand over Deb's hair. "Does your father get home late very often?"

"Yeah," Deb said with a shrug. "He's trying to find someone for me to stay with. He gave me an air horn to blow if I need help." Her face brightened. "Daddy's gathering data on killer whales. Did you know that they stay here virtually all the time, rather than migrating? That's because the fishing is so good. It's important work, helping the whales."

"Very important," Ariel agreed.

She watched from a distance as the girl knelt on the dock and emptied the rotten fish into the water.

"My daddy says that nothing gets wasted in the ocean." Deb scrunched her nose as she watched the slabs of meat sink in the clear, shallow water. "Some creature will even eat *that.* Yuck."

Ariel couldn't leave Deb kneeling there with nothing better to do than watch a fish rot. "I wonder if you'd do me a favor."

Deb bounded to her feet, picked up the smelly bag and thumped along the dock to where Ariel stood. "Anything, Miss Johnson."

"Help me bake some cookies. You can stay at the teacherage until your father gets home."

"I'd be glad to help."

"Good," Ariel said. "Without your help, I wouldn't get around to baking today at all."

"Without me, you probably wouldn't need to bake."

Ariel laughed softly and put her hand on the girl's shoulder. "I can't fool you, can I?"

The girl smiled as she looked up at Ariel. "I'm willing to do most of the work, Miss Johnson. I'm real good at cooking and baking. Sometimes I cook the whole dinner for Daddy and me."

She began skipping up the ramp. The ravens squawked their disappointment and scattered at her approach. "I was going to surprise Daddy by scraping paint off the office cabin so he can start painting soon, but I can do that tomorrow.''

"It sounds as if you like helping your dad."

"Sure," Deb answered as if that went without saying. "If I get my chores done, he says he'll even let me paint.''

As Ariel walked down the soft forest path, she tried to reconcile this girl's enthusiasm, helpfulness and intelligence with her image of a drunken, debauched Scott MacKenzie. She failed miserably.

"Deb, I was wondering..." Ariel paused, unsure how to proceed. "Does your father have any beer in the house?"

The girl blinked. "You want a beer?''

Ariel felt a warm flush creep up her neck. "Well, no. I just wondered."

Deb shook her head emphatically. "Daddy says alcohol is bad for you. He never drinks except sometimes at a party. He says I shouldn't drink, either."

"You father is a much wiser man than I'd thought."

Together they cleaned up the classroom, then went to the teacherage to bake chocolate-chip cookies.

As they worked, Ariel discreetly asked about the girl's mother. Deb responded easily, as if the question was no more important than the weather. She spoke in an eerily detached voice that sent shivers along Ariel's scalp.

One day while her father was away on business, Deb had waited at kindergarten for her mother to pick her up. A brief hint of life crept into Deb's voice as she described to Ariel the swirls of green in a finger painting she'd made to represent mountains and the sea. She was eager to show the painting to her mother, who was an artist working on backdrops for a movie company then filming in B.C.

Deb had waited. All the other children left, but her mother didn't appear. She waited until the teachers grew concerned and tried to contact her mother.

She continued to wait.

A teacher from another class took Deb home with her when the school closed. The teacher had been nice but worried and had fed her spaghetti with burned sauce. Deb waited some more, clutching the painting into an ever-tighter wad. Eventually Aunt Sharon had arrived and said that her mother seemed to have disappeared.

After Scott had hurried back from Ottawa, he got a letter saying that Deborah needed freedom for her art, and so had accompanied the movie company to Hollywood. Deborah MacKenzie may have found her art, Ariel thought, but she'd lost her daughter. Aside from Christmas and birthday cards, she hadn't contacted Deb in nearly two years.

And the most heartrending part of the whole sad story was that Deb never looked Ariel in the face, nor showed the least sign of emotion.

"Daddy doesn't like to talk about her," Deb said as she placed cookies into a tin. "He gets this weird look on his face like he wants to hit something. When I talk about Mommy, he defends her and says she loves me, so I don't talk about her much. If she loved me, she wouldn't have left me like that, would she? We need another tin, Miss Johnson. This one's full."

Ariel didn't know what to say. She got out another cookie tin, then hugged the girl. Deb looked at her with a shy yet eager smile.

The girl seemed less affected by the tragedy than Ariel. Within seconds Deb was copying the cookie recipe in her very best handwriting to surprise her dad.

The girl's love for Scott was obvious. The only thing more obvious was her loneliness. As Ariel walked the girl home, she put her hand on Deb's shoulder and pulled her close.

Scott's boat still wasn't at the dock when they got to the cabins, but Deb insisted she wanted to start her father's dinner. Ariel thanked her for the help with the cookies, then went to her knees to look Deb in the face.

"Any time your father isn't home after school, I want you to stay with me."

"I don't know." With her toe, Deb scratched a zigzag across the path. "I'm not supposed to go anywhere unless I tell Daddy in advance. I'll catch heck if he finds out about today. You won't tell, will you?"

"It'll be our secret. I want…that is, I need to talk to your father, anyway. Here's a note for you to give him. I'll explain about your visits when he comes to see me."

"Okay." Deb beamed. "Tomorrow I'll help you eat some of those cookies."

She skipped up the steps to the cabin.

"I'm sorry I couldn't come sooner," Scott said. "I was busy, and today was my first chance to come right after school."

Ariel nodded.

"Of course I didn't dare come by the teacherage at night. After all, you might have a shotgun."

"No shotgun." Ariel's voice was soft, almost a whisper.

Scott had expected a sharp, witty rejoinder rather than meek civility. He eyed Ariel warily as he sat on the wooden school chair opposite her desk. She appeared very professional, almost patrician. The image of breeding and quality was emphasized by the sweep of her fashionable hairdo and the prim navy blue dress, whose white collar lent an air of sophisticated authority.

He hoped Ariel was as professional as she looked. Since getting her note about wanting to discuss Deb's schooling, Scott had worried. His daughter's education was too important to leave to chance, and unfortunately he'd come to expect the unexpected from Ariel. Beyond that, he had no idea what to expect.

Ariel returned his gaze without expression. "Deb told me you've been studying the local orca pod. Perhaps you could explain your work to the students. I'm sure they'd be fascinated."

"There isn't much to explain. You can't think up research projects overnight, at least not valuable ones. Whale watching in itself isn't research." Why was he telling Ariel, of all people, that he was wasting his time and the taxpayers' money? She'd probably make a wisecrack, and the situation bothered him enough already.

"The children aren't critical," was all she said. "They'd love to hear about whale watching."

"Well . . . certainly." So far the meeting had started exactly the way he would expect a meeting with a teacher to start—which was the opposite of how he'd expected a meeting with Ariel to start. She had him waiting and wondering, as always.

"Would you care for tea?"

"As long as you don't slip any poison in it."

Ariel plugged in an electric kettle, then looked down at her lap. Her reaction surprised Scott. His muscles grew tense, wondering when the bombshell would fall.

"No poison," Ariel agreed. She shifted her gaze from her lap to the papers on her desk. "Before we get to personal matters, I'd like to talk about Deb."

"In other words, my tea is safe until we finish dealing with school?"

"Something like that." Ariel handed him two sheets of paper. Her voice became brisk and impersonal. "These are informal tests I've given Deb. I'm sure it doesn't surprise you that she scored exceptionally high in both reading and math." She pointed out scores and interpreted them clearly and concisely.

Ariel's informal tests rated Deb much as had the standardized tests in Victoria, and Ariel's conclusions about what should be done were also similar. Yet Deb had been in this woman's class only a few weeks. Scott began to regret his remark about the tea.

"No," he said, "I'm not surprised that Deb scored well. She's an exceptional girl."

"I have her school records, and I've written Deb's teacher for specific information about last year. Obviously we don't have a class for gifted children like the one in Victoria, but a multigraded classroom is the next best thing. I tentatively have her working with the grade-five students."

Scott glanced from the paper to Ariel's aristocratic features and back down to the paper. He was impressed but not quite ready to let it show. "According to these test scores, she works above a grade-five level."

"I know. But socially even grade five is advanced. Deb's only seven years old, remember."

"Nearly eight." But Scott knew what she meant. At the end of last year, the teacher had commented that Deb didn't seem to relate to other children. Ariel had given him nearly as much information after mere weeks.

The teakettle shrieked. As Ariel rose to pour the water, Scott studied the strong, feminine curves of her back. He fanned himself with the test papers. This woman was good.

"You seem to have learned a lot about Deb in a short time," he acknowledged.

Ariel accepted the compliment with a confident nod that showed neither surprise nor false humility. Scott's assessment of her wavered still more.

She handed him a mug and a tea bag. "Deb's only playmate is Parmijeet Singh, who just arrived from India. It's a positive sign, even though Parmijeet doesn't speak English. If possible, encourage Deb to play with other children."

They continued discussing Deb's work and social adaptation. At the social level Ariel had noticed little things about his daughter that showed she cared. Scott found himself wanting to take notes. This was, he thought, exactly the way an interview with an outstanding teacher should be.

He was amazed when he saw the clock. He'd been here nearly an hour.

"I'm sorry for taking so much of your time," he said as he stood. "If there's anything I enjoy discussing, it's Deb."

"I can tell." Ariel rolled a pencil in her hands. "Scott . . . I'd like to get around to those personal matters I mentioned before. Can you stay a few more minutes?"

"Personal matters?" Scott warily sat back down. To provide a reason for a getaway if needed, he added, "Deb said she'd have a surprise baked for me when I got back."

Ariel mouth curved at the corners as she laughed softly and enchantingly. Scott felt like a mouse in the paws of a cat.

"You're doing it again," he said.

"Doing what?"

"Putting me off balance so I don't know what to expect."

She laughed gently. Scott almost found himself smiling back. Almost, but not quite.

Ariel laced her fingers together. "Do you remember the morning when you came to the teacherage?"

"Vividly."

Ariel seemed to study the empty school desks behind him. "You might have noticed that I acted a little strange."

"I seem to recall something like that, yes."

"Uh, yes." Ariel looked him in the eye. "I had what I thought was good reason. You see, the night before, I had heard footsteps outside my bedroom window while I undressed. It turned out to be Angus."

Scott leaned forward. "That dirty old...do you need help or protection, Miss Johnson?"

"Please, call me Ariel." Her shoulders rose and fell as she took a deep breath. "Angus was working on the garbage cans. I've spoken to him, and it won't happen again."

"I think I understand. You thought it was me."

"Well...yes."

A chuckle lightened Scott's mood. He leaned against the back of the chair and folded his arms. "And the next day, you thought—"

"I treated you terribly," Ariel interrupted, "and I thought even worse things about you." Her shoulders rose and fell again. "I was wrong. I hope you'll accept my apology."

Sincerity shone from her face. Scott found himself yearning for her to gaze at him like that forever—or at least, he amended, for as long as his Blackfish Bay exile lasted. "You reacted reasonably, under the circumstances. You don't owe me an apology."

Ariel's lips softened. "Thank you, but I do."

"Since you feel that way, I accept your apology."

Ariel hid her smile behind her mug as she took a sip of tea. "This was so much easier than I feared. Thank you very much."

"You're welcome, Ariel." Scott raised his cup to his lips. For several seconds they shared a peaceful silence.

"You're different from what I imagined," he said.

"So are you. And the differences are all for the good, I assure you."

Scott raised one eyebrow. "Same here."

"Oh." Ariel kept her gaze on her cup as she placed it on the saucer at the edge of her desk. Her neck colored, as if she were imagining what he thought of her. Scott wondered if she would turn and run, as would a startled deer.

But instead, she looked him squarely in the eye. "Deb tells me you haven't found anyone to watch her after school."

"Not yet."

"She's come to the teacherage the last few days. She wanted me to explain, because you've told her not to go anywhere without okaying it first."

"It was good of you to keep her company, but you didn't have to do it."

"I wanted to. I also want her to stay with me whenever you'll be late getting home."

Scott swallowed the last of his tea, then nodded. Since child care wasn't working out, he'd begun to fear that Deb might have to live with his sister, Sharon, in Victoria. Two years ago, when he doubted he could parent alone without doing irreparable damage, the prospect of Sharon's taking Deb would have been almost a relief. Now it loomed like a death sentence.

"That would help," he admitted. "How much would you want?"

"Want?"

"To be paid."

"Why, nothing."

"Hmm. Then I'm afraid I can't accept your offer."

Ariel stood abruptly and began straightening the bookshelves underneath the windows. "Let me understand this," she said without interrupting her work, "you won't let me help unless you pay me. Is that correct?"

"Well . . . yes."

"You can't simply accept a neighbor's help?" Ariel sounded impatient. "Not even for your daughter's sake?"

Scott took several steps toward Ariel. She turned and folded her arms across her chest. He stopped and stood there, wondering how the relaxed mood had evaporated so suddenly. "What's wrong with paying you for your trouble?"

"If you don't know, I'm sure I can't explain it." Then her face brightened. "You still need someone to look after Deb until you find someone to pay." She emphasized the last word as if it was mildly obscene. "That person is me."

Rubbing his hand along his jaw, Scott pretended to be considering her words. Yet his only thoughts were of the shadows highlighting the curves of her high cheekbones and how wonderful she smelled, like wild strawberries.

"You have a deal," he said when he could stall no longer. He held out his hand. Ariel shook it with almost no pressure, as if wary of his touch. She pulled away quickly.

"It seems," he said, "I will be seeing a lot of you after all. No innuendos intended."

Ariel's expression grew gentle, and she let out that quiet, caressing laugh that seemed so typical of her good moods. "None taken. And I apologize again for the way I acted."

"I'm just glad we understand each other at last."

A few minutes later Scott strode across the playground toward the band of trees that hid the fisheries cabins. Ariel was intriguing in ways that went beyond the physical attraction that had transfixed him when he'd first seen her.

On the other hand, Ariel's outlook was different from his, more emotional. A long-term relationship probably wouldn't work. That was all right, of course, since he wasn't interested in a long-term relationship anyway.

He was glad everything was straightened out between them. Scott began whistling. Yes, he definitely intended to see more of her.

Ariel stood at the open door of the classroom and watched Scott saunter away. He'd let her off the hook fairly easily, considering how badly she'd treated him.

But it was over. They understood each other now. She could continue to regard his obvious interest in her sensibly—as a minor annoyance to be strenuously ignored.

She shut the door on the sight of him.

Chapter Five

Ariel opened the door slowly. It was Scott.

"Good evening," Scott said. In the dim light of dusk he appeared as a shadow against the sky. He brought with him the brisk odor of fresh after-shave.

"Hello."

"May I come in?"

"Well, I haven't turned on the generator yet. It's dark inside." Ariel stepped onto the porch to forestall further requests, feeling that she wanted to meet Scott on neutral, open ground.

"I wanted to thank you again for looking after Deb. I'm afraid I don't have anyone else lined up yet."

"That's hardly surprising. It's only been two days since I volunteered."

"I haven't forgotten about finding someone else."

"I don't want you to find someone else."

Scott moved closer, chuckling. "When you say that, do you mean you want to be mine? That I should give up trying to find another woman to share the long winter nights?"

"No, I . . ." His laughter took some of the boldness from his words, but Ariel nonetheless suspected they signaled his true intentions. As she laughed softly, a treacherous breathlessness warned her that she didn't object as much as she should. "I mean that I enjoy helping people, and I enjoy being with Deb."

"She loves being with you."

"I like her." Deb was a much safer topic than the length of winter nights. "You seem to be doing a good job of parenting."

The sound Scott made was halfway between a chuckle and a sigh. "It doesn't always seem like it."

"Being a parent isn't easy, even when there are two."

"Sometimes it isn't, like when you're torn between leaving her alone after work or sending her to live with her aunt."

Scott moved to stand in front of her.

Ariel's skin seemed to spring to life. A tingling warmth bathed her torso, as if she were basking in front of a wood stove. She looked up at his face, confused by the abrupt assault on her senses, yet aware that she'd felt this way before—when she'd let him touch her cheek, back in the woods.

Scott reached out and cupped her shoulders in his hands. Her muscles twitched. She cautiously lowered her head. Was he going to kiss her?

"I want," he said slowly, then paused. "I want you to know that I won't take advantage of you."

Ariel looked up at him. "And you plan to convince me of that by holding me?"

The warm shadow that was Scott laughed. Ariel felt the laugh as a slight yet vivid wavering of his hands on her shoulder, and her nerves.

"I mean I won't take advantage of your baby-sitting." Scott tightened his grasp ever so slightly. "Beyond that . . . well, I never make promises I don't intend to keep."

But he removed his hands.

Bereft of their support, Ariel held herself rigid to keep him from sensing her reaction. She wanted to get away from Scott, to think, to examine. To get away.

"Am I interrupting anything? You're looking at the door."

"What?" Ariel hugged her elbows as if to ward off his unexpected physical effect. "No, I was just fixing dinner."

"In the dark?"

Ariel moved away from Scott. "There was light by the window. Don't worry, I was going to turn on the electricity before I sliced carrots. Is there something you wanted to discuss?"

"Dinner. Saturday night, at my place."

"I see." Ariel looked through the murkiness, trying to read Scott's expression. She'd already decided to avoid him, of course. His blatant interest and her confusing reaction made avoidance even more prudent, at least until she figured out what was going on. "Will Deb be there?"

"That's the beautiful part. I took your advice about encouraging Deb to have friends, and she's spending Saturday night at Parmijeet's house."

"I see."

"How about it, Ariel?"

She did the only thing she could. She stalled. "How did you manage to arrange an overnight stay at Parmijeet's?"

"Her father works at the logging camp, and he knows enough English for me to arrange it. So, what about dinner? We can celebrate Deb cementing her first new friendship."

"I don't think so, Scott."

He was silent for a few seconds. "You're sure?"

"Quite.

"Even if you're condemning me to an evening of loneliness? Without even television to keep me company?"

"So read a book," Ariel said. "And if you want noise, tune in your shortwave radio."

"I'm not *that* desperate."

Ariel laughed, and the soft sound seemed to release her from the spell he cast. "Are you implying that spending the evening with me is an act of lesser desperation?"

"Well . . . I am kind of desperate to be with you."

Ariel continued laughing as she went to the door. Banter transformed Scott's interest into an innocent flirtation, and she could handle that. "Thanks for stopping by, Scott. I have to check that my dinner doesn't burn, though. Good night."

"Good night, Ariel."

She shut the door again and locked it.

Deb floundered noisily through the forest. It mystified Ariel how a girl who was so quiet in class could make so much noise simply walking.

"Do you know every trail on the island, Ariel?"

"Hardly. Mowitch is twenty miles long." Ariel crawled over a massive cedar that had fallen across the trail decades ago. The bark felt spongy under her knees. "I used to hike a lot, but the last time I backpacked in the Rockies I sort of lost my taste for it. Still, this trail is special."

"Why? Where does it lead?"

"You'll find out soon." Ariel helped Deb over the fallen cedar. "Would you like to learn to walk like an Indian, so quietly that the forest creatures can't tell you're here?" Ariel began exaggerating the way she avoided shrubs and watched where she stepped.

"The social studies book," Deb said skeptically, "says the Indians around here used dugout canoes because the rain forest was so thick." Nonetheless, she tried to walk more quietly.

They heard the ocean before they saw it. Dense underbrush hid the beach until they reached pebbly sand that shifted underfoot. Ariel led Deb to an overgrown clearing at the edge of the rushing waves. Several tall stumps rose from the bushes.

Ariel put her hands on her hips and turned to Deb. "Well?"

The girl looked at the waves and cloud-misted islands that rose in layers to the vague, frosted mountains of the distant mainland. "It's okay, I guess."

"Not out there. Look at the stumps."

Deb walked toward the closest stump, which rose six feet. The stump ended in a shattered top covered by a bush growing like green hair from the rotting wood. She glanced back at Ariel, then leaned forward to touch the log. Excitement began to show in the way she examined it.

"This is a totem pole!"

Ariel laughed quietly. "A hundred years ago this was a village. There were probably a lot of poles, but only a few still look like anything."

Deb dashed over to another stump, which she abandoned quickly because of its advanced state of decay. She darted to a log that lay on the ground and reverently traced the carved eye of a totem creature. "Did all the other poles rot?"

"I guess so. Either that or they were taken to museums."

Ariel followed Deb from stump to stump, telling the girl the little that she knew about the ancient village. None of the poles were intact, but that gave the place an even stronger aura of antiquity, of mystery, of holiness. Ariel was glad that Deb seemed to feel it, too.

Deb sat beside the remains of a fallen pole. "Can this be our special place, Ariel?" She looked up with a yearning expression. "Just ours, so you don't bring the class here?"

Ariel nodded. She wouldn't dream of dragging twenty-one children over such a steep, tangled trail. Besides, she understood the urge behind girl's request. In the weeks that Ariel had been looking after her, Deb and she had grown close. The girl wanted to be more than someone whom Ariel taught and looked after.

"It's our special place." She sat beside Deb and put her arm around the girl. Deb said nothing, but she rested her head against Ariel's shoulder.

"Ariel," she said hesitantly, "my daddy wants you to have dinner with him."

"I know," Ariel answered with a laugh. "He's asked me at least six times in the last two weeks."

"But you said no."

Ariel opened her mouth to explain, but she didn't know what to explain. She knew that she felt something physical whenever Scott came near her. A purely physical relationship wasn't what she wanted, though. It certainly wasn't what she needed.

How could she explain that to Deb? She said nothing and held the girl more tightly.

"Are you..." Deb paused, then sat straight so she could look Ariel in the face. "Are you going to be my auntie?"

Ariel dropped her arm to her side. "Your what?"

Sensing Ariel's reaction, Deb shifted her gaze to her lap. "My auntie. You know, like Auntie Amy."

"Is that the woman you stayed with in Victoria before you moved up here?"

"No." Deb spoke as if Ariel had said something silly. "That was Aunt Sharon, daddy's big sister. She tries to boss him around a lot."

Ariel had a hard time picturing that.

"An auntie," Deb continued, "is your daddy's girl-friend."

"And this 'Auntie Amy,' she's your father's girl-friend?"

Deb shook her head. "Not for a long time. She used to be at our house a lot, though. She laughed a lot, and she was a terrible cook. Are you a good cook?"

Ariel shot an edged look at the girl and rose to her feet. Deb followed. Together they walked toward the shrill, salty breeze pouring from the open water.

The waves were loud enough that Ariel raised her voice slightly. "Did your father want to marry Auntie Amy?"

Deb shook her head emphatically. "I heard him say that the best thing about Amy was that she didn't want to get married."

Ariel took a deep breath and hugged the little girl. Her grip was strengthened by annoyance. Didn't Scott see how desperately his daughter wanted a mother? Yet he had the girl trained to think in terms of "aunties" instead. Men and their biological urges! Scott was a selfish jerk after all. The thought made Ariel feel stronger.

"I told my daddy what you said."

Ariel went to her knees to look Deb in the face. "What was that, hon?"

"About you never having been married. I told him that probably meant you'd be a good auntie."

"Uh, thank you."

"You're welcome."

The wind blew strands of black hair across Deb's face. Ariel gently smoothed them back. "Hon, there's a lot more to being an auntie than that."

"Yeah, there's sex." Deb scrunched up her mouth. "Daddy told me about that, and I think it sounds yucky."

"I'm glad your dad's told you about sex, but has he told you about love? About the special feeling that two grown-ups get for each other, a feeling so strong that they never want to be apart? A feeling that makes them want to marry and spend the rest of their lives together?"

Deb lowered her gaze. She moved her head, but Ariel wasn't sure if the motion was a nod, a shake or merely random. "And you don't feel that way about us."

"Oh, Deb. I like you a lot."

"Yeah." Deb slipped from Ariel's grasp and went to sit on a rock, gazing out to sea.

Ariel gave Deb time to assimilate her disappointment. As she waited, wind gusted off the water, loud in Ariel's ears and cold on her hands and cheeks. She huddled with her hands under her arms. Something would have to be done about Deb's hopes. She'd have to talk to Scott.

"Deb, does your father ever take you to watch the whales?"

The girl glanced at her through a veil of windblown hair. "Sometimes."

"Do you think he'd be willing to take the three of us out some day after school? I'd like to see the orcas again."

"Sure. I'll ask him." Deb broke into a wide smile that relaxed her whole body.

After several minutes of companionable silence, Deb's posture changed. She glanced toward the nearest totem pole, then squatted with her hands raised to her chest in the same position as the carving. She stared out to sea, her eyes as wide and unmoving as if carved from cedar.

"You make a good totem pole," Ariel commented.

Deb didn't answer, but she smiled.

Ariel looked from the pole to the girl, then walked to stand in front of her. "That's a beaver on the pole. Put your top teeth over your lip... that's right."

Deb still said nothing, though she looked pleased at Ariel's ready acceptance of her game. But Ariel's impatience with Scott returned. In many ways he'd done a good job with Deb, but in other ways he'd failed. He'd nurtured her intellect but not taught her about people, about love, about relationships. Oh, she had no doubt that Scott loved his daughter and that she loved him, but the language and primacy of love simply weren't there.

Ariel went to stand behind Deb and stared at the totem pole. With a sigh she wrapped her arms around Deb in the same way that the upper totem figure wrapped its arms around the beaver. Deb giggled, realizing what she was doing, but Ariel couldn't share her enjoyment.

Ariel stared uncaringly out to sea for as long as she could. That wasn't nearly as long as Deb managed.

"Goodbye, Flopsy." Deb waved in the direction of the disappearing black dorsal fins.

From her seat on the engine cover in the middle of the deck, Ariel watched as the ocean breeze whipped Scott's light brown hair back from his face. Her own hair was in a simple ponytail, because anything more complicated made little sense for a Sunday afternoon outing on a boat.

Scott's hair was getting long. Mrs. Fearson would trim women's hair—until they uttered a word of complaint, at least. Where, Ariel wondered idly, could a man get a haircut without having to get on a floatplane?

Scott turned toward her. Now hair blew into his face.

"You need a haircut," Ariel told him.

"I told you so, Daddy."

Scott reached out to ruffle his daughter's already unruly hair. "Where's the nearest barber?"

"Probably Alert Bay, if they even have one there," Ariel said with a shrug. "Mrs. Fearson might give haircuts, though. I know she cuts women's hair, and she's always looking for ways to earn money. She and her family live on the small island at the mouth of Blackfish Bay."

"Tammy's mother?" Deb asked.

Scott again ruffled his daughter's hair. "Who's Tammy? Someone you'd like to invite to your birthday party?"

Tammy Fearson was one of the most popular girls in the class. Ariel doubted that Deb had ever braved a word to Tammy, as much as she yearned to be accepted and liked. The girl looked down at her hands and didn't answer directly. "I want Ariel to come to my birthday party."

"I'm flattered," Ariel answered.

"It won't be for a couple of weeks," Scott said. "She wants to have a picnic—"

"In November?" Ariel stared at Deb with mock seriousness. "Not even the ants will come to a picnic in November."

Deb giggled. "No, silly. A picnic on the *Simoom Queen,* while we explore some of the islands for buried treasure."

"Shall I bring a shovel, then?"

Deb giggled again. "That sounds great. You can do the digging, and I'll get the treasure because I'm the birthday girl."

"I'd be honored to come." Ariel turned to Scott. "How's your research coming? Have you thought of a project yet?"

He shrugged his shoulders. "At least I've gotten a start. I'm recording orca vocalizations and trying to correlate them with their activities."

"Trying to learn their language?"

"Something like that." He looked toward the open water where the orcas had disappeared. "Some of their vocalizations are easy, such as the clicks they use for sonar. Others are more complex, like when they're circling a large school of fish or when they come to a fork in a channel between islands. They chatter for a while and eventually all take the same channel."

"You mean they actually *talk?*"

"They communicate," he agreed cautiously.

Deb wandered over to stand by Ariel. "Daddy has to spend a lot of time tracking down the pod so he can record their songs. Most of the time he sails around just looking for them. That's why he's away so much."

Ariel took Deb's hand and squeezed. There'd been no accusation in the girl's words, only resignation, but it bothered Ariel. "Scott, why don't you position underwater microphones—"

"Hydrophones," Deb corrected.

"—hydrophones at key positions in the area, such as forks in channels? You could use radio transmitters to bring the signals to you, rather than having to search aimlessly."

Scott stared at her, his brows knit in concentration. He didn't move a muscle as he considered her suggestion. He looked, she thought, rather like he was posing for a portrait, *The Thinker on a Fishing Boat.*

"Has anyone ever told you," he said at last, "that you're a genius?"

A soft laugh curled up from Ariel's belly. "You're the first person today."

"Thank you, Ariel."

When he looked at her like that she felt so... Ariel jerked to sit upright. What she felt was tingly and feminine and aroused, and that was the exact opposite of her reason for inviting herself today. She came to warn Scott about Deb's matchmaking, since nothing would come of it.

"I'm glad you agreed to come with us," he said as he sat beside Ariel.

Deb spoke up. "It was because of me, Daddy."

"Thanks, kiddo. Now try to convince her to have dinner with me."

Ariel shook her head. "I'm more stubborn than you are, Scott."

"Not necessarily." Scott settled back on his elbows, his arm deliberately touching hers.

Ariel stiffly pulled her tingling arm away, then sighed. "You may be right, at that."

"A man who should know once said that my persistence sometimes edges into stubbornness. Not that I believe him, of course."

When Ariel began to glare at him, Deb spoke up quickly. "I like your hat, Ariel."

Ariel slipped off the Australian bush hat and put it on the girl's head. Half of her thin face disappeared under the brown hat. When Deb pushed it back so she could see, she was grinning.

"Have you been to Australia?" Scott asked.

"On a visit, the year I spent in New Zealand on a teacher-exchange program."

"So this isn't your first foray into adventurous living?"

Deb handed the hat back, and Ariel put it on her head. "The people in Dunedin consider those who live in a far-away place like staid old Victoria adventurous. Still, one of the compensations of the single life is that you can follow your whims."

Deb jammed herself between the two grown-ups, which was fine with Ariel. Her goose bumps, which had nothing to do with the salt breeze, slowly settled down. After a minute she began to enjoy herself again.

Moments like this, full of quiet, meandering talk and companionship, made her feel at peace. She stared across the wide expanse of water between Vancouver Island and the maze of islands near the mainland. Mowitch Island was lost to her in the multitude of steep, carpeted hills.

"Too bad the orcas wouldn't come any closer," Scott said.

"I still enjoyed seeing them," Ariel replied.

Deb popped up and went to the side of the boat to gaze at the sea. "Especially Flopsy. I hoped I could show you how I pet her with an oar."

"Another time," Scott said.

"Yeah." Deb brightened considerably at the prospect of future outings with her father and Ariel. She looked at the two of them with a look of angelic simplicity. "I'm going down to the cabin and take a nap."

"A nap?" Scott let out an incredulous laugh.

Deb nodded solemnly. "Wake me if the whales come back."

Ariel braced herself. The chaperon was leaving.

As soon as Deb closed the wheelhouse door, Scott began chuckling. "She hasn't taken a nap since she was ten months old. I think we have a matchmaker on our hands."

"I've noticed." And in a way it seemed a shame that the girl's dreams were wasted. Nothing, however, had changed. She wasn't willing to get involved with someone like Scott. She walked over to the wheelhouse and leaned against it, her arms crossed. "What are we going to do about it?"

"About Deb's matchmaking? Don't worry, her attention will turn to something else."

Ariel shook her head. He didn't understand his daughter's need. "It hurts when you get your hopes up. I'm an expert on that, Scott."

"You could have dinner with me and not dash her hopes."

On impulse Ariel walked to Scott, put her hand on his shoulder and leaned her head close to his. "Do you want to marry me, Scott?"

He burrowed his hand into the hair at the back of her neck and broke into a deep, rolling laugh that sent lines of good nature radiating from his eyes and mouth. After a second, however, he looked at her curiously. He dropped his hand, eyeing her warily. "You're joking, aren't you?"

"That's what I thought." Ariel returned to the wheelhouse wall. "No, Scott, I wasn't proposing. But that's what Deb would like."

"Do you really think so?"

"Yes."

He rubbed his hand through his hair, then gave an unconvinced shrug. "I'll talk to her."

"Good. And while we're on the subject of dashing hopes..."

"I don't like that look in your eye."

"Scott, I think we should be open and honest with each other." Ariel paused to take a deep breath. Deb wasn't the only one whose hopes could get raised painfully high. "I want to be your friend, but I'm not interested in having dinner with you or in doing any of the other things your mind has been busy imagining."

His eyes widened innocently. "How do you know what I've been imagining?"

"You're a man. I can guess."

"I see." He walked slowly toward her, his eyes glittering. "Then you already know the one about us, the school swings, thirteen pillows and a Tarzan costume."

Ariel felt her lips curving into a smile. "I hadn't counted the pillows, but yes. And you should be ashamed of yourself."

"I am." He stood in front of her and placed his hand on the wheelhouse window, just to the left of Ariel's head. "Thoroughly ashamed."

"Scott..." Her body reacted to his closeness by accelerating both her breathing and pulse. An errant, unwelcome question flitted through her mind. What forbidden things could two people do with thirteen pillows? Scott stared at her with eyes that could burn holes through the ocean, as if trying to tell her the answer through telepathy.

Ariel dragged her gaze away from his face. She couldn't stand there gaping at him with doe eyes. "I said I wasn't interested."

"I don't believe that." He slowly raised his hand.

Ariel felt trapped as she saw his hand approach her face. The touch of his thumb along her jaw was light and teas-

ing, yet it held her as effectively as a wrestling grip. She
swallowed, hard.

"I propose an experiment," he said.

"No."

"I kiss you," he continued as if he hadn't heard, "then,
if you feel nothing, well . . ."

"Well, what?"

"Well, I'll have to try harder. But in the meantime you'll
have proved your point."

His face approached hers.

"Scott, I . . ."

He silenced her with a kiss.

She wasn't ready. It wasn't fair.

His lips were soft, pliant and warm, and since she was in
the middle of talking, her mouth was wide open. It wasn't
fair of him to take advantage, to tease her with his tongue,
to steal past her words so that she had almost no choice but
to kiss him back. It wasn't fair.

His tongue flicked against the tip of hers, and Ariel stopping complaining. A gush of energy shot through her,
bouncing crazily from her lips to her tongue and down to her
heart. Somewhere along the way, it steamrollered her reservations. She made a soft sound that was far too close to a
whimper as he probed her mouth for resistance and found
none.

When Scott pulled away, her lips reached out to maintain contact—not for long, but undoubtedly long enough
for him to notice. Ariel braced herself against the wheelhouse wall. Actually she more like lolled helplessly against
it as she brought her gaze up to his.

His lips curled in a smile whose smugness returned her to
her senses like a slap across the face. "Well?" he asked.

Ariel forced her hands to stay at her side, rather than
touching her lips to see if they were really hers. "Nothing,"
she said. "Not a thing."

Scott's lips curled more. "I don't believe that. Experi-
ments have to be repeated in order to verify results."

Oh God, he was going to kiss her again. He was leaning toward her, and her lips were already parting...

Panic swept through Ariel. "Do you believe *this?*" She stomped on his toe.

She wore soft runners while Scott wore thick-toed hiking boots, but he hopped back regardless. Ariel seized the opening, hurrying into the protection of the wheelhouse, where their conversation could be overheard from below in the cabin. She needed Deb's chaperonage desperately. That, and a strong drink.

"We've drifted quite a way." Ariel didn't care if her voice was ragged. At least it came out. "Don't you think we should head back now?"

"It's a good thing I don't have to walk back," Scott complained as he pretended to limp into the wheelhouse.

"Poor little boy. Did I break your toe?"

Scott winked at her. "Don't worry. I'll get even."

Ariel stopped at the edge of the trees. Scott's and Deb's voices filtered through the evergreens, though they were nowhere to be seen. They must have started painting at the front of the cabin.

The old blouse Ariel had put on for painting was from ten pounds ago, so she checked that the buttons hadn't popped open. Scott already had ideas. She didn't need to give him more.

Her exercising must be starting to take effect, though, because the buttons didn't gape the way she remembered. Still, she zipped her windbreaker for good measure.

It was a glorious Saturday, with clear skies and a hint of autumn in the air and in the yellowing leaves of the bushes. It was too good a day not to enjoy. Softly singing a melody from a Beethoven piano sonata, she headed toward the cabins with a bounce in her step.

Scott heard singing and paused in the act of bending over to refill the paint roller. The sound was beautiful.

He looked at Deb, who had the tip of her tongue between her lips as she concentrated on brushing without getting a single drop on her hands. Deb didn't sing that well.

"Hi."

Scott turned in the direction of the path. It was Ariel. Her hair tumbled out from under the Australian bush hat, and faded jeans stretched snugly across her hips and thighs. Yet despite her casual attire, she carried with her a dignity that proclaimed her a lady.

After greeting Deb, Ariel turned to him. "Good morning, Scott."

"Hello," he said. He wiped his hand on a rag, but not all the paint came off. He held up his palm. "I guess this isn't the best time to shake hands."

"Nonsense." Ariel slipped off her windbreaker and slung it over her shoulder, then stepped forward and shook Scott's hand. "I came here to paint."

Scott brought his mind off Ariel's plaid blouse, which molded her powerful curves as closely as did her jeans. The remembered taste of her lips seemed more vivid than her words. "Paint?"

Ariel stepped back to survey what they'd done so far. "Deb mentioned that you'd be painting the office cabin today, and I came to help."

"It's nice of you to offer. I think we have everything under control, though."

Ariel looked at the clapboard cabin and squinted her eyes skeptically. "That's a lot of painting for two people. Each of the overlap joints has to be brushed, not rollered."

"We'll manage." Scott turned to his daughter. "Deb, are your hands still clean?"

The girl beamed and held up her palms. "Yes, Daddy."

"Run inside and get a chair for our guest."

Ariel put her hand on the girl's shoulder. "Make that a paintbrush, not a chair."

Deb looked at her father.

"Maybe," he said, "Miss Johnson needs a hearing aid more than a chair. She's our guest."

Deb looked at Ariel.

"Maybe," Ariel said sweetly, "your father is the one who needs a hearing aid. I said I was here to help."

Scott shook his head impatiently. Why was she making such a big deal about this? "I can do this job without help."

Deb swiveled her head from one of them to the other. "When you two get your act together, let me know, okay? Till then, I'm going to paint."

Ariel followed the girl. "Since your father doesn't want assistance, I'll help you, instead. You'd like that, wouldn't you, Deb?"

The girl glanced back at her father, then nodded.

Ariel knelt beside Deb. "Tell me what you want me to do."

"Ariel," Scott said in a low, growling voice that had lost all trace of amusement, "let's talk." He jerked his head toward the inside of the cabin. "In private."

She studied him with a surprised look on her face, then joined him in the office. "What's the matter?"

Scott's jaw muscles moved rhythmically. He closed the door, then leaned against the edge of the table that held the radiophone. "Don't ever do that again."

Ariel swallowed. She didn't understand Scott's stern expression. "Do what?"

"Try to get my daughter to choose sides between us."

"Scott, I wasn't doing that."

He glared at her, his eyebrows forming a single line across his forehead.

"Well, I guess I did, but I...I just want to help, that's all."

He looked at her for a long time. Finally he edged back to sit on the table and ran his hand through his hair. He looked at the wet paint on his hand and swore under his breath.

"I'm sorry," Ariel said softly.

"Maybe I overreacted." Scott took a deep breath and looked again at his hand. "You're giving me gray hair, woman."

He seemed approachable again. Ariel sat on a swivel chair by the radiophone and put her hand close to his on the table. "Did your ex-wife try to turn Deb against you?"

He glanced at her sharply, paused and then nodded. "Sort of. When we quarreled, she'd spend the next day trying to get Deb to choose her side. Deborah put down my attempts at parenting, sometimes in front of Deb. Yet when she left, she had the audacity to write that she knew Deb would be better off with me than with her."

Ariel moved her hand so her forefinger brushed Scott's thumb. "I'm sorry."

"Yeah." Scott took her hand in his and smiled. "I'm sorry, too, especially about jumping you like this. I guess I have a few buttons that are better off not being pushed."

"The divorce must have been hard on you."

"Not as hard as restructuring my life afterward." He rubbed his thumb up and down Ariel's palm. "I wasn't prepared for being a full-time father. At first I felt guilty taking time from work for Deb. Then I felt guilty about the reverse. It's been a mess at times."

Ariel's attention was evenly divided between his words and the sensations his touch spread across her palm. This moment of quiet, intimate sharing spread a comfortable warmth through her.

"You're doing a good job," she said softly. "Deb loves you very much."

"Yes, she does." Scott nodded at Ariel with an expression that increased the warmth she felt. Something stirred inside her. There was a long silence that needed no words.

"I just hope," Scott said, "that Deb isn't too badly hurt by this year in purgatory."

"What do you mean?"

He spread his hands to indicate the office. "This. My stubborn mouth landed us here, with liberal help from a supposed friend. She's without companions, without conveniences she's always taken for granted, without—"

Ariel rose quickly to her feet and interrupted Scott's words by pressing her forefinger to his soft lips. He blinked in surprise.

"Don't punish yourself, Scott," she said. "You're doing the best you can, right?"

"Yes."

When his lips moved under her finger, Ariel realized she was still touching him. She became aware of his closeness, aware that their faces were now on the same level, aware of his knee touching hers. Yet she didn't back away. Instead, she slid her hand to his shoulder.

"As for Deb," Ariel said, "she'll be enriched for having sampled a different kind of life. How many people can say they've lived in the wilderness without television or telephones or cars or pollution?"

Scott looked in her eyes till Ariel became even more aware of their closeness. He draped his arm casually over her shoulder and pulled her closer. She stood between his legs, thigh to thigh, their chests nearly touching.

He's going to kiss me. Ariel remembered what his kiss was like. A thick, salty dryness filled her mouth.

But he didn't kiss her. Instead, he leaned forward till his forehead touched hers and his face became a pink blur. The hat slipped back on her head.

"I like you, Ariel Johnson."

Ariel didn't know how to answer that simple statement, so loaded with complications. Her heart would have been safer if he'd kissed her.

He still might. His breath teased her cheek. Her mouth became drier still.

"Ariel Johnson," he repeated. "It's a good name. Ariel *what* Johnson? What's your middle name?"

She lifted her forehead away from his, far enough that she could focus on his face. "My middle name is Ariel. Jane Ariel Johnson."

"Jane. That's nice, too, but I think I prefer Ariel. It suits the magic in you."

Ariel smiled yet pulled from his embrace. This situation was making her feel things too quickly, before she was ready. She pushed her hat in place, then hugged her elbows and spoke with her back to him.

"The name Jane made me feel old—though it's exactly the sort of name I'd expect my parents to choose." She walked to the door and put her hand on the knob. She needed fresh air. "I've always been somewhat amazed they'd consider something as fanciful as Ariel even for a middle name."

Scott followed her into the dappled sunlight. Deb didn't bother to pretend she wasn't curious about the two of them. He winked at her. She smiled, then walked to the far end of the cabin and continued painting.

Ariel was also smiling. "So, how about it? Will you let me paint?"

"You never give up, do you?"

She added an impish twist to her smile. "No."

"Will you have dinner with me?"

"Don't *you* ever give up?"

"Let's just say we're well matched."

Ariel's smile twisted further, into a small frown. "I don't understand this situation, Scott. If you want to eat with me, why won't you let me help?"

"The two things are completely different. Unconnected."

"No, they aren't. Building a relationship and getting involved with someone—which is what you want, not me— means a lot more than a dinner date."

Scott winked. "A lot more," he said as he stared into her face.

Instead of getting flustered as he'd half expected, she laughed softly. "I feel as if you're willing to let me be a guest in your bedroom, but not a real part of your life. That's not much of a relationship."

"And I feel that you're only willing to be my buddy. That's not much of a relationship, either." Scott softened his words by putting his arm over her shoulder. He was surprised when she didn't pull away. "We're a mismatched pair, all right. You know what that means, don't you?"

The amused yet wary way that she looked at him from the corner of her eyes was thoroughly captivating. "No, what?"

"That we have a ticklish relationship." He punctuated his words by reaching out and tickling her in the ribs. Except that she didn't laugh. She just looked at him, her eyes dancing with amusement. "You aren't ticklish," he said.

"Not a bit."

"People who aren't ticklish are no fun." Scott picked up the roller, filled it with paint and returned to work. After several seconds he heard a twig snap right behind him.

"It's just me," Ariel said almost in his ear.

Scott turned his head, surprised at her closeness. He said the first inane thing that came into his head. "We never did give you that chair, did we?"

"No," Ariel breathed, "but I'm going to give you what you deserve for not letting me help."

She tapped him with her palm—first on one buttock and then the other. After the second touch, her hand seemed to linger for a fraction of a second.

Too startled to react, Scott watched numbly while Ariel pranced down the path. When she had a good head start, she turned and walked backward. "Goodbye, Scott. Goodbye, Deb." She waved with a hand that was painted white.

As he twisted to look at his backside, Deb put her hands to her face and began shrieking. "You have hands painted on your bum, Daddy!" The girl was so scandalized and delighted that she didn't seem to realize she was holding the paintbrush against her jaw.

Though Scott twisted farther, he couldn't see much. So, the proper Miss Johnson had a devilish, improper streak. He'd suspected as much during their kiss, since there'd been an ocean of passion hidden under the demure waves of her brown hair. He hoped she wouldn't hide it again, because he liked this side of her.

"I think," he said, "I'll frame these pants."

Deb swayed from side to side as she laughed uproariously. The prank obviously appealed to the humor of a seven-year-old.

"What are you laughing about?" he asked in a mock-threatening voice.

Deb opened her mouth to speak, but no words came out. She laughed harder.

"I'll teach you, young lady." Scott stabbed out with the roller and dabbed her wrist with white. Still laughing, Deb wielded her brush like a sword. After absorbing several messy thrusts, Scott seized his daughter in a hug that was no less sweet for the paint fumes.

When their mutual laughter finally unwound, Deb pulled back and looked at hem sternly. "Enough horseplay," she said. "Back to work."

Scott saluted. "Yes, ma'am."

"And Daddy..."

"Yes?"

Deb spoke in a voice that seemed almost shy. "It's good to hear you laugh again."

Scott stared at the empty trail. After a moment a lopsided smile spread across his face.

Chapter Six

Deb braced herself against the door frame between the wheelhouse and the cabin. "Daddy, look what you made me do!" A curl of pink birthday-cake icing adorned her nose. She glared at Scott, though a solitary, high-pitched giggle spoiled the effect.

Scott managed to look at his daughter without laughing. "I didn't make you do that, a wave did."

"Besides," Ariel said, "whose idea was it to have your birthday party on the boat?"

Deb disappeared back into the cabin. Within seconds girlish giggles danced from the open doorway. The language barrier between Deb and her friend Parmijeet was disappearing. Besides, giggles were universal.

Deb reappeared in the doorway standing behind Parmijeet, who now wore an identical clump of icing on her nose.

As soon as Scott looked at them, the two girls dissolved into laughter and disappeared again. He shook his head and smiled at Ariel, who sat on the seat on the opposite side of the wheelhouse with one leg curled underneath her.

"Deb's sense of humor is on a par with the Three Stooges," he said. "For example, she loved it when you left your handprints on my rear end."

Ariel made a noncommittal sound.

"In fact," he continued, "I kind of enjoyed it myself."

Ariel looked regally out the window. "That was temporary insanity. I'd appreciate it if you'd forget it happened."

"Not a chance, Ariel."

"Then at least be enough of a gentleman not to bring it up again." She cast a meaningful look toward the steps leading down to the cabin. "Especially not in front of my students."

"Deb was there," he pointed out, "and Parmijeet doesn't understand what I'm saying."

She frowned at him, then paused. "It's good to see Deb acting like a little girl rather than a miniature professor, the way she does at school."

Scott accepted her change of topic with a grin. "Fine for you to say. You don't have to clean the cabin if this degenerates into a food fight."

"I will, though. I'll be glad to help."

"Hey, I was kidding." The hoarse hum of the engine seeped into his bones as he scanned the channel. He'd trained himself to be on constant alert for signs of orcas, but none were to be seen. "I'm already more beholden to you than I care to be. Don't you have anything better to do than clean up after other people's children?"

He meant his words to imply that of course she had more important things to do, but when her jaw tightened he realized she'd taken it as criticism.

"Have I made it clear," she asked, "that the only reason I came today was Deb? There's nothing between you and me."

"You've mentioned that once or twice."

"We understand each other, then. Since you know I'm here to help with the party, you should accept my help gracefully." She turned to study the rugged hills that plunged without a pause into the ocean. "Scott, if we have time, you should check out the cove over to port."

Scott looked at the green hills where she pointed. As they'd explored, going wherever Deb wanted to go, he'd been watching for a suitable location for a whale-watching camp. Blackfish Bay was too closed-in by cliffs to receive radio signals from remote hydrophones. As he'd explained to Ariel and the girls, an ideal lab site would be deserted yet large enough for a float house and close enough for easy commuting. It needed a hill with an unobstructed vista to the most-frequented channels to the north and east, both for antennae and for literal whale watching. Fresh water would be convenient, but not essential.

Scott steered toward the cove. It faced the right direction, at least. "Do you know this spot?"

"I followed an old trail there once. It's less than a mile from the school. Quite a bit farther by water, I'd guess, since you have to go around a peninsula. There's a stream, but I don't know if it runs in the summer."

"By summer I'll probably be gone."

Ariel paused before answering softly, "I know."

After they anchored close to a small beach bisected by a stream, the four of them rowed ashore in a dinghy. For half an hour they explored the bay together. It seemed, Scott thought, like a good whale-watching campsite. The tiny cove was protected from storms, and the water was deep enough for the *Simoom Queen* to enter even at low tide.

"I'm going to climb up there," Scott said as he pointed to a small hill at the mouth of the cove, "to see if it's feasible to mount antennae. Anyone care to tag along?"

Deb cast her somber glance from Scott to Ariel. "You two go. Parmijeet and I will hunt for seashells on the beach. You can keep an eye on us from up there."

Ariel cleared her throat.

"I'm not trying to be a matchmaker," Deb protested. "We want to collect shells. Right, Parmijeet?"

The other girl nodded, though Scott doubted she knew what was going on.

Ariel went to her knees to look Deb in the face. "Are you sure, hon?"

Deb nodded, though her face remained serious.

For a moment Scott thought that Ariel would stay with the girls, but to his surprise she headed up the hill. He followed, his senses heightened by the gentle swaying of her hips.

At the top of the hill he put his hands on his waist and turned in a full circle. "It's rocky up here. That makes it easy to anchor the antennae. It also means fewer trees to clear."

Ariel sat cross-legged on the ground, studying a book of marine charts he'd brought to check the line of sight to the places where he wanted to mount hydrophones. As he often did when she wasn't aware of it, Scott took his time watching her.

Suddenly she laughed—not her usual soft, intimate laugh, but a sharp burst of surprise. "Do you know the name of this place? Honeymoon Nook."

Scott felt the brisk wind on his face as he turned to look at the tiny beach where Deb and Parmijeet strolled with their heads bent to the sand. "Not exactly Niagara Falls, if you ask me."

As he checked the surrounding islands and channels against the charts, Ariel's mind strayed to the name of the cove. Who had spent their honeymoon here?

Conjecturing wasn't wise, she realized. Maybe she wasn't as resigned to spinsterhood as she'd thought.

That was a frightening thought. Her optimism, her readiness to bounce back were normally considered strengths, but they were weaknesses where her love life was concerned. Before she had accepted her fate, she'd grown desperate and downright pitiful. Scott wasn't the right one. She had realized that the first moment she saw him. Why, then, should she let him tilt her whole world?

She shouldn't. It was that simple.

Still...Ariel watched as Scott stared to the east. His freshly cut hair was rumpled by a day on the water. His face and posture were solid and unmovable, almost heroic in an unselfconscious way. This scene would make a good portrait. Man, with a capital *M*, facing the wilderness.

Her skin seemed to buzz. Scott's thick Indian sweater emphasized his broad shoulders. His legs and thighs supported him in perfect masculine proportion....

"Perfect," he said.

Ariel felt her neck grow warm. It was a couple seconds before she could reply. "What's perfect?"

A glimmer in his eyes told her he'd noticed the pause—and the color creeping up her neck. Warmth spread up her cheeks with increased speed.

"This spot," he said, "is perfect for a whale-watching camp." He went on to detail the locations of receiving antennae, standing in place and facing in the appropriate directions. He explained how he'd run the wires down to the sophisticated recording equipment he would put on a float house.

As he talked, Ariel got herself back under control. From the picture Scott painted, Honeymoon Nook would lose little of its appeal. "Can you get all that equipment? It sounds expensive."

Scott chuckled grimly. "I radioed my boss early this morning."

"On Sunday?"

"I got him out of bed, in fact. There are some advantages to having the boss's unlisted number." Scott chuckled again, but the sound carried little humor. "Phil owes me, and he knows it. I'll get the equipment, if it takes every loose cent out of his budget."

Ariel nodded. Though she'd never heard this hard edge to his voice, she somehow wasn't surprised that Scott could be tough. He was easygoing, yet this hint of ruthless determination underlying layers of good humor suited him.

"Getting a float house for a lab will be easy, though it will take work to get it ready." Scott held up his palm. "And no, I don't need help." He sat in front of her and draped his arm over her shoulder.

Ariel hugged her elbows and turned toward the open water. His touch was so... well, so *male* that she had to force her mind not to replay the sensations that his kiss had generated. "Scott, find someone else to fill your lonely nights, okay?"

He stood, leaving her shoulders cool and empty. "There aren't exactly a lot of eligible women up here, you know," he said in a light, teasing tone. "According to actual count, there are four single women within a fifteen-mile radius—and one of those is old dragon-lady Shalyeskiw from the general store."

"Then try twenty miles," she said briskly. He'd *counted?* "Obviously any warm body will do as long as it's single and female."

"But you're the closest."

"Gee, Scott, you say the most flattering things."

"True. I fancy I have quite a way with words when I choose."

When he said nothing for several minutes, Ariel looked at him. He was gazing down at the beach with a soft expression. If his previous pose had epitomized the rugged pioneer, now he typified the loving parent.

Ariel linked her arms around her raised knees and rested her chin in the valley between them. Scott turned to her, his expression bathing her in its warmth.

She cleared her throat. "You actually counted?"

"Counted what?"

Ariel shrugged and tried to appear casual. "You know."

"No, I..." Scott paused. A smile—no, a leer—spread across his face. "Mrs. Fearson counted for me while giving me a haircut. We had quite a little chat."

"I can tell."

"Not about what you think, either. Or at least, not only about that. Ariel, Mrs. Fearson is willing to baby-sit Deb."

"Oh." Ariel felt no other words inside her at first. After spending so much time with Deb, she'd almost begun to feel that... Well, never mind what she'd begun to feel. "I'm glad for you. I hope she charges you too much, though."

"Worth every penny," Scott said with a low chuckle. "What do you think of the arrangement? Will this be good for Deb?"

"It's a little late to be asking me, don't you think?"

"I want your opinion." He came to sit beside her.

Ariel braced herself for his nearness. "Mrs. Fearson," she said with slow deliberation, "has a lot of common sense. She's a warm, giving person. Spending time with Tammy Fearson, though, might cause more problems than it solves."

"Why?"

"Because before Deb arrived, Tammy was the smartest child in grade five. Now a little grade-two girl has shown her up. Tammy's a good kid, but this could build into a real rivalry."

"Should I cancel the arrangement, then?"

Ariel wanted to say yes, but she couldn't lie. If Deb made friends with Tammy, her social isolation would be over. "No, but perhaps you could encourage Deb to tone it down a little in front of Tammy. And if Tammy can help her in any way, Deb should be sure to express her gratitude. You get the idea."

"That makes sense. You're a wise lady."

"No, I'm stupid. I should have lied so I got to keep Deb to myself."

"You're too honest to lie."

That was her, all right. Honest, dependable, helpful—and alone. Ariel shrugged against the wintry feeling that was settling over her.

Scott was studying her, his hazel eyes scraping away the outer layers of her defenses. Ariel filled her lungs with air tinged with the rich perfume of balsam. He looked, she thought, as if he knew that this was the perfect time to bring the focus of the conversation back to the two of them. Well, she could take the offensive, too.

"I don't understand you, Scott. Why do you keep pursuing me when I keep turning you down?"

"I thrive on rejection."

"I'm serious. Why?"

"Seriously?" Scott moved closer to her and mimicked her position. "This is too beautiful a spot for serious, but if you insist..."

"I'd like to know."

"So would I," he said quietly. He spread his palms. "Ariel, do you believe in love at first sight?"

"Of course."

"There's no 'of course' about it. You see, I don't."

"So why did you bring it up?"

He rubbed his jaw. "Damned if I know."

A laugh bubbled out of Ariel. "What, no logical explanation?"

"Look," he muttered, "I don't like doing things without a reason."

Ariel felt something stir inside her heart. She stomped on it before she could examine what it was, because she didn't want to know.

Dangerous territory.

Scott cocked an eyebrow at her and ended on a lighter note. "The scientist in me insists that I investigate this phenomenon thoroughly. How's that for an explanation?"

"Weak, MacKenzie."

"How about this, then?"

He kissed her.

Ariel's cheeks felt his lips first, nuzzling and caressing and stirring embers that had been banked since his previous kiss. He touched her hair and threaded through its fullness. Her scalp came alive to the sensations of his touch and the gentle, insistent tug on her hair.

Ariel drew away and rested her weight on one arm. She breathed heavily as she glared at him. "This isn't a good idea."

"I happen to think it's a stroke of genius."

Her new position gave him better access to her mouth, almost as if her treacherous body had made plans. The next assault of his lips demanded rather than teased, commanded rather than asked. His touch fanned the embers inside her to a glowing red heat. Though she refused entry to her mouth, her strength weakened as he nipped at her sensitive flesh. Her arm buckled and she sank to the ground with Scott on top. Weight—warm, vibrant, masculine weight—flattened her breasts.

There was too much to resist. Her mouth opened. Her lips moved and writhed. Her tongue danced with his. A honey-like melting swept through her, warm enough to turn her flesh into a quivering liquid that yearned to boil.

When his hand stroked her waist, then moved higher to nudge the bottom of her breast, she felt the first bubble of full-fledged arousal percolate from the core of her body. One shiver of delight. Another. Then a seething torrent of passion and readiness. Nothing in her previous experience had prepared Ariel for the speed and strength of this desire that roiled through her, warm and moist. Even through a sweater, blouse and bra, the feel of his fingers was devastating and delightful.

Too delightful. Ariel groaned.

Scott pulled back to look at her face. "Are you okay?"

I would be if you removed your hand. Ariel stifled another groan. "As you said, it's rocky up here."

"Sorry about that." He didn't move.

Now that she'd mentioned it, Ariel noticed the uneven ground under her back. The sky behind Scott's ruffled hair was cloudy, yet with gaps in the grayness that seemed to invite her to reach through to grab the blue and hold it to her bosom. She closed her eyes.

When she opened them again, Ariel felt in control. She glared down at Scott's hand and positioned her fingers in a playful shooing gesture. "Move, please."

He did, but only after squeezing her breast enough to give her second thoughts. Ariel rolled quickly to her feet, crossed her arms over her chest and wandered to the edge of the hilltop clearing. The girls waved at her from the beach. Ariel didn't have the energy to wave back.

"I must be crazy," she muttered.

"Quite possible."

"You don't have to agree so readily."

"Sorry," he said cheerfully.

His tone grated against her nerves. She couldn't let him get to her like this—and, especially, she couldn't let him see how he got to her.

"I'm not crazy, you know," she said lightly. "Actually I consider myself one of B.C.'s last bastions of upper-class English respectability."

Scott took her change of subject with an easy smile. "Tell me about yourself."

"You know the stereotypical British colonel who retired to Victoria to raise roses—who acts as if Great Britain still has an empire and this is the colonies? He was my grandfather."

"Your grandfather was a stereotype? At least there's a reason for your craziness."

She laughed, though it took an effort. "You haven't even heard about my parents yet. I love them dearly, but I can sum them up in a couple of clichés—*Keep a stiff upper lip,* and *Children should be seen and not heard.*"

"Not very affectionate, eh?"

"No," Ariel again put her chin between her knees. "I remember dusting my father's office and washing the car and doing the dishes without being asked, trying to earn a hug or a pat on the head. I used to fix breakfast in bed for my parents on Saturdays and Sundays. It was a ritual, starting when I was about seven."

"Deb did that for me last week," Scott said. "I bet they enjoyed it."

"I guess they did." Ariel shrugged. "I used to hope for an invitation to climb in with them and talk as they ate."

"The invitation never came, eh?"

"Wrong." Honesty forced the next words from her, though she would just as soon have deflected the look of sympathy on his face. "Once or twice."

"You can serve me breakfast in bed any time, Ariel. I promise you that I'll be properly appreciative."

A sharp image of climbing into Scott's bed pierced Ariel's thoughts. Keeping her hands linked, she ran them from her knees to her shins and back. The physical sensations were distant and vague compared to her unbidden imaginings.

She rose to stride across the clearing on the pretext of checking the girls. They seemed to be having a skipping race along a complex track of sand, rocks and driftwood logs.

Ariel rubbed her hands on her upper arms, though she wasn't cold. She wanted to flee from Scott's scrutiny and also to signal her submission by lowering her gaze. Yet she felt that to do so would be submitting to more than she knew.

She raised her chin and kept her gaze on his. It was difficult. The texture and lines of his skin, the unkempt wildness of his dark eyebrows, the probing intensity of his hazel eyes . . . These filled her mind and pasted themselves into a jumble of visual memories that seemed more real than reality. Ariel rubbed her upper arms again, trying to reconnect to a world where Scott's face was only a minor part.

She spoke with forced decisiveness. "We should get back to the girls and then head home. It's getting dark, and I have papers to mark."

Nodding, Scott rose to his feet. After a moment's hesitation when she thought he was going to say something more, he led the way downhill.

For some reason Ariel didn't feel that the day was coming to an end. It felt more like a beginning.

"Hello?" Ariel leaned in the open doorway. Crisp streamers of late-afternoon sun seemed to emphasize the emptiness of the room.

Ariel pulled her head back. Today at school Deb had said that the float house for the whale-watching lab had been towed to Honeymoon Nook. The *Simoom Queen* was tied to the float, so Scott had to be around somewhere.

Her heart was beating faster now than when she'd hiked the trail from the school. It had been over a week since Deb's birthday party. Over a week since she'd seen Scott.

She knew he'd been busy directing technicians from Vancouver who were installing hydrophones and cables. Still, she'd missed him.

Coming here was undoubtedly a mistake. She shouldn't pursue him in any way, given her track record. She didn't want a casual relationship. So why was she here?

She considered leaving, but instead stepped into the room. "I'm here," she said firmly, "to see if a neighbor needs my help."

And, she added to herself, to prove that she could deal with him when Deb wasn't around. She liked Scott and his daughter too much to avoid them. Keeping him at a distance should be relatively easy. After all, what were a few kisses between friends?

An earthquake, unfortunately.

The room was empty except for a bed whose neatly made, checked spread seemed out of place. Two doorways led to other rooms.

A moving shadow blocked the light from the door. Ariel whirled toward it.

"Well, hello." Scott put down the cardboard box that he carried and wiped his hands on the thighs of his well-worn blue jeans. He wore a tattered plaid jacket, boots and work gloves, yet her heart beat faster regardless.

"Hi." The quiet word echoed in the barren room.

"I didn't expect to see you today. How did you get here?"

"I walked."

Scott glanced at his wristwatch as he leaned back against the wall. "You must have left right after school got out."

"I guess so. It doesn't take long to get here. Now that Deb is staying with the Fearsons, I have time on my hands. Can I help you carry anything from the boat?"

He dismissed her offer with a wave of his hand. "Let me show you around."

Resting his hand on her elbow, Scott showed Ariel through the three rooms of the float house and explained what would go in each. Tapes and equipment would be stored in the first room, with the bed for Deb when Scott worked late. The tiny kitchen was immaculate, with several boxes of food piled on the floor of its walk-in pantry. The large room at the back of the float house would be the main laboratory, with computers and monitoring and recording equipment lining three walls.

Scott pointed to a massive Franklin wood stove that radiated a friendly warmth from a corner of the large room. "This will have to go, I suppose, since I'll have electronic gear that doesn't like smoke. At the moment it's the only heat, though."

"I've always loved stoves like this that open into fireplaces."

Scott nodded, as if taking her words heavily into account. "I won't get rid of it right away, then. I'll see if high technology can coexist with wood heat."

Ariel refused permission for her smile to go out and play. "Don't endanger your equipment on my account, Scott."

"To be honest, I like fireplaces, too." He returned his hand to her elbow as he leaned closer. "They're romantic," he added in a confidential voice.

Ariel agreed, but she'd be darned if she'd admit it. He might install a fireplace in every room of the float house and of the fisheries cabins.

Without asking, Ariel went to the *Simoom Queen* and carried a box of food into the pantry. Scott joined her a minute later with several more boxes. Together they began stocking the shelves of the pantry.

The door kept swinging shut, blocking out the light, so Scott brought in a kerosene lantern. He found himself concentrating not on a system of stocking the cans, but on Ariel. He was fascinated by the shadows she cast as she worked, and by the play of light and dark around her cheeks and eyes. Combined with the closed-in air, still rich from pine-scented cleaner, the light created an aura of mystery and intrigue that flowed and shifted with each move Ariel made.

"What's wrong?" she asked.

"Nothing."

Ariel bent for another can. When she straightened, she looked him full in the face. "You're staring at me. And don't tell me there's a smudge on my cheek."

"Have I ever told you you're beautiful?"

"I'm overweight."

He gratefully took the excuse to study her figure. "You look fine to me."

He reached toward her. She leaned away from the hand that touched her hair, hair that felt like an angel's kiss on his palm. She swiveled her gaze from his hand to his face. The movements in her neck as she swallowed were magnified by the shadows.

"Scott . . ."

He lowered his hand.

Ariel swallowed again. She raised a can as if to put it on the shelf, but instead clutched it to her chest. Her face was turned toward the shelves, but her gaze darted in his direction every few seconds.

"Scott," she began again, "don't stare at me like that.

"I can't help it. You're too beautiful for me not to stare."

"I'm not beautiful. At most, I'm attractive in a mature sort of way. And besides," she added as she put the can on the shelf, "I feel self-conscious when someone stares at me."

Scott edged closer. "You shouldn't be so modest."

Ariel edged away from him, till her back was against the shelves. Her laugh was nervous, yet it still carried that quality of gentle softness that he loved. She had the laugh of a lady, and the body of a fantasy woman.

He stopped mere inches from her. She had to tilt her head to look at him, which she did once before glancing away. Scott reached for the lantern. He turned down the light till the flame flickered and died. The darkness was broken only by a harsh line from the crack of the door.

Scott matched his tone to the darkness—hushed and velvety. "Is that better?"

"Worse." Ariel's tone copied his, with the addition of an uncertain quaver at the end. "Scott, I really think—"

"Don't think." He reached his hand toward where her waist had been, but she had shifted position. He touched instead the top of her stomach, with his thumb resting against the voluptuous swell of her breast.

Both of them froze. Scott heard Ariel swallow, the gentle sound seeming loud. Her head was raised toward him.

When she didn't move away, Scott slowly shifted his hand. His knuckles skimmed her soft roundness, first one breast and then, when she still hadn't moved away, the other. He was breathing harder. So was she. He cupped her breast.

Ariel made a soft sound that blended a sigh and a protest. "No," she murmured. Yet she leaned into his hand and grabbed his shoulder for support.

Scott brought his lips to her forehead as he kneaded her pliant flesh. The hardness of her nipple against his palm drove caution from his mind.

"Yes," he said.

When he kissed her forehead, she made another sound that might have been "no" or might have been a murmur of pleasure. She tasted clean and female and very desirable as his lips worked their way down her temple to her cheek.

Scott withdrew his mouth while he tilted her head upward. His thumb traced slow circles on the soft underside of her chin as he looked at her. "You are so beautiful."

After a moment's hesitation she tried a tremulous quip. "In this light, maybe."

"In any light." He tilted his head to one side as he lowered his lips toward hers.

Ariel evaded his kiss by edging backward to sit on a shelf. Scott closed the gap effortlessly. Her knees touched the outside of his thighs.

A sense of panicky anticipation crowded into Ariel's heart as his mouth descended toward hers. She tried to turn her head. Futile. His lips trapped hers and, unprepared and unwilling, she was thrust into the fierce heat of the kiss. His lips touched the corner of her mouth and satisfied themselves there with a slow, lingering massage.

He dragged his lips across hers. She was expecting arousal, was girding herself against it, yet was helpless when it engulfed her. Every muscle in her body became instantly weak. Her mouth opened to his tongue. Greedily she sought the nourishment of his mouth. Her hand pulled him toward her, deepening the kiss.

Gone so easily? Every good intention, whisked away after mere seconds of a kiss? What kind of power did this man have over her? Though her mind cringed from the answer, her body ached to learn.

And then thought was gone, submerged under sensation. She leaned shamelessly into his hands as they roamed her neck, her back, her waist, her breasts. His touch was sure and forceful, gaining boldness from her moans of encouragement. She continued to feed on the taste of his mouth as his hand first sought the buttons of her blouse, then released the catch of her bra to free the flesh of her breasts. Cool, dark air caressed her chest, replaced quickly by warm, expert hands.

Desire was trapped inside a cocoon, struggling and yearning to stretch its wings and soar. Scott's lips branded her breasts; the silk of the cocoon stretched. Her nipples grew hard and fiery under his touch; the silk began to tear. His hands sought the snap at the waist of her slacks; the silk threatened to burst asunder in a riotous confusion of joy and trepidation.

"No." Her voice was too soft to be a word.

Not here, she thought, not like this. Not on a bare wooden shelf in a dark pantry, with the smell of disinfectant haunting her nose and the bite of wood chewing into the back of her thighs.

"No."

The word came out this time, though not as loud in the stillness as the burr of her zipper being lowered. The cocoon peeked out through the rents in its husk and shuddered at the glimpse of the outside world.

"No, Scott. Stop."

He paused. After breathing heavily for several seconds, Scott shifted position. He remained a looming, indistinct shadow. Ariel pulled the edges of her blouse together. Her mind slowly began to clear.

"Let go of me," she whispered raggedly.

"I'm not touching you."

"Oh?" She looked around, then up at his face. "I thought . . . I mean, I assumed that . . ." She exhaled loudly, then marched toward the door of the pantry, still clutching the edges of her blouse. The sudden wash of light splashed her like a cold shower, leaving only embarrassment in its wake.

Ariel kept her back to him as she straightened her clothes. Then she stood stiffly with one hand resting on a kitchen counter, looking at nothing in particular.

"I was just beginning to think about eating dinner," Scott said. "Care to join me?"

A groan eased from Ariel's lungs. "Give up, Scott. This—" she gestured toward the pantry "—wasn't supposed to happen." And then, more feebly, she said, "I like you, but only as a friend."

"Sure." His lively tone conveyed far more meaning than the terse word—skepticism, unconcern, determination. "What sort of things do you do in a pantry with someone you're attracted to, then?"

"That was you," she said sharply, "not me."

"That was *us,* Ariel. Both of us."

"Scott, it isn't wise for us to pursue anything more than friendship."

"Why not?"

Taking a long, deep breath, Ariel gathered all her determination around her like a fortress. It was far less substantial than the silk of a cocoon. "Auntie Amy."

"Amy Radling?" There was surprise and pleasure on his face. "You know her?"

Ariel shook her head.

"Then what does she have to do with anything?"

"I'm not interested in any man who's interested in a woman like her."

"But you said you didn't know her."

"I know enough." Ariel stuffed her hands into her pockets. Now that the sun had disappeared behind the hill, there was a definite chill in the air. "Scott, I'm not some floozy looking for a good time."

"Neither is Amy," he said with a laugh. "She'd just gone through a divorce, true, but she's a professor at the University of Victoria and a deaconess in her church."

"Oh." Ariel had the strong suspicion that a man like Scott would be effective medicine to heal the scars of divorce. "Okay, but the best thing about her was that she didn't want to get married, remember."

"Of course. She was one of the few women I've known who demanded nothing of me except companionship and pleasure."

Hearing him speak so positively of a sterile relationship pricked Ariel's resolve to greater strength. "And that's the kind of relationship you'd like to have with me."

"There's nothing wrong with a relationship based on mutual respect, good conversation and good sex."

"No mention of love, I notice." Ariel clenched her fists inside her pockets.

"Love?" Scott's face became still, as if he'd wiped all emotion off it. "Ariel, right about now I'll settle for survival. My personal life revolves around an eight-year-old who needs more than I can possibly give. My professional life is sinking faster than the *Titanic*. Can you blame me for at least trying to salvage a sex life? Give me a break, Ariel."

"Is that all I am to you, a sex object? I don't believe you're that calculating, Scott. You feel *something* for me."

"Desire, Ariel. I like you, but what I feel is desire."

"No," she said with a shake of her head. "I'm not saying it's love, but there's more. Why can't you admit it?"

"Because there's nothing to admit."

Ariel turned away from him and braced her hands against the edge of the kitchen counter. "You're impossible."

"Probably." His voice was close behind her.

She didn't turn, but she imagined the fire burning in his eyes, a fire that, no matter what he said, was fueled by more than lust. He was close. He would reach out and touch her, and her womanly instincts would thaw under his touch....

She had to stop him before she melted completely. "I'm an old maid, Scott."

"Hardly," he said with a laugh.

Ariel turned. "I am. I'll never get married, not at my age. It was hard—you'll never know how hard—for me to accept that. I'd started to become desperate and pathetic, though, so I had to come to grips with it. Don't undo all that hard work, Scott. I can't handle casual affairs. Unless you want to torture me by getting my hopes up, leave me be." She squeezed her eyes shut. "Please."

There was a long silence in the empty cabin. A log crackled in the fireplace.

When Scott finally spoke, his tone was gentle yet teasing. "If I propose, will you have dinner with me?"

Ariel tried to match his lightness, recognizing it as an acceptance of her words. "Maybe. Then again, maybe I'd save dinner for the honeymoon. I am a Victorian by birth, after all."

Scott folded his arms and advanced toward her. Amusement had won out over the other emotions on his face. "This isn't fair. You should have a kid, too, so I could learn a few of the juicy details from your past, like Amy Radling."

"I haven't lived in a cave, but there are no 'juicy details' in my past."

"Then I feel sorry for you. You have a lot of catching up to do."

Ariel glanced away. "You're looking for someone who doesn't want commitment. We'd make each other miserable."

For a heartbeat Scott stared into her eyes. Then he broke into a grin. He began walking toward her, the dangerous glint in his eyes proclaiming that he intended to kiss her again.

Ariel stood straighter and edged backward. She'd given him her best arguments. If he kissed her again, she doubted she could stop him from doing whatever he wanted with her. "What are you going to do?"

He stopped. Ariel got the impression it wasn't her words so much as the look in her eyes that stopped him. Could he tell, she wondered, that she'd enjoy his kiss and everything else he yearned to do to her body—and yet still didn't want it?

Scott closed his eyes and ran his hand through his hair. His expression was that of a man battling his conscience.

Ariel watched as he stood so close that if she reached out she would touch the firm muscles under his jacket. The dim light from the window turned him into a shape without detail, a larger-than-life male whom she didn't know how to handle.

"Come on," he said at last, "I'll give you a ride home." He headed for the door.

Ariel followed him outside but stopped halfway to the *Simoom Queen*. Something nagged at her, warning her not to get on the boat with him. "Can I trust you?"

Above the sharp silhouette of evergreens the tumultuous clouds were smeared with the reds and grays of sunset. Against this backdrop Scott turned to her with one foot resting on the gunwale. She wished he hadn't chosen such a masculine pose.

"Probably not," he said cheerfully. "But I'm trustworthy, if that's what you mean."

The premonition of change hovered over her thoughts, yet it seemed to have no foundation. With hesitant steps Ariel boarded the *Simoom Queen*.

Chapter Seven

Scott felt like growling as the *Simoom Queen* pierced the calm waters. If he'd kissed her again, she'd have been his. It was as simple as that.

And as complicated. If he'd kissed Ariel and made love with her, he might also have lost her friendship. That mattered. Somewhere along the line he'd come to care about her. He wasn't prepared to admit it to her, especially when she seemed to be asking so much of him, but he did.

Making love might have been bad for her. She was right; they were looking for different things from a relationship.

How had he gotten himself into this bind?

"Are those whale spouts?" Ariel pointed out into the open channel to the east.

"Looks like it. Want to take a closer look?"

"Yes." Her guarded expression had vanished. Excitement and curiosity lit her pale complexion to a soft luminosity. "I wonder if Flopsy is there."

Ten minutes later Scott set the *Simoom Queen* on the same course as the orcas and cut the throttle back to idle.

"They're playful today." He pointed out the window at an orca who showed them its white belly as it spy-hopped, or stood partway out of the water to look at them.

Ariel hurried out to the open deck at the stern. Scott followed.

The waters on all sides showed tall black dorsal fins as the orcas gathered close to the boat. "This is the B pod," he said. "The locals."

Two orcas glided half out of the water as they passed on the starboard side no more than fifty feet from the boat. From the port side came a rush of sound that always reminded Scott of a steam engine—a spouting whale.

He grabbed Ariel's shoulders and jostled her in the direction of the magnificent sight of an orca lifting its entire twenty-five-foot length out of the water in a startling leap. At the height of its leap the creature seemed to hang in the air, watching them, its sleek, strong body poised in a curve that proclaimed its power. Its reentry splash was like an explosion, sending spray over Scott's cheeks.

Ariel's hair was dark with spray, but she didn't seem to notice. She grabbed Scott's forearm and held it with strength born of excitement. "Was that Wavy?"

"No, that was Max."

"Max?" She turned to him slowly, a wide grin turning her face into an even more beautiful sight than usual. "What kind of name is that for a whale?"

"B-3," Scott said quickly.

"I prefer Max."

"That doesn't surprise me."

"How did you come up with the name Max?"

"Uh, the name seemed appropriate, that's all." Scott wiped the spray from his hair as he sheepishly explained. "The local Indian name for the killer whale is *Max'inuth.* B-3 is the largest male in the pod, so he seemed to deserve the name."

"Is Max—" she leaned slightly on the name "—the big boss of the pod?"

"No, he's just somebody's henpecked son. Our best guess is that orcas mate outside their own pod."

"Who'd henpeck something that big?"

"His mother. Killer whales stay in their mother's pod for their whole lives, unless the pod grows too large and gradually splits. From the similarities in their dialects, I'd say the B pod split from the R pod, which is also related to several other pods. All indications are that orca social structures last for centuries."

"You can tell all that from their squeaks?"

"That and more, once I get the project up and running."

She leaned over the side of the boat. Flopsy had come back, poking its rubbery black head out of the water.

"Hi, girl," Ariel said. She looked at Scott, her face aglow. "She remembers me."

"I'm sure," he said dryly.

Ariel stretched her hand toward the calf. It was almost, but not quite, close enough to touch. She leaned farther.

"Careful, Ariel."

She flashed him a look of quick annoyance. "Hold on to me, then."

Scott watched the long, smooth curves of her legs, which seemed to stretch to the beginning of his imagination. She couldn't be serious. Hold on to her legs, after that impassioned speech about keeping his hands off her? Was she a sadist trying to tempt him to death?

"Please, Scott."

"Torturer," he muttered under his breath.

He laid a gentle hand on her waist, then held on in earnest as she leaned dangerously far. The wool of her jacket teased his palms. The firm curves of her thighs and buttocks teased his arms and eyes as she stretched and strained. She was so intent on the calf that he doubted she'd notice if he caressed the enticing roundness that loomed just inches from his face.

On second thought, she'd notice. If he didn't hold on tightly, he'd drop her in the ocean. With an effort he dragged his gaze to the baby whale.

After a minute Scott had endured all the enticement he could take. He hauled her back onto the deck. "Enough. You're going to pull me into the water with you."

Ariel nodded, her eyes still on the calf. "I petted it."

Flopsy lowered its head almost under the water. A string of high screeches and whistles shot from its blowhole.

Ariel laughed and grabbed Scott's leg. "She's talking to me."

Ariel seemed oblivious to her hand on his thigh. Scott wasn't. He wanted her to touch him, but he preferred that she be aware of what she was doing.

He moved. Ariel didn't seem to notice his departure. "Underwater, orcas sing through their mouths," he explained in a classroom voice. "On the surface they use their blowholes. They hear through their jaws, by the way. Would you like to listen to them? I have a portable hydrophone on board."

Ariel leaned out to watch Flopsy lower itself under the waves. "I'd love to."

Scott went to the wheelhouse to kill the engine, then brought out a roll of thick electrical cable attached to a tiny microphone. He lowered fifteen feet of cable over the side and attached it to a power supply. Down in the cabin he put on headphones and made a few adjustments to an amplifier, then handed the headphones to Ariel.

Soft furrows appeared on her brow. She said nothing for several minutes, while Scott enjoyed the sight of her.

"It *is* singing," she declared as if daring him to challenge her. "They use rhythm and pitch and volume. I took enough piano lessons to recognize music when I hear it, even if the instrumentation is unusual. I'm surprised their voices are so high and squeaky."

"Like a rusty door hinge being closed quickly."

"Do you understand any of it?"

"No. I'm hoping that by recording their calls I'll be able to..." Scott stopped as a flash of inspiration hit him.

Ariel slipped the earphones off her head and looked at him. "What is it?"

"How good are you?"

She looked at him strangely. "What do you mean?"

"On the piano."

"Well, I used to be pretty good, for an amateur. Now I mostly play by ear because I'm out of practice at reading music."

"Don't worry. That's no problem. Have you ever played a synthesizer? It's a lot like a piano, I gather."

She laughed gently. "No, but what—"

"Ariel, orcas are as sound oriented as we are sight oriented. That's well documented. They're also curious about human music."

A soft, patient smile lit Ariel's face in the grayness of the cabin. "I still don't understand what you're getting at."

"Ariel, I need your help. I want you to play for the orcas so I can record their responses."

She laughed again, covering her face with her hands. She looked out at him from behind their shield. "You're kidding."

He shook his head vigorously.

"You're sure this is science, not an excuse to hang around me? I mean, would I do any good?"

"You might do a lot of good." He avoided answering her first question. "You'd have to work, too. I mentioned a synthesizer because it can approximate whale tones. You'd have to learn to use one."

"Well…" Ariel hesitated, but he could tell she wanted to be convinced.

A realization hit him. Ariel wanted to be convinced not that this would be fun or easy, but that she'd be needed. Looking at her gleaming eyes, he suspected that to Ariel, unlike most people, the idea of labor was an enticement.

"You'd have to work *hard*. Your music could become a keystone of my research, so I'm looking for a real commitment."

Ariel's face sobered at his use of that word.

"You'd have to play every weekend," Scott plowed on, "and some evenings during the week, too."

"Why, Scott? Why are you suddenly so eager for my help when you've turned it down every other time except when you were desperate about Deb?"

He sat down beside her and resisted the urge to take her hand in his. That, unfortunately, wasn't the proper approach with Ariel. "This is science, not personal."

"Not personal." She looked at him skeptically. "That means no funny stuff like back in the pantry?"

"You thought that was *funny?* I'm insulted."

"Promise me, Scott."

"Okay, okay. I promise I won't touch you in the pantry."

"You won't touch me anywhere. You have to give your word."

Scott gazed toward the vanishing pod of whales, though his mind wasn't on the cetaceans. "You have it," he said slowly. "Unless—"

"No exceptions, Scott."

"Unless," he insisted, "you want me to."

Her look of distress was entirely satisfactory to Scott's ego. She took a deep breath. "If I have your word, I guess I'll try."

"Thank you."

A soft laugh filled his ears. "Maybe you should save your thanks till you've heard me play. I don't know how discerning an audience of orcas are, but . . . well, I'll try."

"I'll take that," Scott said, "as a promise."

" . . . so I know you're right, mother, but I've only managed to lose five pounds so far."

Ariel stifled a yawn, being careful not to jab herself with the pen. Letters to her parents were a duty, not a joy, and even though it was early evening she found herself getting sleepy. She forced herself upright to a less relaxed position on the couch.

She wanted to write about Scott's whale research, which was fast becoming one of the most important things in her life. How to bring it up casually, though?

She suspected that her parents did care about her. Their reticence, however, had bred a similar reserve in her. Ariel knew it was unfortunate, but by now her parents were the last ones to learn of anything important in her life.

School has been going well. The class is livelier than last year, because of the big group of grade sevens—all but one of whom is a girl. Needless to say, all the girls have their eyes set on Damien, which makes for a lot of bickering. All in all, I've been busy lately because ...

Ariel tightened her grip on the pen. Why was it an effort to write to her parents about the whale research?
Because it was important to her, of course.

... because I've gotten involved in a government research project. It involves killer whales. The man in charge has put a lot of people on the island to work in the last two weeks, organizing everyone effortlessly. He had a squad of technicians from Vancouver installing hydrophones and monitoring equipment.

Scott had also hired locals to fix up the floating lab, install antennae and two generators and improve the trail from the school to Honeymoon Nook. Ariel didn't bother going into details, though. She didn't think her parents would care that the trail was now an easy ten-minute stroll.

Putting the end of the pen in her mouth, she smiled. One of the men clearing the trail had answered her question about the origin of the camp's name. Fifty or sixty years ago, when the island had more people, the cove was a favorite anchoring place for young couples having the honeymoon before the marriage.

Ariel dragged her thoughts back to the letter.

The whale-tracking equipment is mostly in place. This week I got the loan of an electronic synthesizer, which has a piano keyboard but can be programmed to produce an incredible range of tones and sounds. I've been studying tape recordings of killer whales and experimenting with reproducing their tone quality. I'm not good yet, but all those years with Mrs. Driscoll are paying off. Now I wish I'd listened to you and practiced even harder.

Her parents liked the chance to say "I told you so," and Ariel obliged by giving them as many opportunities as possible. What would have encouraged her to practice harder—though she'd practiced a lot and had even dreamed of a musical career—would have been words of praise from her parents.

Ariel pulled the quilt from the back of the couch over her legs. When she finished the letter she'd turn up the oil heater, because her fingers should be warm to practice. In a few days Scott was going to take the synthesizer to Honeymoon Nook, and she wanted to live up to Mrs. Driscoll's claim that Ariel had been her best student.

The man in charge of the project is monitoring the whales' movement pattern and trying to associate their songs with their activities. I thought I knew a bit about computers, but seeing what Scott...

Ariel made a clucking sound with her tongue. Reaching to the end table behind her, she obliterated the last word with correcting fluid.

...what the scientist is doing to catalog and analyze the sound patterns makes me feel...

Ariel rubbed her left hand along the thigh of her corduroy slacks. She shifted position, trying to ease a vague ache.

...makes me feel ignorant. All in all, I'm looking forward to playing for the whales.

And, she admitted to herself as she snuggled under the quilt, to spending impersonal, nonthreatening time with Scott. The more she saw of him, the more impressed she was with his humor and his effortless ability to organize and lead.

Being with Scott made her feel less lonely and more lonely at the same time. He still gave her the impression that he was pursuing her, but he hadn't tried to kiss her again. She was glad but surprised. Of course, she was careful not to be alone with him.

An image of Scott's face, lit by the amber glow from a computer monitor, brought a smile to Ariel's lips. The smile was still in place when she resumed writing.

> Thank you for the birthday money. I won't get to a store before my birthday, though, so I'll get something from the Eaton's catalog.

Ariel already had the birthday present selected—a powerful battery lantern for traveling the trail to Honeymoon Nook.

> Yes, Father, I'll try to write more often. I know you've heard me say that before—and I'm afraid my habits are firmly entrenched by now.
>
> > Sincerely,
> > Ariel

As Ariel folded the letter, put a dab of perfume on it and sealed it in an envelope, she wondered how her working relationship with Scott would turn out. The next few weeks would apparently reveal a great deal.

The whales turned out to be an elusive audience. The first Saturday Ariel sat expectantly at the keyboard, more aware of Scott's presence than she wished. Nothing happened. The speakers linked to the hydrophones carried a multitude of vague, watery sounds—the ocean was a much noisier place than she had imagined—but no orcas.

The next day was the same, so Ariel looked around for things to do. When she began straightening the kitchen, Scott took hold of her arms and led her back to the lab.

They talked. Scott showed Ariel oscilloscope printouts of whale calls and played tapes to familiarize her with the distinctive calls of the local dialect. They played gin rummy with Deb. Aside from numerous smoldering looks, Scott behaved himself. It was more like a family weekend than a scientific experiment.

Even when the orcas did appear, Ariel didn't accomplish much. She played a few tentative notes. The orcas paused their "talking" as if to listen, but then start chattering again, paying no attention to the music.

After this had happened several times, Ariel began to feel useless, even guilty.

The guilt was because of the enjoyment she got from these evenings and weekends. The closeness and sense of family triggered deep responses of belonging that she knew were inappropriate.

One evening the orcas finally arrived just as she prepared to leave. It was late. She'd had a long day of teaching, a dark trek through the forest following dinner and several hours of waiting. Nonetheless, she sat at the synthesizer keyboard and played a fast and glittering Chopin waltz.

"That sounded good, Ariel."

She jerked her hands off the keyboard and balled them in her lap. "But they're ignoring it again."

The eerie whistles and buzzes from the speakers were growing more faint. As usual, the whales had paused their songs briefly. The synthesizer had been eerily quiet in the room, though Ariel knew that it blared through the underwater speakers. As usual, the orcas continued on their way.

"They don't pay any more attention to Chopin than to jazz." Ariel closed her music book noisily. "I'm wasting my time. I should quit before I make even more of a fool of myself."

Scott padded across the wooden floor in his moccasins. He rested a hand atop hers. "Patience is the trademark of experienced researchers."

Ariel lowered her gaze to her lap. Scott's hand easily engulfed both of hers, his tanned flesh covering her paleness like a blanket. "I'm less experienced than you, remember?"

He squeezed her hand before letting go. His wrist grazed her thigh lightly as he removed his hand. "We're making as much progress as can be expected. It would be great, of course, if they'd leapt into our arms the first time."

Ariel looked up at him, aware of the possible double meaning of his words.

"If it doesn't happen that way," Scott continued, "well, we're still making progress."

"In what way?

"They're getting used to us," Scott said as he threw a log on the fire. It crackled and popped as flames licked and nudged it. He sat on an office chair and leaned forward with his elbows on his knees.

"You mean," she said, "that just by being around them, you think we're wearing down their resistance?"

"Something like that. We're becoming part of their world." His gaze seemed to bore into her soul. "We're preparing them to let us become even more important."

Ariel moved from her piano bench to a chair closer to the sparkling warmth of the fire. "Why do I feel as if you're talking about me rather than the whales?"

He spread his hands and filled his face with a look of innocence. "Coincidence."

Ariel raised her eyebrows.

"There are parallels," he admitted, "but you're rather more important to me than whales."

Ariel looked down at her hands. She gradually closed her eyes. "Scott, I'm not doing any good here."

After a minute of uncomfortable silence, Scott spoke. "If you want to back out of the research project, I'll understand."

"You wouldn't mind?"

"Of course I'd mind. Your help is important to what I'm trying to accomplish. But I'd understand."

The songs of the orcas faded from the speakers, as if the whales were leaving them alone to finish their private conversation. Scott turned down the volume on the hisses and bumps of undersea background noise.

"You make it sound," she said, "as if I'm accomplishing something. I'm not."

Scott turned off the overhead light. The flickering glow of the fire cast prominent shadows that were only partly overridden by the small lamp beside the synthesizer. Ariel liked the room like this. The oscilloscopes and tape decks and speakers seemed softer and more sympathetic in this light. How easy it would be, she thought as her eyes closed again, to lower her guard completely.

"You're tired," Scott said softly.

Ariel murmured a quiet sound of agreement.

"I am, too. In fact, I'm tempted to curl up on the bed here rather than going home," he said.

Would he ask her to join him? The thought was tempting. Maybe she could sleep in the other room with Deb.

"Do you want me to rub your shoulders, Ariel? Sometimes that releases tension."

Ariel's eyes flew open as Scott padded over to stand behind her chair. "It would release tension if you stayed at the opposite side of the room."

"Not for me."

Ariel sat upright. "I should be going. It's already my bedtime."

"That's why I moved an extra bed into this room."

Ariel stiffened and took a long, deep breath. "Scott," she began ominously, "I—"

"Even researchers need rest," he interrupted.

As she gathered her music books, Ariel shook her head. She wished he'd move away from her so she could think clearly. "Look, I'm too tired for this now."

"There might be more whales passing by."

Ariel paused in the act of rising. Scott was probably right. She'd become familiar enough with the sounds of the orcas to know that the group that had just passed wasn't the entire pod. The rest could come any time—or not at all.

She jerked when Scott touched her shoulder. His hand rested there briefly, then began kneading her flesh slowly. "Relax," he said. His other hand sought her nape, searching through her hair, whisking over the warm flesh underneath. His fingertips spread delicate promises along her skin. "You can trust me, you know."

Ariel felt her eyes closing of their own volition as her head leaned into his touch. "No, I don't know."

"Yes." He continued kneading her neck and shoulders, melting away not only tension but willpower, as well. He leaned close and spoke urgently. "I want you, Ariel."

"Don't say that."

He gripped her shoulders firmly, his fingers on her upper chest. When he moved his hands in strong, kneading circles, she felt pleasure stir in her breasts. "I want you," he repeated, "and I think you want me, too."

"No," she whispered.

"And one day you'll be ready to admit it." His face was close to her temple now, an added distraction and enticement for her senses. His fingers traced her collarbone, then slipped under the veil of her blouse. He stopped just before she cried out.

"You can trust me," he said, "to wait for that moment, and to do everything I can to hasten it."

Scott removed his hands.

After a heartbeat Ariel jerked to her feet. Her forearms pressed against nipples that were taut and sensitive. "I'm leaving," she announced.

"Okay."

Ariel turned away from him and tried to calm her ragged breathing. "You think that you just have to be patient, and I'll fall into your arms."

"I know it isn't that simple."

"But still, that's what you think. Scott, I..." Ariel's shoulders slumped. She faced him and sighed. "I resign from the research project. It wasn't supposed to be personal."

Scott's eyes narrowed. Analyze the situation, he commanded himself.

His mistake had been touching her, he realized. When he touched Ariel, her defenses went up while his went down. He said impetuous things, things that he meant but that set Ariel prancing away like a startled deer.

"I won't touch you," he said.

"That's only part of it." She shuffled to the door to the outer room and rested her hand on the doorknob.

"I won't give up, you know."

Ariel smiled at that, though her eyes were sad. "No, I don't suppose you will. Not right away. But it's better this way."

Scott took a step toward her. He saw her grip tighten on the doorknob. "Why, Ariel? Why is it better this way?"

She shook her head. "You don't understand."

"Then explain it to me."

Her gaze strayed in his direction but stopped short of meeting his face. "Scott, I..." Ariel shrugged her shoulders and opened the door. How could she explain what she didn't *know,* but only *felt?* Without a backward glance she picked up her lantern from the floor and stepped into the dark outer room.

In the skewed rectangle of light from the door, Scott saw her approach the bed where Deb slept. Scott imagined Ariel's soft expression as she tucked a blanket around Deb's neck and then leaned forward to kiss the sleeping girl on the forehead.

When Ariel straightened, she stood for several seconds with her back to him. Abruptly she looked back, her face more vulnerable and appealing than he'd imagined possible.

Yes, Scott thought, she was vulnerable. Was he willing to risk hurting her? Maybe it simply wasn't meant to be. No matter what he thought or wanted, maybe this was one of those inexplicable things that defied his logic. The unaccustomed thought rattled harshly through his mind, resonating with the vibrancy of a truth revealed through some indefinable transcendent process.

Ariel turned to leave.

A high-pitched moan escaped one of the speakers. Ariel glanced back, wondering if he had made the mournful sound.

Scott shook his head and motioned toward the speaker. "The rest of the pod," he said.

"Oh." Ariel paused again, listening.

A burst of whale chatter sounded quietly in the painful silence, with one voice rising over the others. "Waaa-AAAaaaup!"

An evanescent smile graced Ariel's lips. "That's Flopsy."

Scott shrugged, saying nothing. Ariel seemed to have a special rapport with the baby whale, and perhaps she could recognize the calf's voice.

"One last song for Flopsy?" He held his hands open. "No tricks, no strings."

Ariel stared into his eyes. "All right."

She sat at the synthesizer and turned it on. For several seconds she just sat. She flipped several switches that controlled tonal quality, then sat still.

"What are you going to play?"

With her fingers poised over the keyboard, Ariel shrugged.

Another low moan came from the speakers. The sound swooped up in a modulating, otherworldly melody that wandered through a string of snorts and mockingbird trills before ending on a high note that went almost beyond human hearing.

The synthesizer echoed the low moan. Scott turned to see Ariel hunched over the keyboard, her face barren of expression. One hand was far to the left of the keyboard. The other flipped tone switches with quiet haste. Suddenly Ariel's hands moved over the keyboard, swooping in imitation of the whale's call. She ended on the synthesizer's highest note, which wasn't as high as the whale's.

Instantly the speaker repeated a variation of the song Ariel had just imitated.

"Oh, my God," she whispered. She darted a glance at Scott. "Did you hear that?"

"Yes." Scott hesitated, watching the awe on Ariel's face. "Or maybe not. What was so special?"

"The last note was different. She also copied the mistake I made on a series of runs and changed the glissando to a series of steps like I did on the keyboard."

"You mean Flopsy copied you that quickly?"

"Yes!" She turned back to the keyboard and fiddled with a switch. "I wish I played guitar so I could match the glisses better. In theory, if I hold down one key till I press the next, the tone will slide, but . . ." Her voice faded to silence.

Ariel repeated the tune again, though her fingers slipped in the middle. Immediately the speakers returned an exact copy, complete with the mistake.

Scott turned on several tape recorders, then pulled a chair close so he could see both the keyboard and Ariel's shadowed face. Her features were outwardly placid, yet they glowed with an inner excitement. Her eyes sparkled from within the deep shadows that gave her a stark, exotic beauty.

Maybe, Scott thought, it *was* meant to be. The orcas had kept Ariel at his side. For a moment he savored the thought of the giant sea creatures watching over Ariel and himself as if they were truly the powerful, benevolent spirits of Indian legends.

He shrugged away the fanciful thought and assigned the occurrence to the nonscientific category of lucky coincidence.

"Scott, I'm teaching music to a whale."

Then a new voice boomed through the speaker. Another whale had joined the communication—and Scott had to think of it as communication. The newcomer repeated Flopsy's original tune. Ariel began to repeat it, but before she'd finished, the newcomer interrupted—impatiently, it seemed to Scott. He shook his head, trying to clear it of such unscientific thoughts.

Light shimmered off Ariel's hair, and she bent her face parallel to the keyboard. Again she repeated the song. Again the newcomer interrupted.

Ariel looked up at Scott. Perspiration beaded her brow. "Wavy is a critic," she said with a faint smile.

Scott didn't bother to ask if she knew for certain that the newcomer was Wavy, or was guessing. Instead, he nodded to her. "You're doing fine."

Ariel's face glowed brighter. She smiled shyly and returned her attention to the keyboard. With her fingers poised above the keyboard she glanced back at Scott and smiled again, this time more broadly.

The newcomer—Scott decided to think of it as Wavy, for convenience' sake—stopped a third of the way through the call and waited for Ariel to repeat it.

She did. Scott noticed a small difference in her version. Ariel tried again. Apparently satisfied, Wavy began the second section of the call.

Ariel looked up at Scott. Her lip quivered, though her eyes danced. She looked like a different person, or like an angelic, spiritual incarnation of herself—like the ethereal vision he'd glimpsed in his weakened condition, the first time he'd seen her. He reached out to touch her cheek with one fingertip.

Ariel smiled beatifically. "Dear God," she whispered. "Who's the teacher and who's the pupil?"

Then she bent once more to the keyboard and repeated the second section. Back and forth went pupil and teacher, the orca giving Ariel no time to rest. Her hands flew over the keyboard and the tone switches, searching for a combination of slides and tone qualities that would satisfy the orca.

When he noticed a drop of sweat fall to the keyboard, he wiped Ariel's face with a handkerchief as unobtrusively as possible. Other than that, he sat and observed, trying to burn into his memory the concentration and inner joy that infused Ariel's being.

Wavy repeated the entire passage, adding a single downsweep note at the end. Ariel followed suit, but inserted her own triumphant flourish at the end.

Then the speakers were silent. They both sat for a long time, waiting, poised.

After several minutes Ariel's shoulders abruptly slumped. She looked like a rag doll about to slide off the piano bench. Scott seized her arm, worried that she was about to fall.

"I'm all right," Ariel said.

She didn't protest, though, when he swept her into his arms and carried her to the bed in the opposite corner of the room. He knelt beside the bed and brushed aside hair that had stuck to her temples and forehead.

"Are you sure you're all right?"

"I feel magnificent," Ariel said with slow emphasis. "A bit drained, as if I'd swum from here to Vancouver Island. But magnificent. Do you know what I mean?"

Scott nodded, unconsciously bringing his head closer to hers. "Ariel, that was one of the most amazing things I've ever seen. You were unbelievable."

Her face glowed for a second, then she sobered. "Wavy was the one who was incredible, not me. I'll be better next time. I've never had a lesson on the synthesizer—" she laughed softly "—until tonight, that is. Scott, just how smart are orcas, anyway?"

"A lot smarter than I ever thought." Even if tonight had witnessed nothing more than the instinctual teaching methods of a mother whale, Scott was impressed beyond anything that could appear in his official reports. How could he answer Ariel's question, though, when he didn't know the answer? "The best I can say is that they're smart in different ways from us."

"If nothing else, they're musical geniuses."

The scientist in him began to reemerge. "Perhaps," he said hesitantly. "I don't exactly know how to interpret what happened tonight."

A throaty, gentle laugh mocked his caution yet included him in its warm pleasure.

"Maybe," he said, "you managed to trigger an instinctive mechanism that the orcas use to teach their young."

"Instincts nothing. That whale was smarter than me." Ariel turned on her side, facing him. Her lips were mere inches from his mouth.

They kissed.

At first only their lips touched. Aware of Ariel's reluctance, Scott held back. Ariel, however, dragged her lips from side to side across his. When they reached the corner of his mouth, her lips opened to tantalize him with her soft moistness.

He seized her lower lips between his, drawing an audible breath from Ariel. Her tongue flicked against his lip, then met his tongue when it demanded entry to her mouth. Scott explored the hidden recesses of her mouth, her tongue always hovering near his. Together, they probed, they danced, they advanced and retreated. Ariel was uninhibited and forceful, shameless in the ways she sought pleasure from his mouth.

Scott's desire threatened to overwhelm him. Taking the lead, he thrust at her. She yielded before his insistence, rolling onto her back without ever letting their lips part. He loomed over her and drank of her sweetness, slaking nothing, building only a greater thirst.

The kiss had to end and it finally did, leaving Scott dazed with passion. He opened his eyes as he reached for her.

He froze with his hand hovering over her chest. And then he remembered where his persistence had led him last time....

Ariel's eyes were still closed. A smile brushed her mouth with the soft innocence of a kitten's fur. Scott stared at his hand, looming over the prominent nipple of her breast. He imagined the firm feel of her flesh and her sigh of pleasure.

Instead, he moved his hand to his side and knelt upright. His fingers twitched.

Ariel's eyes fluttered halfway open. A wisp of hair caressed her cheekbone and wandered languorously to the gentle indentation at the corner of her satiated mouth. A log crackled, sending a gush of light glittering off her dark pupils just before her eyes closed again.

Scott knew then that he would always remember her this way. It wasn't a matter of memorizing the way she looked. Ariel had just moved into a corner of his soul and would live forever in this moment.

"I'm so tired," she said.

Scott closed his eyes. He could still see her.

He was shaking as he stood up. His frustrated desire was so strong that it was painful. Ariel remained limp on the bed.

"Don't fall asleep there," he said. *If you stay there all night there's no way I could refrain from making love to you.* Scott dragged his hand through his hair. "You have school tomorrow."

"Mmm."

"If you wait for me to carry Deb out to the boat, I'll give you a ride home."

Ariel nodded without opening her eyes. "You're a good friend, Scott." Her voice was a sleep-softened mélange of sultry femininity and trusting ingenuousness.

"Sure," he said as he struggled to draw his gaze from the hypnotic rise and fall of her chest. "A good friend."

Chapter Eight

Balancing a bag of garbage in each hand, Ariel closed the teacherage door with her foot. She hummed a whale call, cocking her head from side to side in time to her humming. Her fingers crinkled the paper bags, mimicking the keystrokes of the call.

As soon as she stepped from under the roof, she noticed the mist and the ominous sky, both of which made her happy. But then, almost everything in the past week and a half had seemed happy.

A movement caught her attention at the corner of the school. She headed across the brown, spongy grass. Angus was huddling under the eaves and holding the garbage cans from the classroom. He edged away from her.

"Angus, why are you hiding?" Emptying the garbage was his job, after all, even if he didn't always do it.

"I'm not hiding, just getting out of the rain."

The frizzes of hair springing from under his toque glistened with moisture. "You're already soaked," she pointed out.

Angus bolted from the eaves and stomped toward the trash barrels at the back of the school. "What do you know about soaked?" he muttered as he stomped. "You with your designer raincoat, you can't even handle this kind of weather." His voice faded, though he continued muttering.

Taken aback, Ariel didn't move until Angus had disappeared behind the school. What was wrong with him?

She was eager to finish her Friday schoolwork so she could get to Honeymoon Nook after dinner. Since the breakthrough a week and a half ago she'd gone there every day, hoping for another lesson from the whales. None had come, but that didn't matter. She'd also become deeply involved in recognizing and cataloging the types of calls the remote microphones recorded. She was needed.

A weekend of playing for the whales loomed in her mind as brightly as the sun streaming through a break in the clouds. Still, she could spare a few minutes for the old man.

Angus clattered the small garbage cans against the metal barrel with unnecessary vigor. Ariel stopped a few feet from him. "Is something the matter, Angus?"

He didn't look at her. "Big lot you care."

Ariel thrust her bags into the barrel, lowered the lid and turned as if to leave. "If that's the way you want it, fine."

"Lass, I..."

She turned back just in time to see his hand stretched out to her. Angus shoved the hand back into his pocket and returned to banging the garbage cans.

Ariel huddled under her cape, waiting for him to say something. When he didn't, she said, "Angus, can we discuss this inside, away from the rain?"

He lifted his face to the sky, stubbornly blinking away the drizzle that fell in his eyes. "I've got work to do here." He slammed one garbage can inside the other. "But you run along. You've got more important things to do than talk to me."

"Is that what this is about?" If the old coot missed her, he sure had an aggravating way of showing it. "I know I haven't visited you often lately, but I've been busy with the orca project.''

Angus snorted. ''Don't you mean you've been busy with the fishy man?''

''No,'' she said slowly, ''I mean that I've been busy with the orca project.''

Still, she knew Angus was partly right. She'd become entranced with the whales—and also with Scott. During the past few weeks she'd learned that she and Scott fit together perfectly in so many ways. Their tastes in music and reading. Their affinity for adventure and out-of-the-way places. Their politics and daily routines.

''Orcas.'' Angus made a face. ''Killer whales, you mean. Killers they are, too. I don't believe all this newfangled talk about them being overgrown puppy dogs of the sea. Back in my day they were known as killers, and killers they are.''

''That's not true, Angus.'' Ariel's hand curled into a fist. ''Orcas don't attack people. As for their hunting, well, they have to eat. At least they don't kill for pleasure like humans.''

Angus wilted in the face of her displeasure. ''Take it easy, lass, take it easy. Hey, I'm not like some of the fishermen who carry rifles to shoot at killer whales on sight.''

Ariel grabbed the damp wool of his jacket sleeve. ''They do *what*?''

Angus's forehead rumpled into a tangle of furrows. ''Well, killer whales eat an awful lot of fishies. Fishermen see their livelihoods floating into the teeth of that eating machine and they get a wee bit carried away sometimes. They don't mean anything by it.''

Ariel's voice rose an octave. ''They don't *mean* anything!'' Flopsy, be shot for the sin of romping around the wrong kind of boat? ''Into the teacherage, Angus. Now!''

He jumped, his arms flailing to the sides. With a backward glance he scampered toward the teacherage door. ''What are you going to do to me?''

''Find out everything you know about fishermen and rifles.''

"Hey, I don't know nothing. I mean, everybody knows some fishermen carry rifles. They've been doing it for years. I don't know anything more than that."

Ariel ushered him inside regardless. "Stay there," she ordered as she shucked off her cape and boots.

Shifting from foot to foot, Angus stood on the mat near the door. He removed his toque and held it in two hands in front of him. A drop of water poised on the tip of his nose.

"That's real pretty." The drop fell when he nodded hopefully toward a glass flower resting on a newspaper in the middle of the kitchen table. "Did it break?"

"Yes." Distracted against her will, Ariel cast a long glance at the rose, barely shining in this light. "I'm trying to glue it back together, but I lost a few pieces of the leaves."

"What kind of glue are you using?"

Ariel jerked her attention back to Angus. "Don't try to change the subject." She folded her hands on the table and fixed the old man with her sternest schoolmarm stare. "Tell me," she said, "everything you know about fishermen and rifles."

Ariel emerged from the softly dripping forest and threw back the hood of her cape. Despite the storm clouds she'd seen when emptying the garbage, the rain had lessened rather than intensified. It cooled her face, just as her hasty plunge along the trail had cooled the worst of her anger at hearing about the fishermen. The anger was still there, though, ready to spring to life when she told Scott.

She rarely arrived at Honeymoon Nook during daylight, but Angus's news wouldn't wait. The nook looked different under the gray clouds, more somber and yet more connected to the real world. Her evening vigils sometimes seemed to take place in an alternative universe, sealed off from the rest of her life.

Ariel continued toward the ramp that led to the orca lab, but her footsteps slowed as she glanced around.

Dark evergreens and underbrush formed a wall around the cove, broken only by the small beach and outcrops of bare rock that plunged into the water. The float house hid the smaller utility float, which held a generator, woodshed and storage.

The echoing crack of ax hitting firewood, muted by trees and the misty air, told Ariel that Scott was by the woodshed. She headed that way.

When she rounded the corner of the float house, Ariel jerked to a stop. Scott, bare to the waist, was in the act of raising an ax over his head. He hadn't seen her.

Spellbound, Ariel followed the glistening ripple of muscles as the ax fell with a sharp crack. The piece of wood trapped the ax. Undeterred, Scott swung both the ax and the captive piece of wood back, then up, over his head and down again with stunning force. The sound made Ariel jump.

With one easy scooping motion, Scott tossed a shattered piece of wood under the cover of the shed and placed another round of wood on the chopping block. Again the ax rose, propelled by muscles that seemed to hypnotize Ariel through sheer virility. He wasted no motion. Every move was controlled, effective, precise, overpowering.

Ariel's mouth went dry as a disturbing speculation insinuated itself into her consciousness. Was Scott, she wondered, this masterful and potent in...well, in other physical activities?

The ax soared in a crescendo of power and skill. Wood yielded to Scott's thrust with a sharp, enthusiastic cry.

Ariel swallowed, her throat sticky and uncomfortable. She allowed herself one last look at the corded muscles of his arms before she stepped forward. She let out a wolf whistle rendered feeble by the dryness of her mouth.

Scott glanced up from gathering split pieces of wood. He smiled as he stood. "Well, hello. You're here early." His eyes traveled the length of her body. "You look good today."

Ariel glanced down at her legs and the hem of her dress, poking from the bottom of the rain cape. Usually she changed to jeans or bulky woolen slacks before hiking here. Today she hadn't taken the time.

"Look who's talking," she answered belatedly. Her vague gesture in the general direction of his shining torso—with him watching her, she found she couldn't look boldly at him—weakened her riposte. She forced energy into her voice. "Don't you know it's December?"

Scott gathered an armful of firewood. "The Indians used to go naked all winter, because wet clothes are worse than none at all. Don't you agree?"

"Sorry to short-circuit your fantasies," she said briskly, "but I'm into neither nudism nor wet T-shirts."

Scott's gaze roved her body from head to toe, making her feel underdressed despite the shapeless cape.

"Don't you dare say it," she warned.

His eyebrows rose in overstated innocence. "Say what?"

"Whatever you're thinking." Ariel pulled the hood over her head, then glanced at him. "And stop thinking it, too."

Scott's deep chuckle was unrepentant. "Well, if you aren't into wet T-shirts, are you into lazing in front of warm, romantic fires?"

"That depends who I'm with."

"I see." The light in his eyes made Ariel suspect that he was seeing *her,* stretched in front of a fire while wearing rather less than this modest cape. "So you have experience in front of fireplaces, eh?"

"Fireplaces are very handy," she said with a sweet smile, "for roasting pigs."

Scott's mouth curled into a tight, winking grin. He held out several pieces of cedar and balsam fir. "Here."

Ariel took the aromatic wood without comment. When Scott had filled his own arms, they headed toward the float house.

"Did you get your papers marked already?"

"Papers?" For a moment Ariel wondered what papers he meant. Then she shook her head, angry with herself. She hadn't marked the children's schoolwork. On top of that, she'd forgotten her lantern so she'd be unable to walk back in the dark. Worst of all, she'd temporarily forgotten why she'd stormed out of the teacherage. "No. I had to discuss something Angus told me."

Scott nodded. The mention of the name Angus had brought a dismissing smile to his face. "Could it wait a few minutes till I shower? It wasn't bad while I worked, but now that I've stopped I feel cold."

Ariel glanced at his well-defined biceps, then stared across the cove. She nodded mutely.

The float house felt cool while Ariel waited for Scott to shower. She sat at the synthesizer keyboard for a while, but she soon went into the kitchen because the hiss of running water was too loud, too insistent, too evocative.

Scott joined her in a few minutes, buttoning a plaid flannel shirt. His hair was damp from the shower. "I was going to have dinner," he said as he put a package of hamburger meat back in the fridge.

Ariel appreciated that for once he wasn't pestering her with an offer of dinner. She took a deep breath. "I'll join you," she said casually. "If there's enough, that is."

He looked at her, his eyebrows moving close together. He waited as if expecting her to say something more, something that would turn her statement into a witticism. Finally he nodded.

"You know you're welcome." His casual tone matched hers, though his eyes glimmered. "The meal is nothing fancy, I'm afraid."

Ariel made a fire while Scott fixed dinner. Once the kindling had caught and the first logs were burning brightly, she put the spark screen over the aperture. The aroma of balsam and the sounds of crackles and hisses spiced the air with a snug coziness.

Dinner was simple, as Scott had warned: frozen vegetables and thick hamburgers fried to a crispy crust, the insides juicy. As they ate, Ariel told him what Angus had said.

"Did he have the names of the fishermen?"

Ariel dabbed her fingers on a napkin. "Well, no."

"Did he know when this happened?"

"He said everyone knows fishermen do it. He didn't have any specifics."

Scott shrugged his shoulders. "Unfortunately he's right. Fishermen have been known to do that sort of thing. It's no news that humans are the orcas' biggest enemy." He took a healthy bite out of his hamburger.

"What can we do about it?"

"Nothing, unless we hear about a specific incident. We can't indict all fishermen because of a few renegades. A lot of the fishermen like orcas and help when we take our census each year. Just be thankful that orcas are too small to interest the whaling fleets."

"When I think of Flopsy out there with all those fishing boats..." Ariel pushed her plate away. "There must be something we can do, Scott."

"There is." He paused while he chewed. "We can learn about the orcas. We can spread our knowledge so people realize how intelligent and peaceful they are. The older generation grew up hearing that killer whales were vicious. We can teach the new generation the truth."

"I guess." Ariel laced her fingers together and leaned forward. "That doesn't seem like enough, though."

Together, they washed the dishes. Between thoughts about what else she could do for the whales, Ariel marveled at the easy camaraderie between her and Scott. He hadn't made a big deal out of sharing dinner with her, as if he knew that would make her self-conscious.

Maybe he did know. In so many ways they fit together well. She felt comfortable around him, though the comfort was liberally interspersed with moments of desire. As if on cue, the memory of his torso filled her mind.

Scott nudged her with a plate. She dried the plate, hoping that desire would never destroy the friendship between them. She didn't want what was between her and Scott to end, and affairs ended. The emotional weight of physical intimacy could be crushing, as well as life-giving.

"Your mind is off in the middle of the Pacific," Scott commented when he had to nudge her again to wipe the silverware. "Still thinking about saving the whales?"

"Maybe." Ariel looked at him out of the corner of her eye. When he turned away for a moment, she snapped the dish towel at his backside.

"Hey!" Scott put his hand on his buttocks and looked at her with raised eyebrows. "What was that for?"

Chastened, Ariel put away the silverware. She forced airiness into her voice. "Revenge for all those females whose hearts you've broken."

"Kind of a class-action slap?"

"Something like that." Ariel turned from him and faced the flickering warmth of the fire.

Scott stood close behind her and slipped his hands around her elbows. Ariel felt his nearness with every nerve on the back of her body.

"And what," he whispered close to her ear, "would you think if I initiated a class-action embrace for all the men whom you've tantalized with your sexy body?"

"I'd think no such class of men existed."

"You'd be wrong." Scott rubbed her forearms with a lightness that nonetheless trapped her.

Ariel's eyes fluttered shut. "I . . . I'm not a flirt. I don't tantalize men."

"Wrong again." Scott's voice was close behind her, a physical sensation, as well as an auditory temptation. "By your very existence you tantalize."

Ariel concentrated on keeping herself rigid so she wouldn't inadvertently lean back against Scott's hard, aggressive body. Yet despite her concentration, her buttocks grazed his abdomen with an effect like sandpaper against a match.

She jerked from his grasp, but the fire had already flared. She tried to ignore the heat that could so easily consume her and leave only ashes. Ariel stood irresolute, half-facing the doorway, rubbing her arms where he'd touched. "I should go."

"Stay," he said immediately.

Ariel swallowed and listened to the sound of her own heartbeat.

"You know there's something special between us." Scott's voice was low, seductive.

"No. I don't want there to be."

"I don't think either of us has any choice."

Ariel felt her voice go weak. "We always have a choice. We can choose not to succumb if it isn't good for us. Otherwise we aren't people, we're animals."

"I wouldn't hurt you, Ariel."

She looked at him over her shoulder. "Yes, you would. Saying goodbye forever . . . that hurts."

"Every relationship has to end—"

"No!" Ariel whirled to face him. "That's the difference between us, what makes us likely to hurt each other. Look, if I were to say that it hurt to be deserted, would you agree?"

Scott didn't answer at first. "You mean Deborah?"

Ariel nodded.

Leaning back against the countertop, Scott took his time answering. "That hurt," he acknowledged. He paused. "Relationships don't have to end in pain, though."

"Ending *is* pain."

Scott pushed himself away from the counter and began walking toward her. "Ariel . . ."

She backed away. "No," she whispered.

Scott stopped no more than a foot from her pounding heart.

She lowered her gaze to his chest. "You're a good man, Scott. I know you don't want to hurt me." Her voice faded to a sound unheard as she walked into the lab room.

His eyes narrowed to dangerous slits that seemed to distill the essence of his masculinity. "In other words, I'll keep my hands to myself because you think it's best?"

She shook her head once, then met his gaze with a wide-eyed stare of her own. "Because you *know* it's best. An affair has no future, Scott, and I'm no one's plaything."

He covered the distance between them in two slow, deliberate steps. Ariel's heart pounded, yet she didn't lower her gaze, not even when he touched her cheek, flooding her skin with a delicious bath of sensations. Her lip quivered, but she never looked down.

"It isn't fair," he said, "for you to trust me this much. I never asked for that kind of trust. I don't want it."

Ariel raised her chin and widened her eyes. A muscle below Scott's left eye moved. The scent of soap and clean masculinity seeped into her consciousness. It mingled with the pressure of his palm on her cheek in a mixture that threatened to overwhelm every shred of restraint and caution. She said nothing, because she couldn't trust herself to speak.

"I don't want this kind of trust, damn it."

Ariel's eyes widened still more. Her knees were rubbery.

"Don't look at me like that. Say something, Ariel."

She managed to shake her head. "Please . . ."

"Please what? Please hold you?" With his eyes boring into her soul, Scott pulled her toward him, one hand claiming her waist and the other resting at the side of her breast.

"Please, Scott." Her voice was almost too soft to be heard.

"Please touch you?" He cupped her breast, the insistent movements of his thumb brushing the tender nipple to hardness, pouring life and energy and desire into her body.

Ariel splayed her hand against his chest and tried ineffectually to retreat. Her actions only served to heighten the pleasure of his touch.

"Please kiss you?" His face descended inexorably toward hers.

Ariel's lips trembled, yet they opened of their own will.

And then Scott stopped, so close that she felt the heat of his breath on her lips. Though his thumb paused also, the hard peak of her breast pulsed under his fingers.

Scott stayed like that for two breaths, then three. Then Ariel lost count.

Abruptly Scott lowered his hand and turned his back to her. His shoulders rose and fell. A log on the fireplace crackled sharply. Ariel crossed her arms over her chest and tried to relieve the ache in her breasts by hugging them fiercely.

When Scott faced her again, his smile was composed and seemingly untroubled. "If you want, I'll give you a ride back to the bay when I pick up Deb."

Ariel tried to copy his calmness. A smile that should have been more robust crept across her face, then wilted. "I'll stay."

Ariel watched as Scott turned the hydrophone speakers to a murmured hush so they could hear if the whales happened to approach. He stretched out in a chair by the fireplace. How, she wondered, could he appear so calm?

The answer was painfully obvious. That close encounter of the sensual kind had meant less to him than to her.

An inner voice clamored to refute this explanation. Scott simply had an easier time camouflaging his emotions than expressing them. Ariel shook her head indecisively. "When do you pick up Deb?"

Scott glanced at his wristwatch. "I could go now, but the Fearsons expect me a bit later. I have about an hour."

"I see." Aside from being a delightful child, Deb also served as chaperon until she fell asleep on the bed in the other room. After that, nothing roused the girl, not even when Scott carried her out to the *Simoom Queen* for the ride home. But if Scott's self-restraint proved anything, though, it was that they didn't need a chaperon.

Or did they? Ariel didn't wait to think through the answer to her question. She sat on the rug, curling her legs under her with a slow sensuality that lingered from the aborted embrace. Her bones felt as if they were made of molasses. Yet Scott, fingers laced behind his head, appeared unaffected.

The fire crackled, filling a long, healing silence. Ariel had learned during their evenings in the lab that they could share silences. Anyone could share words. Sharing silence was rarer.

Desire still coiled within her. Ariel tried to drive the languor from her flesh with words. "Who'd think," she said, "that you could whale watch in front of a fireplace?"

A quiet smile lit Scott's face. "This is wonderful."

The heat of the fire toasted Ariel's cheek and filled her with a sense of closeness and familiarity. When Scott's eyes closed, she studied the lines and texture of his face. The tension was thick between them, yet she felt she could ask or tell him anything, in safety. She edged closer to him, so that her outstretched fingertips touched his foot.

The casual contact of her fingertips rekindled the deep hunger that Scott barely had under control. Right now he wanted to kiss her, to peel her clothes off, to hear her moan his name with pleasure.

Instead, he sat and talked as if nothing had happened, as if the memory of her body wasn't burned indelibly into the flesh of his hand. This woman, with her talk of trust, didn't play fair.

The conversation wandered into a discussion of books, one of the gentle, nonthreatening byways they both enjoyed exploring. Scott gave the languid talk only half his mind. The other half studied Ariel.

Firelight washed over her face, bathing it in a rippling halo of beauty. Her casual posture was like that of a lithe goddess. Everything about her proclaimed that she was aroused, from the feather-like touch of her fingers to her restless shifting that negligently revealed shadowed thighs under the rising hem of her dress.

And according to her he wasn't supposed to sit beside her, to run his fingertips down her cheek, along her neck, down the swell of her breasts to the firm nipples that beckoned through her dress.

Scott clenched his jaw. He was more deeply involved than he'd ever intended, or he would never have stopped. A kiss, a caress, and she would have melted in his arms. Knowing that, he'd still stopped.

I will convince you, he promised her silently. *My feelings for you*—he hesitated, shocked that he was thinking along these lines—*my feelings don't have to hurt you. The time for patience will soon be over.*

Soon.

Through the classroom window a perfect rainbow arched over the peak of a distant mountain. Ariel turned from her perch on the bookshelf by the window to face the children. "Some people say there's a pot of gold at the end of the rainbow."

"Oh, boy," Ronald said. "Gold." The young boy rose from his seat and took a step toward the door. As the class laughed, Damien laid a restraining hand on his younger cousin's chest, guiding Ronald back to his seat.

"Don't worry, Ronald," Ariel said. "School will be over soon enough, and you can chase the pot of gold."

Ariel let several children share their fantasies about what they'd do with all that gold. This discussion of rainbows, filling the last minutes of the next-to-last school day before the two-week Christmas holiday, had ranged from the physical makeup of rainbows to fantasies about their accompanying pots of gold.

Tammy Fearson shared her hope that a gorgeous boy might come with the gold. Ariel turned to the wisp of shimmering, colored light that soared from the head of the bay. For just a moment she allowed herself to think that this was *her* rainbow, in honor of her birthday. Thirty-five years old today...no longer young, even by her own standards. Ariel shoved the thought aside.

There was a pause in the discussion. Deb, as usual, sat with hands primly folded, saying nothing.

Ariel smiled at her. "What about you, Deb? What do you think is at the end of the rainbow?"

Deb glanced from side to side before answering. "Nothing."

Damien Prescott piped up. "I'll bet she has a scientifically correct reason for saying that, too."

The class tittered, none louder than Tammy, who smiled at Damien with adoring eyes before glancing at Deb with a frown.

"That's right," Deb said with a tight-lipped, determined nod. "My daddy says rainbows are illusions that pretend to be real and beautiful, but when you try to touch them there's nothing there. He says you have to be wary of illusions that are only empty air."

Ariel glanced out the window. Such a glorious beacon of hope and beauty... but by the age of thirty-five, wasn't she finally ready to admit that Scott was right? "What do *you* think, Deb?"

The girl again glanced from side to side. "I can see the rainbow," she said quietly, nodding in the direction of the window. "Something is there, even if I don't know what. Sometimes I think grown-ups are silly."

Deb's face briefly glowed as the children laughed, this time in agreement. Then her face turned serious again. "Still, my daddy knows so much..." She left the sentence dangling.

Ariel returned to her desk, subdued by Deb's words. What kind of eight-year-old wasn't sure whether to believe in rainbows?

Ariel reminded the children to bring their costumes for the Christmas concert tomorrow, then dismissed them ten minutes early and shooed them all outside. Ten minutes of peace and quiet was the only present she was likely to get this birthday.

Ariel silently scolded herself as she sorted the mound of papers on her desk. People with birthdays close to Christmas didn't get many presents. She'd been resigned to that by the time she was in kindergarten.

The birthday cards she'd received cut two ways, as well. The card that arrived yesterday had lifted her spirits at first, then left her with a cloud misting her heart. Grant, the man she'd thought she loved for two years, was now the father of an eight-pound, seven-ounce boy. A baby, soft and smooth and needy.

The aftertaste of the news had been a forlorn tang of aloneness—a sense that while a lot of people cared for her somewhat, no one cared for her with intensity and devotion.

She felt restless. Perhaps she should fly out to civilization over the Christmas holidays after all. She'd rejected the idea before, though, because there hadn't seemed anywhere to go. Victoria? Her parents would greet her politely, but their house didn't feel like home. Clearwater? She'd lived there before Blackfish Bay, but she no longer belonged there, either.

An image of Honeymoon Nook sprang to her mind. She shook her head.

Scott and Deb, and even the orcas, had become a family of sorts. But what, exactly, was her relationship with Scott? What had she dared to allow the relationship to be, and what had her caution kept it from being?

Ariel took a pocket mirror from her desk drawer and looked at herself. She couldn't see her whole face, just round, disconnected sections. As near as she could judge, it wasn't a bad face, though not as attractive as she could wish. Above all, though, it was a thirty-five-year-old face. With her fingertip she traced the lines radiating from the corner of her eye.

She snapped the mirror closed and put it back in the drawer. Was a brief, intense fire better than a long-lasting coziness? Ordinarily she'd answer no. Today she wasn't sure.

She had a good job, security, friends, self-respect, more money than she could spend. She worked with children who mattered to her and who would remember her. She made her own way in life. She was her own person. Wasn't that enough?

Ariel stuffed the remaining papers into an unsorted pile. She gazed out the window, not at the children but at the vanishing rainbow.

It was, she realized, possible to be content for 364 days and on the 365th day be miserable about all the things that ordinarily made you happy.

Drumming her fingers against the bookcase, Ariel waited for the school boat to pick up the children. Even if not a single soul knew this was her birthday, she would pamper herself. She'd take a long, soaking bubble bath and then experiment with a new way of fixing her hair. Salmon steaks—fresh ones, this time—from a student would make a succulent dish to eat by candlelight. She'd dress up, too, before she went to Honeymoon Nook. This navy blue dress was fine for school, but tonight she wanted something more . . . well, more human.

Tonight she didn't want to be a teacher or musician or co-worker or any of the other roles that defined and limited her existence. Tonight she just wanted to be a woman.

Scott glanced at his wristwatch, then muttered under his breath. The hands of the watch didn't seem to have moved.

Ariel might be here any time now.

He tried to continue labeling the oscilloscope printouts of whale calls. This one looked like sonar clicks. Or was it a travel-coordination call? He should know by now—sonar clicks had the most distinctive wave pattern of all orca sounds—but he couldn't seem to concentrate. Scott pushed the printouts across his desk and laced his fingers behind his head.

This was ridiculous. He couldn't sleep. Now he couldn't work. Ariel was driving him crazy.

Metal crashed in the kitchen.

Scott charged in there, finding Deb on hands and knees to retrieve an empty pot.

"What do you think you're doing?" he demanded.

Deb's eyes went wide. "Fixing dinner," she said in a small voice. One finger moved in a meager point toward a box on the counter. "Macaroni and cheese."

Until he saw Deb's expression, Scott hadn't even been aware that he'd yelled. He took a slow, deep breath. "I'm sorry, Deb. It's not you fault. I guess I'm in a bad mood."

"You're an old grouch, all right."

Now he was picking on a helpless little girl. Annoyed with himself and even more annoyed with Ariel for reducing him to this state, Scott glanced again at his wrist.

When he looked up, Deb was watching him. Her thin face had that serious look of ageless wisdom that sometimes made him forget her youth. "She'll be here," the girl assured him. "You know she doesn't come until after dinner."

Scott opened his mouth to protest that he wasn't waiting for Ariel, then caught himself. He suddenly whirled Deb into the air and deposited her, shrieking, on the stool by the counter.

"Let's make dinner together," he said.

Ariel still hadn't arrived by the time Scott had put away the last of the dinner dishes. He considered going back to work, but knew he couldn't concentrate. He wandered through the room where Deb was working on a jigsaw puzzle, then went outside. When he realized that he was scanning the spot where the trail opened to the beach, he slammed his palm against the door.

He went inside.

This relationship, teetering forever on the razor edge of desire, was cutting him to pieces. Simple self-preservation demanded change and resolution. Ariel felt it too, he was sure. That look in her eyes screamed that she *wanted* him, even though her words pushed him away.

Scott shoved several logs onto the fire. He paced the small open area in the middle of the room. When he got to the bed, his footsteps slowed, though he made himself return to the fiercely crackling fire.

The drawer in the bedside table held a new box of birth control, purchased on his last trip to Alert Bay. He hadn't been willing to buy them at the general store, because he didn't want the clerks to speculate about Ariel. He would do nothing to hurt Ariel. Nothing. Surely she must realize that.

Somehow Ariel had managed to get him to accept that a physical relationship would be bad for her. He wouldn't hurt her, though. In fact, he felt . . . well, he . . . he cared for her. Ariel, moreover, was a big girl now. She was responsible for her own heart.

And he was responsible for his. Could anything hurt worse than this unresolved hell?

"Tonight," he said loudly.

Deb was stifling a yawn as she poked her head in the doorway. "What about tonight, Daddy?"

Scott ran his hand through his hair. "You look tired, kiddo. Tonight you're going to sleep early."

Chapter Nine

Deb turned at the doorway. "Will you tuck me in tonight, Ariel?"

"Of course, hon." Ariel stretched as she pushed her chair back from the desk where she'd cataloged whale calls for the past hour. She glanced at Scott as she went to sit in the rocking chair near the fire. He wasn't quite licking his lips, yet all evening he'd watched her like a ravenous orca eyeing a plump chinook salmon.

"Hurry into your pajamas," Scott said.

"Yes, Daddy."

After the girl vanished into the other room, Scott warmed his hands at the wood stove. He raked Ariel with another long, deep look, then opened the doors that turned the stove into a fireplace. The fire roared and flared at the sudden rush of air.

"Isn't it early for Deb to go to bed?"

"She seemed tired," Scott answered. "We'll stay here tonight so she can get a good night's rest."

Ariel stretched and stifled a yawn.

"You look as if you're ready for bed, too." Though Scott spoke calmly, the intensity of his gaze added layers of meaning to the remark.

"I'm only a little tired."

He continued to warm his hands by the fire, standing in a decidedly male posture. Whenever he stood still, he looked like a model for a heroic statue. Or was it her imagination that supplied the heroism? Probably. If he posed deliberately, even a bit, it would turn her off rather than the opposite.

Ariel shifted self-consciously away from his scrutiny. Why had she fixed her hair and worn her best silk dress? And why had sitting for the past hour felt like such a squirming torture?

Many questions, few answers. Ariel put the thoughts out of her head. "Your hands must be like toast," she said.

Scott looked at his palms, then up at her. He walked toward her. The sense of purpose in his step made Ariel's heart jump.

"Scott?"

He didn't answer. He stood behind her, out of sight though not out of awareness.

"Scott?" Ariel's voice was small.

He put his palms on either side of her neck. They were indeed warm. Ariel wondered if they wouldn't have felt hot regardless of the fireplace.

"I get it," Ariel joked. "You're going to strangle me."

Scott's hands stirred, though he still said nothing. His thumbs moved in slow circles behind her ears, teasing the sensitive stretch where her scalp began. She drank the delicate excitement of his touch. It was a potent brew that immediately set her head and heart revolving. She glanced back.

"Don't worry," he said softly. "You're safe with me."

"I wasn't worried. Why would I be worried?" Then she remembered her joke about strangling. How could she have forgotten so soon?

When he was touching her, she forgot everything. Almost everything, that is.

Scott continued kneading her shoulders, igniting tongues of flame that licked her skin. Ariel took a deep breath, then relaxed against his hands as he dragged his fingers along her nape.

"That feels good," she whispered. Was this what she wanted, why she'd dressed up?

Maybe. But she wasn't sure what she wanted, and she didn't want to think about it.

Deb appeared at the door in her pajamas. "I'm ready," she said cheerfully.

Scott dropped his hands as Ariel stood. Without looking back, she followed Deb as the girl climbed into bed and turned off the lamp.

"Good night, Deb."

The girl threw her arms around Ariel's neck and squeezed. "Good night, Ariel."

Deb's smile was so warm and uncomplicated compared with the expression on Scott's face. Ariel pulled the covers up to the girl's neck, then pressed a fingertip against her nose.

Deb giggled. "Your hair looks pretty tonight. I like it when you wear a dress, too."

"I'm glad somebody noticed." Ariel leaned close. "Can you keep a secret?"

Deb nodded.

Bringing her lips to the girl's ear, Ariel said, "Today's my birthday."

The girl giggled again, then sought out Ariel's ear for a return whisper. "Happy birthday, Ariel. I love you."

Ariel sat upright. Her vision of the girl became a watery shimmer of pink against the shadows of the room. She blinked, then smiled. "Me, too."

"I'll make you a card tomorrow."

Ariel squeezed Deb's hand. The girl's affection was so much simpler and easier to accept than what her father offered.

Scott came in and pressed against Ariel's thigh as he leaned over his daughter for a hug. Ariel suffered the closeness for a few seconds before a surging swell in her chest threatened to suffocate her. She rose from the bed and watched from the middle of the darkened room as Scott hugged Deb.

Ariel slipped outside to give them privacy. After all, no matter how much she felt she belonged to this family, she didn't.

Cold air drove the warmth of Scott's house from her lungs as she watched the stars play hide-and-seek behind a lone cloud. The clear sky warned of possible freezing temperatures tonight. She'd have to be careful when she walked home.

No. She didn't want to think about returning to the solitude of the teacherage, or about why she'd come here tonight, or about not belonging to anyone. She didn't want to think, period.

Slow, deep breaths clouded the air in front of her face. With conscious effort, Ariel loosened herself from thought. She was aware of the cold caress of the air, though her nerves still carried messages of warmth and stimulation.

She padded aimlessly along the plank sidewalk around the float house. She stopped when she reached the *Simoom Queen*. The wheelhouse, she thought vaguely, meant warmth.

Ariel climbed on board. She started the oil heater full blast, then sat on Scott's stool and didn't think.

An indeterminate time passed. Darkness surrounded her, as if to shroud her surroundings into unreality. The boat stirred softly on the water, as if alive. Slowly the air grew tolerable, then warm.

Ariel picked up the microphone of the boat's radiophone. Without turning it on, she lifted the cold, silent microphone to her mouth. She had no idea what words would fall from her mouth.

"Hello," she whispered. "Is anyone out there?"

The warmth filling her nostrils clashed with the coldness of the metal in her palm. When she squinted at the glow from the float-house windows, the light fractured into shards.

"I just tucked in someone else's daughter," Ariel heard herself say. "Deb told me she loved me, and I couldn't bring myself to say the words to her. Even though I do love her."

Uh-oh. Those words started her thinking. Ariel slowed her breathing, trying to regain the floating sense of awareness without thought. It wouldn't come. Reality pressed in too heavily, seeping in with the warmth from the heater.

"You know something truly amazing? I think I..." She paused, pressing the cold metal against her lips. "I think I love Scott, too."

Ariel drew a pierced heart in the mist gathering on the wheelhouse windows. She stared at it.

"Or at least I think I do. I'm not exactly an expert on the subject." She rubbed out the heart with the side of her fist. The glass was cold and damp.

"It's so different from what I expected. I mean, I thought I'd been in love before. But if I love Scott, then what I felt before was a pale imitation of love. Does that make sense?" She paused, waiting for an answer that would never come.

Footsteps echoed through the lonesome darkness. Ariel put down the microphone as the boat rocked. The footsteps approached the wheelhouse.

The door slid open with a blast of noise and cold. Scott was silhouetted against the light from a window of the float house.

"Hi," she said.

Scott pulled the door closed. "So this is where you were hiding."

She hadn't been hiding, but she didn't bother to disagree. Ariel blinked as he struck a match and lit the kerosene lantern that hung from the ceiling. Her heart beat faster.

"What are you doing out here, having a sauna?" Scott reached to turn down the heater.

Ariel leaned over his back and blew out the lantern, sending blessed darkness around her once more. Scott jerked upright.

Even in the dark he seemed to fill the wheelhouse. He filled Ariel's mind, too, crowding out everything but awareness of his presence. He was right about the wheelhouse being too hot, but a shiver spun down her back nonetheless.

He edged closer. "Why did you come out here?"

"I don't know." With every breath his essence crept into her lungs, filling her.

"I think I know."

Why, she wondered, was his voice so hard?

"You were running from me, Ariel."

"No."

"Yes." Scott closed the gap between them. His legs branded her thighs with their touch. Flames kindled in her abdomen, flickering and flaring.

"You were running," he said, "the same way you're always running and putting barriers between us."

Ariel nodded in the dark. He was a wise man. She usually did do that. Not tonight, though.

He seized her shoulders and pulled her to a standing position that pressed her breasts against the firm promise of his chest. "Not tonight," he said.

Ariel nodded again, agreeing. The motion brushed her forehead against his chin. She repeated the nod to draw every bit of sensation from the contact, channeling the energy from his flesh toward the leaping impatience in the pit of her stomach. Dizziness buzzed into her ears and along her nerves. She leaned against his chest.

"I won't let you run from me anymore," Scott said. His hands roamed from her shoulders to her back. The contact turned her bones into rubber.

With an effort she pulled away. Scott took a half step toward her. Ariel put one finger against his lips. "Don't say anymore," she said. She took his hand and backed toward the steps that led to the deeper blackness of the cabin.

Scott let their arms stretch between them. "What do you think you're doing now?"

Still facing him, Ariel felt blindly for the step. "The Lord only knows," she said with a tremor in her voice that grew into a throaty chuckle, "because I sure don't. But whatever it is, I'm not running. Not tonight."

Ariel stopped when his unmoving hand tethered her. Silence stretched between them as taut as their joined arms.

Ariel rippled her fingers under his touch. The simple movement was a hint, a promise, a declaration. Electricity seemed to flow between them, making Scott's shadowed face seem luminous in the glow from the windows.

"Ariel," Scott whispered as he stepped toward her and down the stairs, "if I live to be a hundred, I will never know what to expect from you."

Her soft laugh sounded sensual even to her own ears. "Good."

And then his arms were around her and his lips were on hers. His kiss began with overpowering insistence, as if to ensure her cooperation. When Ariel met the thrust of his tongue with her own, the insistence remained but was softened and yet sharpened. She met his determination without hesitation, blending her mouth with his. Their energies fed on each other and doubled, then tripled in power.

The force of Scott's embrace drove Ariel's thighs against a table, unseen in the pitch-dark of the cabin. Without breaking the kiss, she sat on the edge of the table. She put her hands on his buttocks and urged him between her knees so that his torso met hers as they kissed. Weakness and desire melted her as she surrendered to Scott's lips.

A flash of rationality escaped with a whimper. There was a bunk somewhere in the darkness that was more appropriate than this tabletop. The thought disappeared as Scott's roving hand explored the softness of her breast with sure touches that set her body quivering. His fingers circled the peak, surrounded it without quite touching, then withdrew over and over till she thought her chest would explode with unrelieved longing and pleasure. She writhed under his caress, trying to force his hand to complete its journey. When his thumb finally brushed over the swollen pebble, Ariel gasped and threw back her head.

"Ouch!"

"What's the matter?" His breath was warm against her neck.

Ariel felt behind her. The edge of a cabinet. "I bumped my head."

He drew her up to the snug harbor of his arms. "I'll get the lantern."

"Don't." Ariel leaned her cheek on his chest. His heart was pounding, just as hers was. "I like what you do in the dark." The light would be an intruder between them, a witness to what belonged to the night.

She felt his chest rise in a long, slow breath. "In that case," he said, "there's a bed three feet to your right." He took a step, guiding her toward the bed.

"Scott MacKenzie," she said in a voice made husky by the friction of his body as they slowly danced sideways, "are you such a caveman that you'd take advantage of a defenseless woman who's been knocked on the head?"

"Absolutely."

"I was hoping you'd say that."

Ariel's calf touched the bed. She moved out of Scott's embrace, though his hand lingered on her hip. "Wait a minute." She began fumbling with the top button of her dress, wishing for a moment that the cabin wasn't so dark.

"What are you doing?"

Ariel undid the button, then paused. She felt the hint of a blush began to stir along her neck. "Unbuttoning my dress. The material is delicate."

The words seemed to vibrate through her as her fingers sought the next button. Scott was a silent shadow that seemed to absorb all her energy and awareness. The dress slid from her shoulders to her hips, the rustling of the fabric shockingly, embarrassingly loud.

And yet also, Ariel realized, shockingly sensual. Scott moved his hand from under a drape of fabric. She was

aware of his shadow moving, then of the bed sighing as he
sat on it. His eyes were invisible in the dark. He said nothing, yet she was utterly certain of his attention as she flicked
the dress off her hips in a chorus of erotic whispers.

Silent energy flowed from Scott as her hands sought the
waistband of her half slip. "I'm taking off my slip now."
The crinoline rustled with strident sexuality as it joined the
dress at her feet.

Ariel's breathing was ragged as she stepped from the pile
of clothes. In the light, she knew, she'd never dare undress
so blatantly in front of him, but the darkness unleashed a
playfulness that surprised and emboldened her.

"Ariel," Scott whispered. "Come to bed."

His words sent a sweet shudder through her. She took a
long breath before she spoke. "I'm not quite ready yet." She
smiled at his nearly invisible shape. "I wore my best linge-
rie. Do you like it?"

"Yes."

When Ariel felt his hand on her thigh, she stepped backward. "Just look," she chided, "don't touch."

"Look?" His groan held a mixture of amusement,
arousal and frustration. "How am I supposed to do that?"

"I especially like the lace on the bra. It makes me feel
feminine."

"Ariel," Scott said low in his throat.

She reached for the front clasp, pausing to put an instant's silence around the sound of the snap. "Here," she
said as she tossed the bra in the direction of the shadow,
which seemed to quiver and storm. "Isn't the lace delicate?" She faced the shadow boldly, arms at her sides. Her
knees held her upright despite their shakiness.

The shadow made an impatient sound of desire that sent
Ariel's insides churning. His desire was her desire. Her
readiness was his readiness. Without hesitation she lowered
the last of her clothes.

"Now," she said in a voice that trembled through the
silky silence, "I'm—"

She hadn't finished before the growling shadow was on her, kissing her neck, grasping her with a feverish haste that brought the swirling energy in her abdomen to a boil. His face brushed against the soft neediness of her breasts, sought and found a hard nipple. Ariel whimpered and her legs went soft. Together they tumbled on the bed in a jigsaw puzzle of arms and legs.

His clothes were a hindrance. She helped him undress, flinging his clothes carelessly in her eagerness to feel his skin against her skin, his body against hers.

When his hands sought her core, she opened to him without hesitation. "Now, Scott." She grew frantic as she urged their bodies together. "Please don't make me wait. Oh, please, now."

When he thrust into her, the jigsaw puzzle was complete, the last piece lodged triumphantly in place. An exhilarating sense of fullness burgeoned in Ariel's soul and body. Her earlier boldness yielded to Scott's masculinity as he drove everything but need from her mind. She gasped as she bobbed helplessly on a wave of overwhelming pleasure that rose abruptly and peaked resoundingly, leaving her floating on the strong currents of Scott's motions.

Her lips sought his neck and her hands roamed his body, thanking him and trying to give as much as she'd received. As he moved against her in the dark, Ariel's abdomen began to coil again, tighter and tighter. With startling suddenness she felt another wave building inside her, stirred by Scott's hard thrusts. A long cry slipped from her lips as the second wave spiraled, crested and crashed over her in an engulfing bath of pure, everlasting delight.

The cabin was dark when Scott's eyes flicked open.

He was sweating. There was something, in a dream perhaps, about starting to turn down a heater and not finishing. Maybe the heat had roused him. Or maybe the subtle unfamiliarity of his surroundings had kept him from sliding into the full depths of sleep.

He started to rise but was hampered by an arm flung across his chest. His heart started pounding as he turned his head.

It was Ariel, invisible in the dark but undeniably Ariel. Dear God, it hadn't been a dream. This evening had been too good to be real. Yet it was. Scott ran a hand through his hair as he groggily reconstructed the memory of the most incredible sex of his life.

No, not sex. Passion.

Somehow Ariel had loosened all the barriers inside him. Inside herself, too. When this magnificent lady gave herself, she did so without reserve or inhibition. She was as eager to take pleasure as to give it. In the end it was her greediness more than her desire to please that had driven him beyond the limits of passion and into frenzy.

There's been no self-consciousness in their first coupling, only fierce, not-to-be-denied desire. Their second time together had been slower, more directed, more controlled and yet no less overwhelming. She'd made him feel and perform as eagerly as an awestruck teenager experiencing the magic for the first time.

Scott slipped from under Ariel's arm. She made a soft noise as she turned over in her sleep. The gentle sound made him pause in the act of going to the wheelhouse to turn down the heater. A smile touched his lips.

He shook his head as he mouthed her name. His profound pleasure wasn't only, or even primarily, because of what she'd done in bed. It was because of who she was. Scott extended his hand toward her, tempted to wake her and make love again.

She needed her rest, though, what with the school Christmas concert tomorrow. He let his hand fall to his side.

That reminded him that he'd forgotten to help Deb one last time with her lines in the play. Too late for that now. While he was awake, though, he should check the float house. The fire would have gone out by now, and the oil heater should be adjusted so Deb wouldn't be cold.

Scott stretched his mouth in a huge yawn. Sometimes, he thought with a look toward Ariel's dim shape, duty was hard to choose over pleasure. He felt around for his shoes and slacks. His shirt was nowhere to be found, so he took a rumpled blanket from the floor and draped it over his shoulders.

In the wheelhouse he lit the lantern and looked at the boat's clock. Precisely midnight. The beginning of a new day.

Before he left he glanced into the cabin. Ariel, lying with erotic innocence on her stomach, was a sight that melted parts of him he hadn't known were frozen. Aside from a sheet twisted across the back of her knees, her splendor was uncovered. The sight of her curves made blood rush to his loins. Her hair was loose and tangled. He knew she'd claim it was a mess, yet she looked more beautiful now, basking in the golden satisfaction of a woman who'd been thoroughly loved, than ever before.

Scott's breath jelled in his lungs. He knew he should check on his daughter, but he was helpless to move. He gritted his teeth and willed himself to leave. A moment of panic sliced at him. Though he tried lifting a foot, he remained in place, rendered motionless and powerless by this disarming woman who'd slipped past his deepest defenses.

Scott squeezed his eyes shut. Only then did he manage to leave the wheelhouse. Breathing raggedly, he steeled himself against midnight.

Billowing dreams eased Ariel out of early-morning sleep and into a world of gentle shapes and fuzzy shadows. She nuzzled her cheek against Scott's deliciously warm arm, glorying in his nearness in a chaste yet sensuous way.

Not for long, however, did she savor the innocence of near wakefulness. Nature called, probably the only thing that could drag her prematurely from this incredible bed at the side of this incredible man.

Scott didn't stir when she climbed over him and opened the porthole curtain. It was nearly dawn, and December dawns came late. Time to leave for school. Ariel yawned. Even the most magical of nights had to end. Life always began again.

The trace of light from the porthole was scarcely enough to locate her clothes. As she picked the silk dress from the floor, she wondered how the delicate material had fared. There were no dry cleaners on the island.

As Ariel slipped the dress over her head, she smiled at the memory roused by the wispy sound of the cloth. This was the last day of classes before the holidays. Two weeks to explore the byways of love that she'd denied herself for months.

Ariel knelt beside the bunk and rested her chin on the mattress as she stared at Scott's peaceful face. Last night had been remarkable. Scott had been magnificent. He'd opened the doors to whole new levels of satisfaction. Just when she'd thought she could experience nothing greater, he magically opened yet another door. She supposed she should be chagrined at her unprecedented and unabashed responsiveness, but instead it assured her that making love hadn't been a mistake.

A smile warmed her heart as she brushed a strand of hair off his forehead. "Thank you," she whispered.

He didn't stir.

"Scott?" She shook his shoulder gently, wondering exactly what time it was and whether there was enough time before school to make love one more time.

When she shook him again, he still didn't stir.

"I see where Deb got the genes for being a sound sleeper," she said in a normal tone of voice. Scott didn't budge.

A sudden rush of forbidden images made Ariel's mouth go dry. Images of daring ways to waken him. Images that would ordinarily make her blush, but which might be fun to explore with Scott. He made her feel that anything she dared to try—or not try, for that matter—would meet with enthusiastic acceptance. She stared down his body and hesitated. . . .

In the end it wasn't propriety but time that decided for her. She couldn't be late for work.

With a frustrated smile Ariel rose. At the steps she turned and blew a kiss at Scott. "I love you," she said. She wished she could hear him respond with those same three words.

"I love you," she repeated, "with all my heart."

And then she left.

Tammy Fearson wagged her tail.

The audience had laughed the first time she'd shaken the fluffy appendage of coat hanger and yarn, so now she did it whenever she had a speaking line. It was an effective trick, Ariel thought. Tammy had dramatic flair.

Tammy gave her squirrel tail one last shake. "But why, Mr. Woodsman, are you going to cut down our tree?"

Deb, also in a squirrel costume, stood stiffly. Her tail didn't wag and her mouth didn't open, though she had the next line.

Ariel leaned forward, silently urging Deb to speak. Unfortunately Deb had stage fright rather than dramatic flair. Her face was blank, her eyes wide. So far she'd missed every one of her four lines in the play.

Tammy saved the moment by putting her hand—or was it paw?—around Deb's shoulder. "My sister wants to know why you can't cut down the oak next door instead. Don't you, sister?"

When Tammy nudged her, Deb managed to nod.

Ariel relaxed again while the woodsman, played with macho swagger by Damien Prescott, explained that he needed to cut a fir for a Christmas tree. She glanced at the audience, but from behind the props she couldn't see if Scott had arrived in the past two minutes. Ariel stifled her impatience.

The play ended in a swirl of applause and excitement. As the children hustled into place for the carol sing-along that would end the performance, Ariel noticed Deb stiffly facing the chalkboard. Smart, sensitive Deb wasn't used to the humiliation of failure. Ariel took a step toward the girl.

Tammy got there first. She put her arm around Deb's shoulder. "Cheer up, kid. Everybody messes up sometime." Tammy was too well mannered to do more than smile briefly at the knowledge that even the genius had a weakness. "Stick by me during the singing, and I'll make sure you don't get lost again."

A rush of gladness filled Ariel's heart, but she didn't have time to savor it. She hurried to the front of the stage area and raised her baton, which was actually a pencil with a Santa eraser stuck on the end. The children didn't sing as well as usual, but the audience wasn't critical.

After the concert Ariel mingled with parents and relatives, accepting their congratulations and holiday greetings. She kept scanning the crowd, though it was obvious Scott wasn't there. His aura would have shone over the group like a beacon.

One of the Mrs. Prescotts handed Ariel a fruitcake tied in Christmas wrap and left to take her children home. It was, after all, the last afternoon.

Ariel clutched the fruitcake as she gave the room a final look. She tried to restrain her imagination, which clamored to supply all sorts of reasons why Scott hadn't come.

She saw Deb near the windows, standing forlornly beside Mrs. Fearson. Pretending she hadn't noticed the approach of another of the Mrs. Prescotts, Ariel walked toward Deb.

"Where's your father?"

Mrs. Fearson put her arm around Deb. "I'll take the girl home with me."

Ariel tried to keep her face expressionless. "Oh?"

"Scott came by about ten and said that some big shots had to meet him in Alert Bay today. He asked if I'd pick up Deb."

"I see." Ariel wanted to grab Mrs. Fearson by the coat collar and demand to know if Scott regretted last night. The image of herself lifting a woman fifty pounds heavier brought a threadbare smile to her face. "It's too bad he missed the play."

"No, it's not," Deb muttered.

"Scott also wanted me to tell you there'd be no research tonight," Mrs. Fearson said.

Ariel blinked and turned away. A whole night to think. To worry. To imagine messages behind Scott's absence.

Mrs. Fearson was eyeing her with a look of veiled appraisal, so Ariel willed her face to blandness. The island was small and gossip spread quickly. "Well," Ariel began aimlessly. Then politeness came to her rescue. "Have a merry Christmas."

Mrs. Fearson said something that didn't need an answer, which was lucky. Ariel wasn't really listening.

Deb watched her closely. Ariel glanced down and realized she was mangling the innocent fruitcake. She shifted it to her other hand.

Tammy ran over and pulled on Deb's arm. "Come on, kid. A bunch of us are going to play outside."

Deb took half a step toward Tammy. "You want *me* to play with you?"

"Come on," Tammy said impatiently.

Deb wore a dazed smile, which faded only briefly when she took a last look at Ariel. She dashed from the room.

Ariel struggled to maintain a neutral expression as a pair of grandparents joined the conversation. The crowd and the small talk seemed to smother her. She tugged at the collar of her dress, wishing for fresh air. Wishing to be somewhere else, anywhere else. Wishing she wasn't such a fool as to always get her hopes up.

Ariel suffered through the conversation, still trying to decide what to do. Each polite word felt like an anvil on her tongue.

She had to get out of here.

The sea was heavy, making the *Simoom Queen* climb laboriously up a wave before sliding briskly down. Scott didn't mind the rough waves, though, because they hurried the boat's pace. Nonetheless, he leaned forward in his seat as if to lend his weight to the boat's progress.

The radiophone hissed out words to which Scott paid scant attention. It was only fishermen complaining about the weather. The darned radio had caused him enough grief today by bringing him a summons to Alert Bay for a meeting with visiting marine biologists from Belgium.

Scott began humming to himself. All he had wanted to do today was stretch out beside Ariel. He could see it in his mind. He could see *her* as she'd been framed in the light from the lantern at midnight. His imagination pictured nothing else but her. There was no room for walls or furniture in a mind brimming with thoughts of Ariel. He could see her and feel her and taste her and smell her.

Maybe they would make love right away, maybe not. They would certainly talk, though. If he shut his eyes, he could hear the music of her voice, filling him with a sense of wonder and trust he thought he'd lost in his youth. He hadn't felt this young in ages.

Well, he didn't feel *that* young. The urges he exercised upon Ariel's imagined body were adult in the extreme. It was more that he felt...hopeful. As if he'd awakened without realizing he'd been asleep. As if he'd rediscovered faith and sharing.

Scott concentrated on the sea. If a wave caught the *Queen* side on, there'd be no warm reunion tomorrow.

He couldn't wait to talk to her. Somehow he knew that she shared his enthusiasm and joyousness. He could feel it in the air, as strongly as the attraction he'd felt that first day he saw her.

Did he love her?

His smile faded when he recalled how she'd slipped away before he awoke this morning. Before now, love had brought him disaster and pain. A niggling spark of skeptical reason warned that the pain might be proportionally greater this time.

Ariel's voice—not her words, only her sultry, seductive tone from last night in the dark—dispelled his dismal thoughts. Scott pushed at the throttle, though it was wide open.

The radio began to squawk again. Scott recognized Angus's voice, calling Alert Bay Airlines. Scott was humming as he turned down the volume before the old man completed his call.

Chapter Ten

The next morning brought wind and rain that turned the teacherage roof into a giant, throbbing drum. Ariel waited for the storm to diminish, hoping that this Pacific gale wouldn't last for days. She paced from the living room to her bedroom and back, then rode her exercise bicycle. When she finished, rain still sheeted across the kitchen window.

Ariel chewed on a carrot, scarcely noticing the taste or the crunching sound as she stared at the soggy playground. She wished the island had telephones. Then she could curl under the bed covers and talk to Scott instead of having to brave the storm. Even worse than the thought of getting chilled and soaked was the possibility of making a fool of herself. Over the telephone he couldn't see tears.

A whole day without seeing Scott had given her too much time to think. She wasn't certain whether she'd made a good decision yesterday after the concert. Visiting her parents for a few days would give both Scott and her the time to digest their new relationship—if he felt they needed the time. On the other hand, the visit would waste precious days—if the relationship delivered on its promise of glory.

Ariel tried to control a surge of hope and its inevitable backlash of gloom. If she really meant anything to Scott, he wouldn't want her to go away for Christmas. It was that simple. She'd find out soon enough where she stood, provided that this abominable storm would ever stop.

Ariel rested her forehead against the cold glass. Dear God, had she made a massive fool of herself yet again? She'd already had too much time to second-guess. Rain or no rain, she had to see Scott. She tossed the remainder of the carrot into the garbage and went to fetch her coat and rain cape.

At the fisheries cabin Deb ushered her into the living room and ran to get her father. The sparsely furnished cabin was less familiar territory than Honeymoon Nook, and Ariel sat on the edge of the chair as she waited for Scott. The wind had toyed with her cape, soaking her clothes and her face. Yet she knew her discomfort sprang from more than cold, clinging clothing.

When Scott came into the living room wearing blue jeans and a plaid work shirt that emphasized his solid physique, Ariel's heart began to pound. He looked magnificent.

"You look like a drowned rat," he said.

"Sweet words," she said with a shaky laugh. "Just what I wanted to hear." She rose to her feet and took a step toward him.

Just then Deb dashed back into the room and flung herself at Ariel. "Here's the card I promised you."

With a nervous glance at Scott, Ariel took the birthday card the girl gave her and began reading aloud.

Scott sensed Ariel's discomfort and found it disquieting. Children, he thought, should be banned from the reunions of wary, battle-scarred lovers. Yet he didn't send Deb away. Instead, he listened to his daughter's happy chatter as he fixed a cup of tea to warm Ariel. When he returned to the living room, Deb was perched on Ariel's lap.

Ariel glanced up at him when he handed her a cup, then returned her attention to Deb.

"What brings you out in such terrible weather?" he asked.

"Well," she began, then paused. She glanced at Deb. "I . . . I just wanted to tell you that I'm going to visit my parents in Victoria for Christmas."

Scott paused with his cup halfway to his mouth. "Oh? I didn't know you were going away."

Ariel didn't look him in the face, which increased his unease. "I just made the decision yesterday."

"I wish I could go to Victoria," Deb said.

Scott put his cup on an end table with a harsh clatter. She'd decided to leave yesterday? *After* that incredible night?

All of Ariel's early protests about a physical relationship cascaded through Scott's mind. So, she regretted making love. A wisp of anger, both at her and at himself for hurting her, began to tighten inside him. His jaw clenched.

"I leave the day after tomorrow," Ariel said.

Scott's muscles felt too tight for speech, so he nodded. She should be ecstatic, yet she wanted to go away instead. The familiar feelings of betrayal gushed over him, yet he tried to look nonchalant.

"I should pack tonight," Ariel continued. "Probably tomorrow night, too. Unless, that is, you need me for the research."

"Would you call my cousins," Deb asked, "and wish them merry Christmas for me?"

"Deb," Scott said sharply, "let Ariel talk."

The girl's head rose in surprise. She looked from one adult to the other and slowly got to her feet.

Scott took a deep breath and ran his fingers across his scalp, trying to calm his quick flush of anger. "Sorry, kiddo. Maybe you should go to your room and let Ariel and me talk."

A subdued Deb wished Ariel a merry Christmas, then disappeared behind a closed door. Staring at the door, Scott rhythmically clenched his jaw. Ariel, he reminded himself, wasn't betraying him. She was just visiting her parents. He had to keep this in perspective.

"Maybe," she said quietly, "we need time to think."

It didn't make him any less angry, but maybe she was right. Maybe they did need time to think. She obviously felt she did, and the least he could do was not crowd her. He owed that much to her—and maybe to himself, as well.

Ariel looked at him expectantly.

He spoke with an effort. "I can get by without you."

"I see." Ariel's face became expressionless, which made her seem even more bedraggled and miserable. She rose quickly to her feet and hurried into her soaked cape. "Well, I...I'll see you. After the holidays. I mean after Christmas. Sometime, I don't know when."

She paused with her hand on the doorknob, then left without wishing Scott a merry Christmas.

As the floatplane descended, Ariel paid no attention to the dusting of snow that turned the scenery into a winter fairyland. Instead, she focused on the *Simoom Queen*, tied to the dock. That meant Scott was at the fisheries cabins and she wouldn't have to wait to see him.

This had been the worst Christmas of her life. Even her father had commented on her distracted state. Her life was a muddle of possibilities, none of them straightforward. Her carefully forged acceptance of fate was in tatters. After days of lonely thought, her only certainty was that if there was any chance that Scott wanted her, she had to give this relationship a chance.

But did he want her? Would he have let her go if she meant anything to him beyond physical pleasure? Ariel clutched her purse to her chest as the floatplane reached the dock.

Deb came running through the slush as the bush pilot maneuvered to the dock. She grabbed a rope from the plane's pontoon and flipped it around a cleat on the dock with practiced skill. As soon as Ariel hopped to the dock,

Deb flung her arms wide for a hug. It was the kind of effusive welcome Ariel had dreamed of from Scott. But he was nowhere to be seen.

They headed up the dock. There was just enough snow to muffle their footsteps and chill Ariel's fear. Her boots, she thought with a rising sense of panic, were in the teacherage. Should she get her boots before visiting Scott?

No, that was stalling. Ariel tried to calm her nerves by concentrating on the dripping white laciness of the trees. "Where's your father?"

"In the cabin." Deb took Ariel's hand and pulled her toward the door of the apartment cabin. "Daddy's been in a terrible mood. I learned a couple of new words, but he made me promise to forget them."

"Great." Ariel took a deep breath. "Just great."

Deb flung open the door. "Daddy! Ariel's back!"

Warm air and the smell of coffee engulfed Ariel. Scott was nowhere to be seen in the immaculate, almost barren living room. Ariel decided that she hated this room.

Footsteps approached from the next room. Ariel's grip tightened on the handle of her suitcase.

She restrained a smile as she caught sight of him, cradling a mug in his hands. His vividly remembered body was hugged by corduroy slacks and a yellow alpine sweater. She took a step forward, ready to throw herself into his arms—

And then caution made her stop.

"Hello, Ariel."

Time seemed to die as Ariel composed her face. The air rolling into her lungs was thick and cloying. "Hello, Scott."

Circles underlined his eyes as if to emphasize his mood. Rather than speaking, he sipped from his mug.

Ariel felt herself shattering into tiny pieces.

Deb turned from one of them to the other with a look of ageless wisdom. Her sigh was full of impatience. She pulled Ariel toward a doorway on the opposite side of the room, away from Scott's impassive, implacable face. "Come on, Ariel. I want to show you what I got for Christmas."

Ariel looked over her shoulder at Scott, but he was drinking from his mug and missed her glance. She allowed herself to be tugged like a rag doll into Deb's room.

"I got this furniture from Aunt Sharon." Deb held up an exquisite dollhouse dining-room set with table, six chairs and matching china cabinet.

"It's beautiful." Ariel sat in a chair and tried to look interested. She jerked a glance at the open doorway. Scott was there, watching. She didn't lift her gaze above the level of his stomach.

"Would you like a cup of coffee?" he asked.

How could he speak so normally? Ariel could scarcely force her voice to work. "Yes, please."

"Some of my presents are over at the lab," Deb was saying. "That's where I keep the microscope—with *real* slides— that Daddy gave me."

Ariel made herself nod, though her mind scarcely registered the girl's words. At least, she thought, she hadn't flung herself at Scott. At least she had that.

"I got a whole box of Christmas oranges, all for myself. I don't think my cousins really bought them, though. I think it was my aunt. Would you like an orange?"

Again Ariel nodded. She accepted a mandarin orange in one hand just as Scott put a cup of coffee in the other hand. "Thank you," she said without looking up at Scott's face. Why didn't he say something about being glad to see her?

Ariel forced herself to listen as Deb cataloged presents, despite her peripheral awareness of Scott leaning against the doorjamb. She rested the saucer on her lap, ignoring its heat on her thighs. The orange scented her fingers as she peeled it and ate several slices without once looking at Scott's face.

The shadow at the edge of her vision stirred. "How was your flight?"

Ariel finished chewing an orange slice. "Fine."

There was a slight pause—nothing impolite, but noticeable. "I'm surprised," Scott said. "I'd have thought with the wind being up today that—"

"It was bumpy," Ariel interrupted sharply. Then, to make amends for her rudeness, she added, "But perfectly safe."

Deb placed a set of thick paperback books on the arm of Ariel's chair. "My other grandmother gave me these. They're the *Narnia* books, like the one you read to the class."

"Stop by the teacherage later," Ariel said to Deb. "I have something for you."

Deb looked triumphantly at her father. "I *told* you."

Told him what? Scott's face gave Ariel no clues, but Deb appeared hugely satisfied. Had he said that while Ariel was gone she'd forget them? That she had abandoned them as Deb's mother had done? Ariel swallowed some coffee, its taste warring with the lingering acidity of the orange.

She couldn't take much more of this. Ariel tried to distract herself from a burning sensation in her eyes. "I don't see anything here from your mother. What did she give you for Christmas?"

The answering silence was thick. Deb was suddenly intent on placing the dollhouse chairs in a meticulous array.

"I'm sorry." Ariel felt almost physically ill about her own insensitivity. "I should never have asked."

"That's okay," Deb said. "It's in there." She waved in the general direction of the living room.

Ariel looked where she pointed, which was right at Scott. "Deborah sent a card that she painted herself," he explained with more animation in his voice than any card deserved.

"I'm sure it's beautiful."

"It's wonderful," Scott said. "She's a professional artist, after all. She's working in Hollywood at a big movie studio."

Deb lifted a doll chair, then replaced it in the exact position it had been in. "She signed it 'Deborah MacKenzie.'" The girl didn't look up from her playing. "I guess she thinks I might have forgotten who she is if she signed it 'Mommy.'"

Silence covered the room like storm clouds off the Pacific. Looking at the youngster, Ariel felt tears sting her eyes. There was so much anguish in this room, and yet Deb played on and refused to surrender to her pain.

Ariel sat straighter. She couldn't be less brave than an eight-year-old girl, even a girl as special as Deb.

"I have to leave." Her voice, she was glad to hear, sounded normal. She handed her cup to Scott, daring to meet his eyes. "Thank you for the tea."

"It was coffee."

Ariel hurried from the room without answering.

"I'll carry your suitcase," Scott said. "We need to talk."

Outside, the cold, damp air stung Ariel's lungs and clouded her breath. She and Scott did need to talk sometime, as unpleasant as the discussion might be. Sometime. Not now.

"Slow down," Scott said. "You can't run from this."

That's what you think. "My feet are cold."

Scott speeded up but otherwise ignored her words. "Ariel, I've had a lot of time to think."

"So have I."

"We need to talk."

Ariel continued to stomp along the trail. "No."

"Why not?"

"Because I don't handle anger well, all right?" Her voice throbbed with a shriek unspoken. "Proper ladies aren't supposed to get angry, damn it, or if they do they're supposed to hide it under sweet phrases and snide remarks."

"Ariel, we can talk about what happened like adults."

The weight on Ariel's heart made her feel as if she were a hundred years old. Was that the same as being an adult?

"These last few days," Scott said in a calm, rational voice, "reminded me how much relationships can hurt. More than that, they made me realize how much risk there was for you. You told me, I know, but I didn't realize it in my heart. Do you understand what I'm trying to say?"

"That you're sorry we made love."

"Look, we got carried away that night, but I hope nothing will interfere with our friendship."

"Scott, we made love. We're beyond mere friendship." Glaring at him rather than watching where she was walking, Ariel stepped into a mound of snow. Ice slipped into her shoe. Muttering dark words under her breath, she stopped to shake out the snow. "Look what you made me do."

"I never made you do anything, Ariel."

She began walking again, quickly. "You made me *want* to do things, though. Now you say we're just friends."

"I need your friendship, Ariel. So does Deb."

But that isn't how I need you to need me, Scott. Not anymore. Ariel didn't answer aloud.

They emerged from the forest into the brighter grayness of the school yard, a snowy sea dotted with islands of tall grass.

"I'll go first," Scott said. He walked ahead of her to clear a trail.

Ariel stared at his back, wishing he wouldn't try to be nice. She filled her lungs with frigid air and began treading in his footsteps. The world was muffled by the snow, leaving the wet crunch of footsteps alone in an aching void.

"Ariel, we both must have wondered what it would be like in bed together. Now we've satisfied our curiosity."

"Curiosity?" The word was a whisper, yet a slap.

"It's simple, really."

"Simple?"

"And now," Scott continued doggedly, without chancing a look at her, "we can settle into being friends." He waited for her small, hurt voice to undermine his logic with a harsh "friends?"

But she didn't speak, and he decided to take that as a good sign. He forced his tense shoulders to relax. Ariel would come around in time. If he had drawn his emotions back from the brink and conquered his disappointment, then Ariel, too, would come to realize they were meant to be friends. Only friends. No more emotional entanglement than that.

They were halfway to the teacherage before Scott spoke again. He kept his voice strictly controlled. Control was the key. "You got your hopes up, didn't you?"

Ariel glanced at the back of his neck. Not seeing his face made it easier to answer. "I drove past your old house in Victoria six times."

"I'm truly sorry." A cloud of vapor swirled around his head as he sighed. They walked the rest of the way to the teacherage in a silence that threatened to suffocate Ariel's heart.

"May I come in, Ariel?"

"What for? Surely you haven't changed your mind already and want to make love?"

"To talk."

"No."

"Ariel, give me a minute of your time."

"No."

"Just one minute."

Ariel pulled keys from her purse and unlocked the door. "Oh, all right. But you can talk to me from there."

Scott stepped onto the porch with her suitcase, but she grabbed it from him. She slung it inside, then turned to him and glanced at her watch. "One minute," she repeated.

"I never meant to hurt you, Ariel."

"You're wasting your minute. Get to the point."

"That is the point." Scott leaned heavily against the porch railing, as if he needed its support. "You were right to insist on keeping our relationship platonic. I'm sorry I hurt you."

"You should be." She hugged his apology to her devastated heart as would a woman wronged. He'd made love without feeling love. She wasn't guilty of that.

"We didn't take precautions, you know."

"You're still wasting your minute. Tell me something I don't know."

"All right. If you're pregnant—"

"I'm not."

Scott paused. "You're sure?"

Ariel glanced pointedly at her watch.

"Well," Scott said softly, "I guess that takes care of what I wanted to talk about. But if you were—well, I want you to know that I would have done right by you."

"How magnanimous." Ariel's throat seemed to constrict, but she kept her gaze level. "How honorable."

Scott crossed his arms and stared at her till she had to glance away. He sighed. "Making love was wonderful, Ariel, but it didn't change who I am. I don't want a relationship. You do. Nothing has changed between us."

Except, Ariel thought, *that I've lost my heart to you.* "Your minute is up," she said without looking at her watch. Yet she couldn't make herself leave. She paused in the doorway, her back to him.

"We can't be lovers," Scott said. "We'd hope the other person would change, and that's no good. We'd end up hating each other. Don't you see, Ariel?"

Staring into the teacherage and its dark bedroom, Ariel saw nothing but emptiness. After several minutes of agonized silence, she heard Scott trudge away.

She whirled around. "Scott—"

He turned.

Ariel looked down at the steps. "That night . . . well, we seemed good together. Wasn't it special for you?"

"Let's just say there's no doubt whatsoever that we're sexually compatible."

"It was good for you, too, then?"

"It wasn't *good.* It was the best ever."

"I'm glad." She turned to the door and stared at him over her shoulder. "Every time you see me from now on, I want you to remember how good it was. Then remember that we'll never do it again."

He laughed, damn him, and then began walking backward, still facing her. "Ariel, you're terrific. I'll see you tomorrow, okay?"

She was too polite to voice the words that scalded her throat.

* * *

"No, no, no, no." Angus shook his head emphatically, just in case Ariel didn't get his message. He sat down on his bed and folded his arms across his chest. "I will not go to dinner with you at the fishy man's house. He's your boyfriend, not mine."

Ariel felt her patience slipping. "How many times do I have to tell you that he's not my boyfriend?"

Not anymore, at least.

Maybe some people could handle a polite, civilized dinner with a former lover. Ariel couldn't. She couldn't handle this entire friendship thing that Scott was pursuing. Maybe if she were a better person, she could smile and disregard her love and her anger, but...

In the ten days since her return from Victoria—since Scott had dumped her—she'd tried to avoid him. Like an airplane on autopilot, politeness had guided her through his visits. Those calls had been eerie, as well as painful, knowing that though they'd shared the deepest intimacy he still considered her nothing more than a friend.

Why did he want to torture her by being a friend? Was it his way of demonstrating that love couldn't touch him? Did he want to convince her—or more likely, himself—that his logic could maintain the moat he'd built around himself, even in the face of love?

Now he'd asked her to dinner. She'd have said no on the spot if he hadn't played dirty by saying how much Deb missed her.

"I'm not going to do it," Angus said. "He doesn't like me."

"Scott doesn't know you very well," she said reasonably. "If he got to know you, he...he might not dislike you so much."

"Thank you for that rousing endorsement, lass." Angus made a sour face. "But it doesn't matter. I don't like him."

"You don't like anybody, Angus."

"And I don't have dinner with anybody, either. I'll bet he didn't even invite me."

Ariel looked at her hands, folded on the cluttered table in front of her.

Angus snorted. "You aren't disagreeing, I notice. You're the only one who wants me to go, lass, and I'm not going to do it."

Ariel heaved a sigh. "Okay."

"I don't know why you'd even think I might go. He'd probably expect me to shave, and—"

"I said okay!" Ariel pushed herself up from the chair.

This settled it. She couldn't face Scott alone. It would be hard, but from now on she'd pretend that Scott didn't exist, that she'd never gotten to be his friend, never experienced the ecstasy of his body.

Never fallen in love with him.

"Lass . . ." Angus looked at her with something like pity etched on his craggy face.

"I'll be fine." Ariel drew herself up straight. As she walked to the door, she summoned her remaining pride and smiled at the old man. She must have been a good actress, for the pity on his face faded. "I'm tougher than I look."

Angus looked her in the eye for a long time. When she proudly held his gaze despite the challenge in his eyes, he nodded. "I know, lass."

Tough or not, Ariel barely survived the following weeks. The winter rains seemed more relentless, the clouds more oppressive. Bleak mists seeped from the ocean to the land, into the boards, into Ariel's bones and finally into her brain. She lost track of when it was raining and when it wasn't. Everything dripped: the eaves of the school, the trees in the forest, her bloodshot eyes.

Scott still stopped by from time to time. She always made him stand outside. She couldn't bear the thought of inviting him in.

At work she went through the motions. The usual winter illnesses hit the school in January. By the end of the month scarcely more than half the students attended on any given day.

Ariel awoke one Friday morning with a knifelike pain in her throat and shivers coursing through her body. Her voice was a guttural croak. Teaching was out of the question.

She'd almost been expecting this. Given the way she felt in her heart, illness seemed appropriate.

Wearing a robe and blanket, she huddled at the kitchen table and prayed Deb wouldn't be sick today, too. Deb came early enough to run to tell the school boat driver to take the children back home. There were no substitute teachers on Mowitch Island, and no telephone to call them even if they existed.

She must have fallen asleep sitting up, for her eyes jerked open when Deb clumped up the wooden stairs of the school. With a combination of croaks and written notes, Ariel told Deb what to do and then shuffled back to bed.

The sounds of children roused her, however. Ariel groaned and lowered the covers enough to venture a peek out the window. Deb must have gotten to the dock too late. As she levered herself to a sitting position, Ariel tried her voice again. It felt awful, and sounded worse.

She was still sitting there when the teacherage door opened. Groaning, she reached for the robe that was miles away at the foot of the bed.

"You look terrible."

"Scott?" Or at least that was what Ariel meant to say, though it came out as a sibilant grunt. She tried to raise the energy to look up, hoping she wouldn't also see a horde of children staring at her. Damien Prescott would snigger for months about having seen the teacher in her nightgown.

But Scott was alone. Walking toward her. Putting his warm hands on her cold arms. Laying her down. Tugging the covers to her chin.

"The boat was pulling away when Deb got to the dock," he said, "but don't worry about a thing."

"The children . . ."

"I'll substitute for you." Scott gave her what he hoped was a reassuring smile. "I've had experience climbing into a pool of sharks. How much worse can teaching be?"

Ariel croaked something that he couldn't understand.

"Here's a pad of paper and a pen. While I'm getting you some water, you can write down what you need."

When he returned to the bedroom, she was detailing directions for running the class. He took the pen from her fingers, then held the glass to her lips while she sipped cautiously. Through the thin cloth of her nightgown, he felt the fever in her body.

"Don't worry, Ariel. I'm not saying the children will learn anything, but we'll get through the day without you."

She opened her lips to speak but instead made a pained face and shut her mouth.

Scott eased her head onto the pillow. She looked so pitiful that it was all he could to keep from embracing her and insisting that everything would be all right. "Cheryl and Eva have volunteered for nurse duty since they've already had this flu, and I'll stop by whenever I can. Will you be okay till then?"

Ariel nodded. Before he rose to face the classroom full of wild animals—he remembered how he himself had taken advantage of substitute teachers—Ariel squeezed his hand. That alone was enough to make substituting worthwhile.

To his surprise, however, Scott enjoyed himself. After testing his limits, the children were sympathetic to his inexperience. He had them "invent" an imaginary fish and write reports about its habits and appearance. After painting their fish, they shared their reports orally. Then Scott started a debate about whether their fish could actually survive in the wild. This led to a discussion of the food chain and adaptation, followed by a revision of their reports and then—

And then the day was over. Scott was almost sorry.

Under protest, Deb went to Mrs. Fearson's while Scott wrote comments on the children's reports. He felt Ariel deserved the weekend to recuperate without worrying about grading papers.

After that he fixed soup for her dinner. She ate in bed, her voice still hoarse though her complexion was a shade better than before.

"You're looking better," Scott commented.

"Better than what? A dead jellyfish?"

"You're definitely on the mend if you're making jokes."

She pushed a bowl of half-eaten chicken soup across the tray on her lap. "Go home, Scott," she croaked. "You have your own work to do."

"The orcas will manage to catch fish without me listening in on them."

She shrugged her shoulders. "I feel so helpless."

"You're making progress. I can understand what you say now." When he picked up the tray, Ariel brushed his hand with her fingertips. He looked at her and smiled.

"Thank you, Scott. You've been better to me than I deserve."

He covered her soft, delicate hand with his own. "That's what friends are for."

Ariel's forehead wrinkled, as if disappointed with that explanation.

"Your hand doesn't feel warm," Scott said. "I think your fever's gone."

"I feel much better, even if I don't sound it."

"Is there anything I can do for you before I go?"

She looked up at him, her eyes wide and wondering. Then she looked away. "Run some bathwater, I guess."

Scott put an extra scoop of bubble bath in the tub, then put a clean nightgown in the bathroom. The simple act of domesticity tugged at his emotions, though he didn't let it show. Instead, he concentrated on the task of proving to her that friendship was not only possible but beneficial.

"You don't have to do this," Ariel said hoarsely as he helped her out of bed.

"Ariel, I meant what I said about being your friend. Friends help each other."

"I mean," she said, "that I can walk by myself."

"Oh." Scott took his hand off her waist, but he still seemed to feel her body, her warmth and femininity scarcely veiled by the nightgown. His thoughts were decidedly beyond friendly as he preceded her down the hall to turn off the bathwater.

"Gee, are you sure you put in enough soap?" Ariel sat on the hamper near the doorway and looked at the mountains of bubbles that threatened to overflow the tub.

"Deb likes a lot of bubbles," he explained as he scooped a handful of bubbles into his palm. He suddenly felt silly holding them, so he blew them off his hand and watched them float to the rim of the sink.

When he looked up, Ariel was watching him. Her throat bobbed.

"You're getting your color back," he said.

Ariel's gaze returned to the tub. "I'll feel human after a bath. Thank you."

Her arm moved, as if she'd considered shaking hands but decided against it. The room suddenly seemed too small and too intimate for mere friends.

Ariel must have felt it, too. Her nipples became hard points that beckoned his gaze. In a translucent nightgown, with her thick hair in disarray, this woman was overpoweringly desirable. Scott took a step toward her before he realized what he was doing. He stopped.

Ariel swallowed again, but not because her throat was sore. In fact, she forgot she was sick. Scott stood there, staring into her eyes, frozen in the act of starting to do something. Had he been going to kiss her? His chest was rising and falling more rapidly, she noticed. But then, so was hers.

The faint hiss of the bubble bath emphasized the awkward silence. Scott's penetrating hazel eyes seemed to search not only her face, but her heart.

And her heart wasn't well. Remembering the pain of the last month, Ariel expelled a deep breath. She cleared her throat and stuck out her hand.

"Friends, right?"

"Of course," Scott said too quickly. He took her hand and immediately released it.

Tension still lingered in the humid air, rising over the faint perfume of the bubble bath. Unsure what to do with her hands, which yearned to reach out to him, Ariel crossed them in front of herself.

Scott winked broadly, and the tension began to dissipate. "Need a hand getting into the tub?"

"I think I can manage," Ariel said with a smile that, she hoped, camouflaged the pause when she'd considered his offer.

"Feel free to call on me to wash your back."

Ariel appreciated his attempt to lighten the thickness of the moment, but his humor struck too close to what she really wanted. What they both wanted, probably. "That's a dumb idea, MacKenzie."

His face sobered. "Sorry. Force of habit, I guess."

"Yes, well ... you can force your habits out of here now. And close the front door when you leave."

Ariel hadn't meant to speak harshly. She swung the door partly closed and leaned her forehead against the frame. "Scott?"

"Yes?"

"I'm sorry if I barked at you. I've never tried to be friends with a one-night stand before."

"One-night stand?" Scott frowned. "Is that what you think you are to me?"

"I can count, Scott." She softened the words as much as she could with a voice that croaked rather than whispered. "Besides, I never had a one-night stand before, and you once said I needed to catch up on juicy secrets. Consider yourself juicy."

"If you put it that way, I'm flattered."

Ariel leaned against the edge of the door and swung it slightly open and closed. "This friendship thing won't be easy, you know."

"No. But it will be worth it."

"I hope so."

She closed the door and put her back against it. When she heard the front door close, she let out a breath she hadn't realized she was holding. "I certainly hope so."

Over the next few months, Ariel found that being friends with Scott was even more difficult than she had feared. The love for him that burned in her soul refused to sputter and die. If anything, it grew to shattering proportions. When they were apart, Scott was always on her mind. Yet when they were together, Ariel was more alone than ever.

She kept waiting for the awkwardness to disappear, but though it occasionally crept from sight it returned when she'd least expected it: when he smiled warmly at her after she'd played particularly well for the orcas; when he caught her staring at him as he played with Deb; when she felt a burst of pride at the way the class responded to his lecture about orcas.

They were polite to each other, so polite that all spontaneity had deserted them. If she was spontaneous, though, she'd probably think up an excuse to grab him as she had that day when he'd painted the cabins. Scott must have felt somewhat the same, for he made sure Deb was present when Ariel was around.

The fact that he used Deb as a chaperon didn't tell her much about his emotions. He could be guarding against his hormones rather than feelings. Or, even worse, guarding against *her* hormones. When Ariel was at her lowest, she wondered if he wasn't simply guarding his independence against entanglement with a meddlesome, overly emotional female.

At other times, though, she was confident that he liked her even if he didn't need her. Was that all he felt, a friendship that was tepid compared with the fierce heat of her own feelings? Ariel began to suspect she'd never know.

In late February Scott asked her to proofread an article, entitled "Ketophonation Among Resident Orcas of the Middle British Columbia Coast," before he submitted it to a professional journal. Ariel not only proofread the article, but she also pointed out where she disagreed about the meanings of whale calls.

The intellectual argument that followed vented many of Ariel's frustrations. Because she felt she had nothing to lose, she held nothing back while defending her interpretations. She abandoned politeness in favor of conviction.

And Scott respected her for it. After initial resistance, he changed the manuscript. He even added ''Ariel Johnson'' as coauthor. His admiration for her intellect touched her enough that she forgave him for not loving her—for about ten minutes.

Scott never took advantage of Ariel's impulses to help out, and she had stood with him on an intellectual level. In some ways her relationship with Scott was the healthiest, most mature relationship she'd ever had with a man.

And also the most frustrating. The only thing that roused her from apathy was the prospect of seeing him again.

Ariel couldn't decide whether it hurt more to see Scott or not to see him.

Someone screamed.

Ariel's eyes jerked open, then darted back and forth. She was sleeping alone, of course. The scream must have been her.

She pushed hair out of her face and squinted at the clock. She flopped back onto the pillow. The alarm would go off in twenty minutes.

Ariel groaned and shut off the alarm. Now that winter had slipped into a soggy grave, April sunshine infiltrated her room earlier and earlier, and it was too bright for sleep. Besides, the panic inspired by her dream had thoroughly wakened her.

Most of the dream had evaporated. She remembered unseen babies crying as she ran for her life but got nowhere. A huge, spokeless golden wheel had been about to run over her.

Though the bedroom was stuffy, Ariel pulled the sheet up to her neck as if to return to the haven of sleep. It wasn't hard to decipher the symbolism of an old maid having nightmares about golden bands.

Ariel stretched away the lingering laziness of sleep. As usual first thing in the morning, she thought of Scott.

She'd last seen him a week and a half ago when she'd played for the orcas. This time the music drew not the locals but a group of strangers that had listened and responded playfully. Scott had told her that in spring, pods often merged. The newcomers would provide a valuable test of his communication theories.

Yet he hadn't asked her back to Honeymoon Nook since then. He didn't really need her, not even for the research.

Ariel impatiently pushed hair out of her face. Her hair was getting too long. She hadn't cut it because Scott had mentioned that he liked long hair, but she couldn't plan her life around him. In a couple of months school would be over. When she returned in the fall, Scott would be gone forever.

She wrapped a strand of hair around her finger. It was time for a change in her life. Would a haircut be enough of a change?

Ariel sighed loudly and spun onto her stomach. She punched the pillow flat and stared at the alarm clock.

She still loved Scott—more now than when they had made love—and she had an overpowering suspicion that she always would. It was as if her life had finally begun that moment when he first touched her cheek.

With an impatient sigh, Ariel flopped onto her back and folded her hands over her navel. She realized how quickly the summer would be here. Then Scott would leave. And when he left, she'd be alone again.

More alone than ever before.

Ariel drummed her fingers against her stomach and watched dust motes dance in a ray of sunshine from the window. They looked far too cheerful for Ariel's mood. Why were they so happy when she was so alone?

The drumming of her fingers slowed. She glanced at her hands. What was there about the tapping of her fingers?

She rested her fingertip against her navel. A strange sensation began to grow in her. She put both palms flat on her abdomen. The feeling spread and became stronger, filling Ariel with a sense of purpose and fulfillment that finally broke into coherent thought.

What would a new life growing inside her feel like?

A laugh danced around the room with the dust motes. Of course. Why not? It seemed so obvious now that she'd thought of it. Humming softly, she began making plans. Not just next week's lesson plans, for a change, but plans for the rest of her life. She'd have to try to buy a basal thermometer, for starters.

Already she felt less alone.

Chapter Eleven

Deb shifted on Ariel's lap. The child's gentle movement, so close to her womb, was a soft, prophetic reminder of her plan.

Not that she'd forgotten it, of course. Today of all days, she couldn't forget the brainstorm of the morning when the dust motes had danced to the beat of her heart. Ariel hugged Deb gently, with all the love that any mother could give.

Scott sat behind the tiller, studying the open channel ahead of the *Simoom Queen*. His profile was a rugged silhouette against the darkening sky outside the wheelhouse window. Ariel smiled, congratulating herself on her good taste. He was handsome, intelligent, strong and witty. He had superior genes.

Her glance caressed the blue material stretched over his muscular thighs. Definitely superior jeans.

It was time. Ariel could feel an eagerness dancing along her nerves. How, though, could she work her proposition into a conversation? This situation wasn't covered in any of the etiquette manuals.

"This was a nice day," Deb said around a yawn.

Ariel squeezed Deb and rested her chin on the girl's head. "What part did you like best?"

"The cemetery." The cemetery at the Indian settlement of Alert Bay was adorned with totem poles, many of them painted on plywood. The natives didn't worry about lack of authenticity because their art was an evolving part of their everyday lives, not something trapped in museums or hawked to tourists. "I've read that the Indians used totem poles like gravestones, but actually seeing it was neat."

Ariel tightened her grip on Deb and stared meaningfully at Scott. "It's been quite a day," she agreed, "and it isn't over yet."

Scott raised his eyebrows. When she said nothing more, he returned his attention to the choppy water.

A few minutes later Deb's chin lolled onto Ariel's arm. "She's asleep," Ariel whispered.

The fiercely proud look that Scott gave his daughter warmed Ariel. How to bring up her proposition? She opened her mouth, then hesitated. She needed privacy. "Could you put her in the bed in the cabin? She's getting heavy."

"Take the tiller for a minute while I put her down. Keep heading to the left when the channel branches."

Ariel studied the maze of precipitous hills and rocks. In the distance she recognized a distinctive stone formation near the general store. "I know my way from here."

As she waited for him to return from the cabin, the enormity of her request overwhelmed Ariel. The reality of what it would mean lit a small glow of anticipation and yearning—and, she admitted, of desire. But then, frustrated desire had been a fixture of her life for months.

"I'll take over again."

Ariel jumped. She hadn't even heard him return. "We're nearly to Blackfish Bay. Can I take the boat in the rest of the way?"

"My poor boat," he sighed. "Okay, but wait for me to put on a life preserver."

"Very funny."

She didn't smile, which surprised him. There were circles under her eyes, too. Something was worrying her.

The urge to comfort her in his arms hit Scott. By now he was a pro at fighting down such urges, though. He leaned back, feeling the throbbing of the engine throughout his body, and watched as Ariel steered into the narrow mouth of Blackfish Bay.

After he tied the *Simoom Queen* to the dock, Ariel was waiting for him in the wheelhouse. She held her hands together and rubbed her fingers against each other. She met his gaze and seemed about to speak, but said nothing.

"Ariel, is something bothering you?"

"Yes." She glanced at the door that led to the cabin where Deb was sleeping.

"Is there anything I can do?"

Ariel squeezed her lips together as if trying not to smile. "As a matter of fact, yes."

"Just tell me and I'll do it. What are friends for?"

"Oh, you'd be amazed." Her lips twitched and her eyes sparkled. "I'd like to discuss it with you this evening, so we can, well, get it taken care of right away, while the time is right."

"Of course. Why don't you have dinner with us?"

"No, I have school work to finish." Ariel glanced again at the cabin. "I'll come by later."

She left without another word.

By the time Ariel arrived that evening, Scott had begun to think she wasn't coming. It was late, almost time for bed. Deb had been asleep for over an hour. Ordinarily Ariel never visited when the little busybody wasn't around. Something was up; that was certain. Scott wondered what.

His interest multiplied when Ariel stepped in the door and took off her trench coat. He'd never seen her wear anything as sexy as this red dress. It was cut low at the front and even lower at the back. When she sat on the couch, the wraparound skirt parted on her thigh before she pulled the ends together. It was a dress for seduction.

Nonsense. This was his buddy Ariel, who was ladylike in both temperament and upbringing. The signals he was getting couldn't be the signals she meant to send.

A friendly compliment on her appearance was in order. "You look as if you've lost weight."

"I told myself I'd lose ten pounds this year," she answered with a pleased smile. "Instead, I've lost twelve."

"Congratulations."

"I put a lot of miles on my exercise bike the last few weeks." She stared at him with a vaguely pleading expression as she smoothed a hand along her hip, unconsciously drawing his attention to her figure. "I've tried hard to get in shape."

No wonder it was more difficult than usual for him to subdue a familiar ache of desire—though he knew that even if she gained thirty pounds the ache would remain his close companion. "What can I do for you, Ariel?"

She opened her mouth, then halfway closed it. "My throat is dry. Could I please have something to drink?"

"Certainly," Scott said as he headed toward the kitchen. "Tea, coffee, soda?"

"You wouldn't happen to have anything stronger, would you?"

Now he knew something was seriously wrong. "I'm afraid not. Ariel, what's the matter?"

She shook her head. "A glass of water would be fine."

Glass in hand, she drifted toward the couch. When she finally sat down, Scott broke one of his cardinal rules for remaining friends. He took her hand.

Immediately he realized it was a mistake. How could he have forgotten that the touch of Ariel's hand was more exciting than any other woman's overt caress? Desire throbbed through his body, temporarily blotting out everything except the blatant fact that she was a woman and he was a man.

No. Ariel wasn't a woman. Not *just* a woman, at least. She was his friend. She needed the comfort of his touch, and by now he was an expert at shielding her—and himself—from his desires. An expert, remember.

"Now," he said calmly, "tell me what this is all about."

Ariel took a deep breath. "Scott, I..." She looked away. Then she drew herself up and looked at him as she might at a misbehaving child.

"Tell me, Ariel."

"Scott, I want you to impregnate me."

He waited for her to continue, but she said nothing more. Too bad, because he hadn't heard right. "Pardon me?"

Her teacherish expression vanished. She was all woman, determined and desirable. "I want to have a child, Scott."

Scott nodded. He stared at her for a heartbeat. Suddenly he jerked his hand away and stood up. He ran his hand through his hair as he paced, turning to face her only when he was on the other side of the room. "What?"

"I'm tired of being alone. I want a baby."

"Yes, but what does this have to do with me?" He resumed pacing, more quickly. "No, on second thought don't tell me."

"It takes a man and a woman to make a baby. I want to have your child."

"Oh, brother." Scott ran his hand through his hair again. "Ariel, I... I don't know what to say."

"How about 'I'd be delighted'?" With an impish, teasing smile she leaned forward with her elbow on her knees and her chin on her hand. The folds at the bodice of the dress separated, creating alluring shadows and feminine depths that drew his gaze like a fisherman's light drew helpless bass to the hook.

"Stop right there." Scott held up his palm. "Now, lean back against the couch."

Ariel laughed, but did as he asked. "Scott MacKenzie, you look like you're having a heart attack."

"I am." Which was nearly true. When she seemed about to stand, he held his palm up again. "Stay right there."

"If you insist." With a smile that left her lips slightly parted, Ariel crossed her legs. "Scott, I'm not trying to trap you. I want only your child, not your hand in marriage."

Concentrate on her words, not her body. He took a deep breath and looked at her face. *No,* he scolded himself, *not her lips, either. The face as a whole.* "Don't be ridiculous, Ariel. That makes no sense."

"It makes perfect sense."

"No, it doesn't. You aren't talking logically. You're talking like a female."

"I'm talking like a logical female," Ariel shot back. She lowered her voice to a husky, humorous tenor. "Would you rather I talked like this?"

She was enjoying his discomfort. That knowledge gave Scott an extra nudge to control himself, at least outwardly. Though he couldn't dispel his disorientation, he tried to ignore it. The come-hither look in her eyes and posture was harder to ignore.

"Let's look at this carefully," he said.

"Fine."

She'd agreed too readily. Uneasiness stirred the confusion inside him. "Ariel, you can't raise a child by yourself."

"You're doing it," Ariel said. "Do you think I'm unfit to be a mother? Is that what you're saying?"

"Of course not."

"So, you think I'd be a good mother."

He shook his head and sighed explosively. "Okay, I concede you have the potential to be a good mother."

"I'm glad." Ariel leaned forward again.

"I'll even concede that you'd be a great mother."

"Thank you. You're a great father, too."

Scott sat in a reclining chair as far from Ariel as possible. He steepled his fingers and carefully considered his next words. "However, it's difficult raising a child by yourself, especially when the child is still a baby. Sometimes people have to leave newborns with sitters, but that doesn't mean it's desirable. You'd have to do that."

"Wrong," Ariel said immediately. "I'm at the top of the salary scale for teachers, and my life-style has always been modest. I invest nearly every cent I make here. Allowing for inflation, I can manage five years off work if I have to."

"You don't realize how much children cost—"

"I know precisely how much children cost." She pulled a stapled stack of papers from her purse. "Here are my figures if you'd like to check them."

The figure he yearned to check wasn't on paper. "No," he conceded, "I believe you."

Ariel's mouth curled in a small, triumphant grin. "Two years off work will probably be enough, after which I'll teach half-time until my child—" the words were a hushed caress "—is in school."

Scott rubbed his thumb along the cleft in his chin as he considered her words. "It seems you've thought this through."

"I have." She studied him with an intelligent expression, a confident smile and a sexy body. The combination was virtually overpowering. "I've been waiting and planning for weeks."

Scott rallied his thoughts. "This is no place to have a child. A pregnant woman needs medical care and—"

"I'll move in June, at the end of the school year. I'm considering either Victoria or Clearwater, where I used to live."

Victoria. After this summer he'd be returning there. The possibility of the baby, *his* baby, growing up in the same city focused Scott's thoughts on his real reservations.

"Ariel, I'm not ready to be a father again."

"I'm not asking you for that."

"No?"

"No." Her smile wavered slightly. "All I'm asking is for you to, well, help me out with the conception end. I think you'd enjoy that. You did the last time."

Irresistible memories made Scott's gaze flick over her body. He managed to drag his attention to the photographs of orcas that covered the wall behind the couch. Ariel was in several of the photos with the baby whale, Flopsy. He looked at the tiled floor instead.

"Do you really think," he said quietly, "that I could father a child and then just walk away and pretend it wasn't mine?"

Ariel had no quick rejoinder.

"I wish I could do this for you, Ariel." When she caught his gaze and held it, Scott experienced a jolt of empathy like an electrical current passing between them. He felt her longing, her need, her loneliness. Yet he also felt his own disgust at the idea of abandoning his offspring. Sadness followed the empathy, washing out other emotions and leaving emptiness in its wake. "As you say, I'd enjoy the effort."

"So would I," Ariel whispered.

"But it can't be. I'd have to be a father, not just a convenient source of sperm. That would mean marriage, and—"

"And you don't love me." Ariel surged to her feet, suddenly panicky with eagerness to escape the indignity of begging. She'd wanted this so badly that she'd tricked herself into imagining that seducing Scott would be easy. Her own embarrassment had seemed the main obstacle. Instead, the obstacle was the same thing that had kept them apart all this time. She loved him with all her heart, but he didn't love her. Simple. Obvious.

Also humiliating, tragic, excruciating and a dozen other words that she didn't care to voice. God, how could she keep making the same mistake over and over again? Would she never learn?

"Ariel, sit down."

"Don't order me around. I'm not your wife." She grabbed her coat and headed toward the door.

Calling her name, Scott followed her outside to the cool, impersonal darkness. Ariel hurried her steps.

Panic budded inside her, hidden by the shadows. If Scott caught her and put his arms around her, she'd crumble completely. The last shred of her dignity would dissolve in tears. She would cry, proclaim how much she loved him and beg him please, couldn't he pretend to love her for a little while? Just long enough to give her a part of himself—that's all she asked. A small part, but enough to make her emptiness less hollow. A baby who would need all the nurturing that she could give . . .

"Ariel, don't leave like this."

The dress opened around her thighs as she hurried through the darkness. She didn't trust herself to answer.

"Come on, let's play." Tammy Fearson stood at the door with lunch kit and homework in hand, trying to hurry Deb and Parmijeet by planting her hand impatiently on her hip.

"I'm coming," Parmijeet said in her oddly cadenced English. She glanced back at Deb, who lingered at her desk.

"You guys go ahead." Deb's eyes darted toward Ariel, then down at her folded hands. "I have to talk to Miss Johnson."

Ariel studied the girl's face with a budding sense of alarm. Now that she thought about it, Deb had been more quiet than usual in class today. Something was wrong.

Deb knew, of course, that Ariel wasn't seeing Scott anymore. Ariel had been so filled with her own pain that she'd neglected to think of Deb. Deb needed her, even if Scott didn't.

Ariel put down the art papers she'd been stapling to the bulletin board and walked to Deb's desk. The youngster didn't look up as Ariel lowered herself to a chair.

Ariel put all the caring and love into her voice that she could. "What's the matter?"

The youngster looked up with one of her heart-stoppingly solemn expressions.

Ariel's pulse grew heavy. "Is it something about your father?"

"No." Deb swallowed and made a visible effort to compose herself. "I haven't let myself think about it all day, till now. I know you'll be upset, though. . . ." Her voice trailed away.

Ariel took the girl on her lap. "That's okay." She stroked Deb's straight black hair, fearing the worst. "You can tell me."

A sigh shook the girl's slight frame. "It's Wavy."

"Wavy?" Ariel almost laughed in relief. "What about Wavy?"

"They..." Deb braced herself with a deep sigh that was almost a sob. "She'd been shot, over and over. Indian fishermen found her floating on her back near Alert Bay last night."

Deb began crying. She cried right until the school boat picked up the other children. Such grief from the stoic Deb unnerved Ariel. The only thing that finally calmed the girl, at least a little, was Ariel's suggestion that they hike to the totem pole beach.

They were quiet during the walk. At the beach they waded in the cool water, then sat cross-legged in the sand and talked.

Ariel probed gently, trying to understand why the girl took the whale's death so hard. Deb couldn't put it into words, but Ariel gradually began to suspect that Wavy's being a mother was crucial. Deb, who had never cried when her own mother abandoned her, cried now when Flopsy was abandoned by its mother.

Ariel stroked the girl's cheek and opened her heart.

"It's not fair," Deb sniffed. "Flopsy needs her mother."

"Flopsy's a big girl now. She can take care of herself."

"That's not what my daddy says. He says Flopsy is too young to be on her own, that she might die."

Until she heard those words, Ariel had been too concerned with Deb to feel the impact of Wavy's death. Wavy was just a whale, but Ariel felt as if she'd lost a friend. If Flopsy was in jeopardy, perhaps she would lose another.

She remembered the first time she'd seen the whale and calf, and the evening when the two of them had given her a music lesson. Despite the warm spring sunshine, a chill rose from the cool sand and passed through her.

"You know how the orcas stick together, Deb. The other whales will help Flopsy."

Deb ran her hand across her nose, then rubbed it on the sand. "Maybe. Daddy's angry, though, and that means he's worried." The girl lifted her tear-streaked face. Her lip trembled, then she glanced down at her hand, which lifted sand and let it slip through her fingers.

"What is it, Deb?"

Dark hair swayed as the girl shook her head.

"Tell me. Please?"

Deb turned to look at the waves that washed over the smooth sand. Her expression held ageless wisdom and pain. "I know how Flopsy feels. She hurts. I wish I could help her."

Heaviness invaded Ariel's chest. Still, she felt relief that perhaps Deb was finally ready to acknowledge her emotions about her mother's abandonment. Ariel stroked the girl's hair. "Yes, you do know. I'm sorry, Deb. I'm so sorry."

"Then why..." Deb looked up at her. "Why did you do it?"

Surprise froze Ariel's hand in midstroke. "Do what?"

"Have a fight with Daddy?"

The heaviness in Ariel's chest swelled until it threatened to cleave her in two. She had no idea what to say.

Deb resumed sifting sand through her fingers. "When school's over I'll never see you again, will I?"

Again Ariel had no answer. She hugged Deb and rocked her under the harsh, unblinking gaze of totem poles whose fierce stubbornness was softened only by the erosions of time, not by compassion.

"The dog diddn no were the cat hide the bon."

Ariel ran her hands over her eyes, then tried for a second time to decipher Ronald's answer. The content of his answer was close to correct even if it was written in a language other than English. Was it close enough, though?

She marked the answer wrong. She wasn't feeling charitable.

Ariel put the papers on the end table and took a handful of popcorn from the bowl on the arm of the couch. As she ate, she stared into the bright bulb of the table lamp and thought about yesterday's soul-searching talk with Deb at the totem pole beach.

The conversation had again made Ariel realize how much she yearned to belong to a family. This need was nothing new, of course. She'd felt it all her life, even back when she'd sought her parents' love by fixing them breakfast in bed. None of her rationalizations about accepting spinsterhood could change the fact that she felt bereft unless she was needed.

As a result she had surrounded herself with surrogate family members. Scott and Deb were the most obvious examples, though there were others. The children in her class. Angus. Even Wavy and Flopsy.

But maybe, just maybe, she'd become selfish about her need to be needed. She'd had no right to give so much to Deb that the girl came apart at the thought of separation. She wasn't Deb's mother, and she should never have acted as if she were.

Her surrogate families were falling apart. And it seemed certain that she'd never have a family of her own.

Ariel folded her hands across her belly and stared at the ceiling. There was no sound in the teacherage. No hint of anyone nearby. She was alone.

Because of embarrassment and anger, she'd avoided Scott since he'd refused to father her child. Now, though, she wanted to talk with him about the mother whale's death. Flopsy's plight symbolized everything that was going wrong. Ariel needed a baby but couldn't have one. Flopsy and Deb both needed mothers but couldn't have them. Scott needed . . .

What did Scott need, anyway? Certainly not her—that was obvious.

Nonetheless, Ariel wanted to hear firsthand about the whale's murder. It was important. More important than it had any right to be.

Someone knocked on her door. This late? With a surprised glance at the clock, Ariel went to open it.

"Hello, Ariel."

"Scott." Ariel's breath caught in her throat. The sight of his rugged face seemed to make the evening brighter and more fascinating. She kept her voice neutral, but fighting down the hope that flooded her heart was harder. "Won't you come in?"

"Thank you."

There was a moment's awkward silence. Scott stood in the middle of the living room while Ariel perched on the edge of the couch, her hands folded on her knees.

"What can I do for you?" she asked.

"Would it be possible for you to take care of Deb for the next two days, starting tomorrow? With all hell breaking loose about the whale's death, I have to be in Alert Bay while an investigation gets under way."

"Of course, Scott." He looked tired. Ariel noticed lines around his eyes that she didn't remember seeing before.

"I apologize for bothering you. Deb specifically wanted me to ask you, though. She didn't want to stay with Mrs. Fearson."

"I understand," she said. "You don't have to apologize."

"That's good of you to say."

He was so polite, so formal. Was this how their relationship would end, in stiff decorum? The thought depressed her.

"Is there any clue," she asked, "about who killed Wavy?"

"No, but the story has hit the news in a big way. Environmental groups are proclaiming this an act of violence as severe as beating baby seals for their pelts. After dinner I was interviewed over the radiophone by a CBC reporter."

"I'd like to hear that."

"I'm not a good interview. Reporters want anguish and thunder, not just facts." He shifted from one foot to another. "I guess I'd better be going."

"So soon?" Ariel realized that her pulse was pouring adrenaline through her system. "I mean, you just got here."

"I think it's best." He turned toward the door.

She couldn't let him leave yet. They had to get beyond this polite stiffness somehow.

"Wait a minute, Scott." Ariel jumped to her feet. In her haste she knocked over the bowl, spilling popcorn across the floor. The bowl bounced with a metallic clang and came to rest upside down.

She was going to ignore the mess—everything else was a mess, why not her living room, too?—but Scott knelt to pick up the popcorn. Thankful for the reprieve, Ariel helped him.

Neither of them spoke as they refilled the bowl. Ariel could think of nothing except Scott's nearness, nothing except the awareness that toasted her skin like heat from a fire.

The cleanup was almost done. They both reached for the same kernel. Their fingertips touched.

Ariel drew back immediately, then sat on her heels and glanced at his face. "Thank you."

"You're welcome." Instead of rising to leave, Scott copied her posture. No more than a hand-spread separated their knees.

Ariel shook her head and stared at the bowl. "This isn't good."

"You'll have to throw it out."

"What? Oh, the popcorn. Yes, I guess I will." She pushed her hair behind her shoulders. "But I meant the tension between us."

He nodded.

"I want to apologize for what I asked you, Scott. I guess I was out of line. I should have known you aren't the kind of man who could walk away from his child."

Slowly Scott put his hand palm-up on her knee. His index finger intertwined with hers. Sparks of energy shot along Ariel's nerves.

"I was surprised," he said softly. "I didn't think you'd be willing to have planned sex, even for a baby, without love."

Ariel pulled away, as his touch had become a feverous sting, and carried the bowl to the kitchen counter. She tried to drive the heat of desire from her lungs with a deep breath. Too late, of course. Desire for Scott had long since infiltrated every cell of her body.

She faced away from him. "What makes you think," she whispered, "that I don't love you?"

She sucked in a breath and held it, waiting. The distant, almost inaudible ticking of the clock in the bedroom was the only sound. She closed her eyes, completing the illusion of isolation.

Her eyes remained closed even when she heard Scott rise. His footsteps approached, making her back tingle with dread anticipation. Softly he touched her shoulder. She turned to him, anguish and doubt furrowing her brow.

He said nothing. The clock ticked away the seconds.

Scott moved. His mouth approached her lips.

Ariel's frown vanished. Without questioning, Ariel opened to him and welcomed him into her mouth. His tongue probed softly, delicately. He held her the same way, as though she might break if he held her too closely.

Blood pounded through her, fueling a soaring ascent of her spirit. Maybe he had meant the kiss as a chaste comfort, but Ariel didn't care. She melted against him and gloried in the heady explosion of sensation roused by contact with his body.

Scott ended the kiss and stared into her eyes. She felt a giddy smile play across her features. "It's been a long time," she whispered.

"Too long." His hands went to her chest, seeking and releasing the top button of her blouse.

Ariel felt her knees wavering, losing strength as all her concentration switched to the voluptuous stirrings in her breasts. His knuckles brushed her chest as he undid the buttons.

Though she yearned to know why, she wouldn't let herself question this moment or his actions. She wouldn't ask if he loved her. Instead, she would remember each motion, memorize each thrusting burst of sensation and clutch them to her bosom for the rest of her life.

Scott was fast losing himself under an avalanche of desire. All of his arguments were swept aside. Every one of his intentions of focusing on friendship was buried. His last shred of rationality warned him that he was taking an irrevocable step, yet he threw himself forward.

Groaning under the eruption of long-suppressed desire, he thrust aside Ariel's blouse and feasted his hands on her breasts. The lacy hindrance of her bra was an annoyance; he hastened to undo it. Her soft hisses of pleasure rewarded his effort. He explored the fervent pleasure of her bare flesh, so warm and willing under his touch.

"I'll give you your baby, Ariel."

Ariel arched her back, pressing her hard nipple against his palm. Her breath on his cheek was sultry. "It ... it isn't the right time for that, Scott."

He paused as her words registered on his brain.

Of course. This wasn't about love, or about passion. This was about creating a child. A child he would never raise, never hold in his arms to soothe away a nightmare. Never even know.

He dropped his hands to his sides.

"Scott?"

He said nothing.

"Please, you don't have to stop, Scott. Really. Oh, God, I take back what I said. Please, Scott."

Ariel's voice faded to a ragged whisper. "Of course, if you want to stop..."

He took a step backward.

Ariel's mouth was contorted, her expression stricken. Did she know how close she'd come to capturing him body and soul, against every shred of reason? Did she know that if they'd made love, he could have denied her nothing? Did she know that her hesitant words had given them both a reprieve?

"When," he asked with tightly controlled composure, "is the right time?"

Ariel's throat bobbed as she swallowed. Her neck turned a dull pink. She pulled the edges of the blouse closed. "A week and a half."

Scott nodded to give himself time to gather his scattered neurons. Would ten days be enough time to prepare to give himself without losing himself?

He doubted it. He feared that his heart would overrule his head once they made love.

Still, all he could do was try.

Chapter Twelve

"We'll probably never know who shot Wavy." Scott rested his eyes as he took a sip of tea. Was it possible for tea to taste better simply because Ariel had poured it?

His watch said that it was past one in the morning. He'd just arrived, exhausted and yet exhilarated, from two days in Alert Bay, and being in Ariel's kitchen felt like a homecoming. Her hair was in complete disarray, and she wore a baggy housedress over her nightgown. She looked gorgeous.

"I tell myself Wavy was only a whale." Ariel whispered even though Deb, sound asleep under a blanket on the couch, was unlikely to be wakened by anything quieter than a gunshot. "Yet I feel as if I'd lost someone important. Do you remember when we first saw her?"

Scott nodded, too tired to speak.

Ariel reached across the table to take his hand. Surprise pulled his gaze up to Ariel's. When had their relationship eased so she could touch him without making a big deal of it? Or were they both too tired to censor themselves? Scott didn't know, but with his mind in neutral, his body's reaction was positive.

"Are you under any pressure, Scott?"

"Nothing I can't handle. Phil Majesky, though, doesn't quite know how to react."

"Is he the one who sabotaged you and took your job?"

"The same. Right now, however, he's torn between being glad he has someone on hand to represent the department, worrying that the exposure will put me back in favor, and trying to figure out if there's a way to blame me. When he sent me here, I think he hoped the world would forget I existed."

"So this is a break for you?"

"If I handle it well, politically." He shrugged. "But that's not important."

Ariel squeezed his hand. "How is Flopsy?"

"Okay, for now." Scott paused to absorb the comfort of her touch. Maybe by agreeing to give Ariel a child he'd dissolved the barriers she'd built around herself.

He veered from the thought of his own barriers. "Flopsy swam around and around her mother's body for a full day. Other members of the pod hung around, too, probably baffled. Nothing hunts killer whales. They do the hunting."

"Do you think the other orcas will take care of Flopsy? She's just a baby."

"It's more a matter of whether they *can* take care of her. And that I honestly don't know."

Ariel's pale skin, so beautiful and smooth, tightened into a frown of worry.

Scott felt protective cravings stir inside him. He urged Ariel to her feet and pulled her to him in a gentle, reassuring embrace. She came without resistance, as if the months of distance and caution had never happened.

Her body was soft, yielding. The feel of her body prodded him to a new level of physical awareness. Gentle reassurance fled from Scott's intentions, and his hands roamed her back. She was vibrant and responsive under his touch.

Even if this wasn't a fertile time, would Ariel resist if he deepened this embrace? And was that what he wanted?

Well, yes, obviously. He wasn't *that* tired. Yet there were ramifications to consider, commitments to qualify. His mind simply wasn't functioning well enough right now. He pulled back a few inches to lessen the pressure on his willpower.

Ariel's eyes were wide, wondering. She seemed ready to take her cue from him.

"I promise you," he said somewhat unsteadily, "that I'll be studying the pod even more closely to see how the group reacts to this loss and to Flopsy. If nothing else, this is a once-in-a-lifetime research opportunity."

"Research? How about helping? Scott, we can't watch Flopsy be orphaned and not do something."

The look on her face tore at him. "We can't do anything this late at night," he said as he brushed his cheek back and forth against her forehead.

Her body relaxed against him, intensifying Scott's burden of yielding, feminine curves. "That feels great," she whispered.

Far too great. Scott felt renewed desire surge from Ariel's body directly into his loins. He pulled away and cleared his throat. "Did I tell you about my research plan?"

"No." Ariel had felt the stirring of his desire. This easy camaraderie and barely cloaked desire left her glowing inside. It was as if they were both too tired for sparring and defenses. All that was left was the truth of their feelings for each other.

The truth? He loved her; he must. In the past four days she'd poured over possible reasons for Scott's agreeing to father her child. The only reason powerful enough to override his scruples was love. Scott MacKenzie loved her.

"It occurred to me," he said, "that the entrance to Honeymoon Nook is narrow. It should be possible to get a fisherman to string a net across it."

Ariel scarcely heard him. She was wondering if he would ask to spend the night. They'd have to be careful handling the morning after, though, what with Deb asleep in the next room.

From Scott's wary expression he didn't seem ready for that yet. Maybe after more cuddling... In the meantime Ariel dragged her mind back to the conversation. "Why would you put a net there?"

"To keep Flopsy in the cove."

It was late. Ariel felt as if she was thrashing through a molasses pool as her thoughts switched from sharing a bed to snaring a whale. "But orcas don't come in there."

"If I move the speakers into the cove, Flopsy might swim in. Especially if you played some of its mother's calls."

"But why?"

"So I can feed the calf for the next few months. After that it should be able to survive on its own."

"Scott, I'm proud of you." Ariel's heart began to beat more quickly. "I'm glad you love Flopsy like I do." She leaned against him and pressed her lips to his.

He kept the kiss short, however, then walked to the counter and picked up his coat. He stared at Deb, asleep on the couch. "I don't love B-18," he insisted, "but children need parents. Even whale children need looking after."

A shadow of concern crossed Ariel's tired mind as she watched Scott cradle his daughter in his arms and walk to the door. "Yes," she agreed, "they do."

Ariel heard hammering from the storage float behind the lab. Good. She'd worried that Scott would be out in his boat this afternoon.

Today was *the* day, though, and everything would be perfect. It had to be. She smoothed her skirt, wishing she had a mirror to check her makeup after the walk to Honeymoon Nook. A raven watched from the nook's small beach, its claws awash in an incoming wave. It gave no hint what it thought of her makeup.

"Don't you dare say 'nevermore.' Please?"

The bird responded to these whimsical words by cocking its head to one side and staring—with, it seemed to Ariel, a mischievous leer. Blackfish Bay, with scant civilization but much wilderness, was slowly making her understand why the Indians attributed powers to animals. Such thoughts seemed to seep in with the fog.

She waved her arms to scare away the dark spirit. With a small squawk the raven flew to the roof of the laboratory and watched her from there.

"I'm not superstitious," Ariel reminded herself. Without looking at the menacing bird, she pushed her hair behind her shoulders and strode purposefully toward the ramp. Her soft-soled runners made no noise on the planks, which suited her mood. She felt as if she should steal up on Scott.

Ariel rounded the laboratory to the utility raft. Scott sat on a stack of thin sheets of foam insulation near a huge wooden crate that could have held a baby killer whale. His back was to her, and he gave no sign that he heard her. He still hadn't moved when she was right behind him. Slowly, tentatively, she touched his shoulder.

He jerked at her touch. "Hello, Ariel."

She didn't give him time to say anything more. She kissed him.

It was intended as a greeting. When he responded by opening his lips to her tongue, it grew to an expression of desire, sweet and daring and intense. Ariel held nothing back. She was the aggressor in this kiss, and as her tongue explored the taste of his mouth, her hands explored his shoulder and back. His muscles were hard under her caress. Warmth began to mushroom inside her.

And then she was no longer the aggressor. Scott met her caresses with demands of his own, demands that carried her to a reclining position on the firm foam. He pinned her under his hard body. His hand roamed her neck and scalp, down to her shoulders and then to the eager swell of her breast. She bobbed on the waves of hunger that his caresses started to pour through her. Amazing, she thought, how quickly Scott's touch turned her on. It was as fast and simple as turning on a tap.

When they broke the kiss, his rapid breath fanned her cheek with warmth. Scott moved his hand from her breast and sat. Feeling bereft, Ariel also sat up and put her arm around him.

Scott lifted her chin with his finger. "Don't you believe in saying hello like normal people?"

"No. Are you complaining?"

"Hardly." A flame danced in Scott's eyes. "Has the great god Estrogen kidnapped your mind, woman?"

Ariel answered his chuckle with a gentle laugh of her own. "What a way with words," she said. "Are you trying to seduce me with your silver tongue?"

Comprehension dawned on his face, and his eyebrows rose till they drew together. "Now I understand the passionate greeting."

Looking past him, Ariel saw the raven on the peak of the roof, staring at her. How could she talk seduction with that *thing* watching her? Ariel cast around her for a new topic. The forest was the same dark green, however, the sea its usual expansive self, the sky a normal, wispy blue. Nothing worth commenting on.

"What is this crate, Scott?"

"It's for fish." In one easy motion he stood and vaulted into the waist-high enclosure. "I'm insulating it so I can store ice with the fish for Flopsy."

Ariel kept her voice light. "Don't you mean B-18?"

Surprisingly Scott didn't smile. "You made me forget the glue gun. Would you hand it to me?"

She gave him the pistol-shaped tool. He knelt down and began spreading glue across the boards.

"When do you want my help luring Flopsy into the nook?"

"Not for a while. Phil's found a way to try to keep me from getting credit for doing my job."

"How can he do that?"

Scott's voice was flat, and he kept working. "He's acting as if my proposal is the same as a marine show trying to capture and exploit an orca. He's organizing a public meeting on the proposal right after school is out, hoping that will give environmental groups time to get upset.''

''I'm sorry, Scott.''

He shrugged as he lifted a foam sheet inside the crate. ''I don't think his ploy will work, so I want to be prepared.''

A lump formed in Ariel's throat. She didn't want to think about the school year ending, or about how to spend the long, lonely summer. ''Where's Deb?''

''At Tammy's.''

Ariel stood at the side of the crate so she could watch him place the foam sheet onto the glued boards. He leaned against the sheet to hold it in place while she held the top edge.

''When do you have to pick up Deb?''

''In a couple of hours. Hand me another piece of foam.''

Ariel gritted her teeth as she lifted the light sheet. At this rate the two hours would be gone before Scott got around to accepting her proposition.

He didn't look up from his work as he spoke. ''I gather from the passion of your greeting that you want me to get you pregnant tonight.''

Ariel's heart began thudding inside her chest. Giving in to impulse, she jumped over the side of the crate. At the top she struggled to get over, but she didn't care how unlady-like she appeared. She had to touch him.

Scott raised his eyebrows. ''Now? Here?''

''Well, I'd rather not have the bird watch.'' She put her arms around his waist from the back and pressed against him. ''But I'll do anything you want, Scott. Anything.''

''Bird?'' He cocked his head to one side. ''What bird?''

She pointed to the roof. ''The . . . well, there was a bird. Honestly,'' she said as he began to chuckle, ''a raven was on the roof, and it was staring at me.''

''Ariel, you've been talking to too many killer whales. I suspect that a psychiatrist would prescribe a marathon trip to a shopping mall.''

''Don't make jokes, Scott. This is hard enough as it is.''

She'd said the wrong thing. She could see it in his face and feel it in his tightened muscles. "I see."

Saying nothing more, Scott continued working. He paid no attention to her arms around his waist or to the kiss she planted on his neck. Despite her ardor, he ignored her. An emotional pain sliced into her heart as Ariel slipped her arms to her side. Being ignored was more hurtful than unkind words.

Scott went back to work, gluing two more foam sheets in place. When he reached for a third sheet, Ariel couldn't stand being ignored any longer. "I didn't say that making love to you would be hard."

"No," he acknowledged, "you didn't say it."

What did he expect, a unilateral declaration of undying affection? She'd already told him that she loved him. The next move was up to him. "I only came here today and greeted you with a kiss," she said, "because you told me that you'd agreed."

He looked at the anxiety creasing Ariel's clear forehead without speaking. Would she kiss him only to expedite having a child? Was a baby the price of her body?

Scott took a deep breath and tried to control his turbulent feelings. This was Ariel. He respected her judgment enough to grant that her decision was correct—for her, if not for him. No matter how uneasy this whole situation made him, he knew she wouldn't prostitute herself even to have a baby.

He ran his fingers along his nape. Things had been more straightforward with his ex-wife. She'd wanted neither him nor their child. Yet from Deborah's betrayal he'd learned the wonder and worry of being a parent. This knowledge would torture him every day that he wasn't part of the life of Ariel's child.

"Do you want out of our agreement, Scott? Is that it?"

"Since you ask, yes."

"I see." Ariel quickly turned her gaze to the roof of the lab. Though she almost expected to see the raven leering at her, it was gone. "You at least owe me an explanation."

"Because of this." He slapped the wood of the crate, his palm stinging from the explosive violence. "B-18's problems made me realize that the world doesn't need another fatherless bastard. If the calf had two parents to care for it, there wouldn't be this potential tragedy."

Ariel raised her chin, though it was obviously an effort. "I love Flopsy, but she's just a whale. It isn't the same."

He shook his head and bent to continue working.

"Scott, how do you feel about me? Do you love me?"

He picked up the hammer and whacked at a loose nail in the corner of the crate. "Irrelevant."

"It's the only thing that *is* relevant. You can't admit you love me. What do you think you are, some sort of human iceberg that's broken off from the ice pack and has to go through life alone until the tides wear you down to nothing?"

"Nice choice of words," he said, "but not logical."

"You're not nearly as logical as you'd like to believe."

No, he thought, at the moment he wasn't logical at all. He wanted Ariel to make love not for a baby, but for him. He wanted her to need him to raise the child. He wanted her to apologize for what she'd asked and then seduce him anyway. He wanted—

No, he didn't. He was just getting carried away. "I'm a scientist," he said harshly.

"And aren't scientists supposed to care?" She took a deep breath and held her hand out to him.

He looked at her hand and said nothing. If he touched her, he was lost.

"Scott, I . . . I care for you."

"Do you really? Or do you just want a child?"

"Both. What can I do to prove it?"

"Nothing." He turned away, then looked back at her. "On second thought, there is something. Give me time to sort things out."

"But I won't have another fertile period until after school ends. I don't have time to give, Scott."

"I see." Scott looked at her, seeing a beautiful face and intelligent eyes that shone with yearning. Weariness engulfed him. "If we were married, you'd have lots of time, wouldn't you?"

The smoldering look of yearning in her face broke into bright, searing flame. "Yes, I would," she said with scarcely bridled ardor. "Scott, does this mean..." She took a step toward him, arm outstretched.

Scott backed away.

Ariel dropped her arm to her side. She looked at him, and he looked at her. If only she'd said that she needed *him* he would have been in her arms in a minute. He couldn't have helped himself, despite all the logic in the world. The harsh croak of a raven interrupted his thoughts, which crumbled into a chaos of uncertainty.

Ariel's face became hard. "I meant what I said about not trying to trap you into marriage. It's cruel of you to play with me like that."

"I wasn't playing."

"Really?" She squeezed and rubbed her elbow so hard that the skin was white under her fingers. "Were you proposing, then?"

"No, I..." Scott rested his elbows on the side of the crate and lowered his head so he could run his hand through his hair. He'd just been thinking out loud, exploring options, not expecting her overreaction. Couldn't she give him time to think? "Look, I don't know why I mentioned it. Forget I said it."

Ariel's eyes began to glisten. "Damn you, Scott MacKenzie." She slapped her palm against the side of the crate. "And damn this box I'm trapped in with you."

"I'll help you out," he said. And then, as he touched the warm softness of her waist, his control broke. "Don't run away, Ariel. Please."

She tore herself from his grip and made an ungraceful exit from the crate. She turned on him with the suddenness of a Pacific gale. Her formidable dignity wasn't diminished by the unshed tears in her eyes. "I won't ever run from you again. I may leave, but that's another matter." She took a deep breath and extended her hand toward him. "I'll always remember you."

Scott slowly unclenched his fists from the edge of the crate and reached his hand toward hers. "You make it sound as if you're saying goodbye."

Their fingers met. The sparks that flew along his arm did little to melt the iceberg of despair that seemed to fill him.

"Not goodbye," she said. "After all, you know where I live. If you change your mind, I'll be waiting."

She trailed her nails along his palm as she slowly withdrew her hand.

"You're a true lady, Ariel. I wish . . . I wish I could give you what you want."

"I'll survive." Her quiet simplicity touched him more than any amount of histrionics. "After all, I've had a lot of experience being alone."

A knock sounded on the teacherage door. Ariel turned from the stove to look out the window, but she couldn't see her visitor. She licked the spaghetti sauce from the spoon as she walked to the door. The sauce, redolent of oregano and tomato, needed more pepper.

She opened the door and then stood motionless, the spoon near her lips.

"Hello," Scott said.

Still staring at him, Ariel lowered her arm.

"Careful." Scott reached for her wrist and held it so the sauce on the handle wouldn't drip on the floor. He took the spoon and carried it to the sink.

"I didn't expect you," Ariel managed to say. In the two lonely weeks since she'd propositioned him, awkwardness had kept them from saying more than a few words to each other. Ariel felt as if they'd said everything there was to say, and there was nothing left.

"Am I early?"

"Early?"

He looked into the living room. "Where's Deb?"

"I don't know. Scott, why are you here?"

"To pick up Deb." A look of concern mixed with impatience tinged his handsome features. "Let me guess. She isn't here."

"I haven't seen her since I dismissed class this afternoon."

With a deep sigh Scott ran his fingers through his hair. "She told me you two had arranged to go hiking to some special place."

"She never said anything to me."

"I see." He leaned heavily against the counter, his voice heavy with regret. "I guess I should have expected something like this. Still, I didn't think Deb would lie."

The urge to comfort him was so strong that Ariel had to lace her fingers together behind her back. "I'm sorry, Scott."

"I don't suppose you have any idea where she is?"

"Well, we do have a favorite place where we hike." And, she thought, the scheming little creature was probably leaning against a totem pole right now, waiting for Scott and Ariel to rescue her—together, of course.

Scott shook his head with a look of long-suffering patience. "Where is it?"

"It's a beach about a mile and a half in the opposite direction from Honeymoon Nook." Ariel turned off the stove and put the spaghetti sauce in the fridge. "Deb wanted it to be our special place. I'll show you."

She went to the closet and slipped on her jacket. Scott reached around her for her digger hat and placed it on her head.

His nearness had its customary effect. A smile warmed her face, and her lungs grew tight. She wanted to fling herself into his arms. She wanted, with equal fervor, to flee from him.

"Don't worry," she said to cover the internal warfare between love and caution. "Deb can handle herself in the woods. I agree that she planned this to get the two of us talking."

"I'm still not happy at the thought of her out there alone."

"I'm sure she's fine." Deb was probably less scared, Ariel thought, than she herself was.

Scott stood by the closet, blocking her way. His gaze skimmed her face. "You look tired. In fact, you look terrible."

"See, it's working. We're talking. I, uh, don't think Deb meant for you to insult me, though."

Scott took a half step toward her. He loomed so large and close that it was as if he blocked out the rest of the world, leaving only the elemental polarity of man and woman. Ariel's heart ached, protesting the increased tempo his presence roused.

"Have you been sleeping well, Ariel?"

"No." She refused to mention that her poor sleep was because of him. He could figure that out easily enough.

He burrowed his hand under her hair to cup her neck, an action that felt as intimate as slipping it under her clothes. Ariel raised her head to meet his probing gaze.

"I never meant to hurt you, Ariel. Everything I've done has been to keep from hurting you. You believe that, don't you?"

Did she? Loving her would have been the only way to keep from hurting her, and he wasn't capable of admitting his love. If he did indeed love her. She was no longer sure of anything. Somehow she found the strength to shrug rather than lean like a cat into the pressure of his hand. "You didn't want to be hurt, either."

A deepening of the creases at the corners of his eyes acknowledged that she was right. "It hasn't worked very well on either count, has it?"

Hope whisked through her like a jolt of sexual pleasure. Ariel steeled herself against it. The effort left her knees on the verge of trembling and her voice on the edge of a whisper. "I guess not."

His fingers stirred on her neck. Ariel pulled back. If she didn't tear away immediately, she wouldn't be able to tear away at all.

She buried her fists in her jacket pockets and moved toward the door with a worried glance over her shoulder at Scott. Though she didn't see how she could spend an hour or two in his company without exploding, the only way to get through the agony was one step at a time, with gritted teeth and no thoughts to what might have been. Which, after loving Scott, was how she'd have to live the rest of her life.

"Let's go," she said quietly.

Chapter Thirteen

The walk seemed to take forever. The sway of Ariel's hips through the dense greenery mesmerized Scott's gaze. Looking away didn't help, because his gaze returned to her body like a compass returning to north.

Not only did he look, but he reacted. No tricks of diversion helped to soften his masculine response to the tight stretch of her jeans as she climbed over a log; to the womanly curves that were within his reach yet beyond him; to the whisper of her scent that teased the air in front of him.

Scott forced his gaze to the shadowy lace where the sun peeked through the evergreens, but his desire didn't diminish. He hadn't had such a one-track mind since he was a teenager.

When Ariel reached to brace herself against a tree, her jacket and blouse rode up to tantalize him with a glimpse of midriff. That set off a whole new train of thought, though it ran on the same track. Scott passed her so he'd have something to see and think about other than Ariel's backside.

"We're nearly there," Ariel said. She waited and looked at him as if expecting a reply.

Scott stepped carefully around a wickedly thorny devil's club bush. "Good."

Ariel pranced around the far side of the bush and waited for him, rubbing her hands together nervously. "Has there been any response to Phil's call for a public meeting?"

"Nothing I can't handle."

"I'm glad."

"A few pickets at the Victoria office," he continued. "Letters to the editor calling for my firing. A death threat. Nothing much."

"Oh, Scott." Ariel touched his upper arm. "I'm sorry."

Scott paused while he hardened himself against the impact of her light touch. "The public was looking for a scapegoat in the whale's death. Looks like I'm it."

"But that's ridiculous. You're just trying to help Flopsy. If you talk at the public meeting about how much you love her, they'll be on your side."

"I've told you before," he said rigidly, "I don't love B-18. My proposal is for scientifically valid research."

She lowered her hand. "Ah, yes, I can see it now. You'll go into the meeting all logical and cold and let them crucify you."

"Emotions are the answer to everything, is that it?"

"No," she admitted heavily. "Sometimes emotions just plain hurt. But it's a crime to pretend you don't have emotions when the pretense needlessly destroys so much."

They walked in silence for several minutes. Finally Ariel stopped and pointed. "There's the beach."

Scott hurried on, calling Deb's name.

"Over here," came an impatient voice. The sound of thrashing bushes signaled the girl's approach. She emerged into view and planted her hand on her hip. "It's about time," Deb said. "I was getting bored out of my mind waiting for you."

"Are you all right?" Ariel asked.

"Of course I'm all right." Deb waved them toward the open stretch along the water. "Come on, you two. We have to talk."

"Young lady," Scott warned, "you're in trouble. I've half a mind to put you over my knee."

Deb didn't bother to look at him. "Oh, Daddy, you know you don't do that sort of thing."

"I'm always open to change."

"Hah!" Ariel said.

Scott glared at her, then at the waving willow leaves that marked his daughter's path. "Trouble, in stereo," he muttered. "Women." His mood growing increasingly dark, he headed through the bushes to the edge of the water.

Deb skipped ahead. Aided by the precarious slant of an old totem pole, she perched partway up it with her feet on a raven's beak. When Scott came close, she held up her hand, a pleading expression on her thin face. "Please, Daddy?"

Scott didn't plan to stop. He planned, instead, to lift Deb off her pulpit and warn her that his love life was his business. Yet when he saw that her eyes brimmed, he paused. Since her mother left, Deb had never cried. The memory of his ex-wife settled over his already smoldering spirits like a lid that concentrated the choking, acrid fumes into a poisonous aura.

He turned briefly toward the gusts that poured in off the sea, then back to his daughter. Females didn't fight fairly. A helpless anger joined the emotions bubbling inside him.

Nonetheless, he spoke softly. "I'm listening, Deb."

The girl's throat moved as she swallowed. "I want..." She looked from Scott to Ariel. "I want a mommy."

"This isn't something that you can solve for us, Deb."

He felt Ariel's touch on his arm, so soft as to deflect any rebuttal. "Listen to her, Scott."

Ariel was right, of course, but he would have listened without her intervention. He stared at the totem figure that stared back at him. He would listen—but he refused to make a decision because of weepy emotionalism. "Go ahead, Deb."

"That's all." Deb shrugged. Her eyes still glittered, but no tears flowed. "I...I need to know if, well, if you two..." Her voice faded.

"The answer is no," Ariel said.

Scott stared at her. "You sound awfully definite, considering what you've asked me."

Deb swung back and forth on the raven, hope in her eyes. "Did you ask him to marry you?"

When Scott crossed his arms and glared at his daughter, Ariel studied his rugged, stubborn face. Had she asked the wrong question? No, she already knew what his answer would be. She'd risked enough already.

"It isn't that simple, hon," Ariel cautioned. "Your father can't admit he loves me."

"Do you, Daddy?"

Ariel went to her knees and hugged the girl. "You might as well ask the totem pole, I'm afraid. He can't say the words."

Deb swiveled to look at Scott. "But you used to tell Mommy that you loved her all the time. I remember you coming behind her when she was painting and whispering it real loud."

Scott turned to stare at the slate gray sea and distant, untouchable mountains.

The bravado behind Ariel's words crumbled. If Scott used to verbalize his feelings, maybe she was wrong. Maybe he didn't love her. Maybe she'd been kidding herself. Maybe—

She squeezed Deb hard, then stood and slumped against the pole, her eyes closed. For several minutes silence wrapped itself around her as close and smothering as plastic wrap.

One word, Ariel thought. If she were right about Scott, then one word uttered into this suffocating silence would make everything right. They were that close. What word, though?

Besides, she might be deluding herself. Heaven knows she'd done that before. This time seemed so totally differ-

nt, though... She pressed the back of her head painfully
gainst the obdurate cedar raven.

What word?

Ariel opened her eyes when she heard Deb sobbing. She
nelt on one side of the girl and Scott on the other. Both of
hem were careful not to let their hands stray too close to the
ther.

Deb spoke through her tears. "I want you to stay with me,
riel. I want that so much, but wanting it doesn't help."
Anger mingled with despair on her face, which for once ap-
eared younger than her years.

Ariel glanced at Scott, but he was looking at his daugh-
er and stroking her hair.

"School will be out in a couple of weeks," Deb said,
and I'll never see you again."

Ariel glanced at Scott before giving full attention to the
irl. "I'll keep in touch, hon, I promise." The promise hurt,
ecause it meant keeping Scott alive in her memories. Not
at she had much choice about that.

"You'll send me cards," Deb said in a ravaged, desolate
hisper. "On my birthday. And at Christmas."

Ariel tightened her grip on Deb's arm. The magic she'd
nce found in this ancient beach seemed to have turned evil,
oncentrating the world's pain into the voice of the inno-
ent girl. "Yes, I'll send you cards, but I'll do more than
at."

A burst of cool ocean wind hid Deb's face behind a veil
f dark hair. "No, you won't. You'll forget about me."

"Never." Ariel smoothed the hair back from the inno-
ent's face. Scott reached for her hair at the same moment.
heir fingers touched, and neither of them retreated.

"Your mother hasn't forgotten you," he whispered. "I
now her pretty well, and I know she still loves you. I think
he was too scared to tell you face-to-face that she was leav-
ig."

Deb shook her head. "Why should she be scared? She
n't the one who got left behind."

"We have each other, Deb. Your mommy is alone, except for the memories of her precious girl. I think she's scared she'll lose even the memories."

Ariel removed her fingers from Scott's. "She should see her mother, Scott. Could that be arranged?"

"Well . . . sure, it could. How would you like to visit your mother, Deb? We could see Disneyland, too."

Deb's lips quivered. "When?"

"I don't know." Scott laced his fingers through his hair. "With all this publicity about the whales I don't know when I can get away. If not this summer, though, then next summer."

The girl's face went blank. "Oh."

Ariel seized Scott's hand. He looked at her, startled. "Can I take her? I meant what I said, Deb. We could have a wonderful trip together. Please say yes, Scott."

He stared into Ariel's face and then, with something very close to surrender in his heart, he nodded. "I think that's a great idea. Don't you, Deb?"

Deb let out a deep moan. She began crying. Adult-sized sobs shook her delicate frame.

"There, there," Scott said.

He held her, looking at Ariel for assistance. She stroked the girl's shoulder, but didn't know what else to do.

"You don't have to visit your mother if you don't want to," he said.

Ariel stared at him, amazed that he could be so far off the mark. She laid her cheek against the girl's shaking back. It was good that Deb was finally ready to cry. "Tell us about your mother, Deb. You can talk about it."

Deb sniffed, but her moans slowly subsided. "With Mommy . . ." She was interrupted by a sob from deep inside her. "With Mommy, I got mad. She'd made me wait before, long after the other kids went home, and that day I hated her for it. I wished she'd go away, because I hated her so. And she did."

Scott continued stroking her hair. "Mommy didn't go away because of you. Not because of you, baby."

Deb sniffed. "No?"

"Absolutely. Not even because of me, really. She just wasn't cut out to be a wife and mother."

"Do you understand what your father's saying, hon?" Ariel leaned close to the girl's face. "You aren't to blame."

Still sheltered in Scott's embrace, Deb turned her head to look at Ariel. With a valiant attempt at a smile, she nodded. Each tear, each sob, knifed into Ariel's heart. She loved this girl nearly as much as she loved Scott, and the girl needed her.

So did Scott. Couldn't he see that?

Obviously not.

Ariel threw her arms around both of them. They huddled together on the windswept beach while the ancient cedar raven watched and chuckled.

After that, there really didn't seem to be anything left to say.

The remaining weeks of school passed in a delirium. Pressure mounted on Scott because of his proposal to capture Flopsy, but he remained adamant. If anything, his near surrender during the emotional scene on the totem pole beach left him more determined than ever.

He didn't change his mind about letting Ariel take Deb to California, however. They made plane reservations for the last week in July. Their brief discussions were polite yet restrained. Deb discussed the trip with an enthusiasm that seemed subdued for Ariel's sake.

The children threw Ariel a party on the last day of school. Parmijeet, the girl from India who hadn't known English, was the spokesperson for the group in presenting Ariel with a present. Tammy cried about Deb not returning in the fall. Ronald Prescott gave Ariel his prize collection of fish scales. Damien, the class troublemaker, astounded Ariel by hugging her and proclaiming that she was the best teacher he'd ever had.

And then it was over. The students left, and Ariel was more alone than ever before in her life. She walked around the classroom and wondered how she'd ever thought that other people's children could fill her life.

Fifteen minutes after the school boat had left, she was already hugging her elbows and staring toward the trees that hid the cabins. Ariel glanced at her desk, but little needed doing. She'd worked every night until she was exhausted. That way she hadn't thought about what might have been.

At least she wouldn't be here much longer. Unwilling to prolong the agony of a chilled relationship with Scott, she'd made arrangements to visit friends in Victoria and Clearwater right after school ended. The floatplane was picking her up tomorrow at noon.

Only a few chores remained. Take down the artwork on the bulletin board. Replace it with a new display for the fall. Sort through the pile of papers that always accumulated at the side of her desk.

Sighing deeply, she picked up the papers. Mostly they were irrelevant now, or not important enough to file. Reports on new social studies texts. Newsletters from the teachers' union. A note from a mother excusing an absence. Ariel flung the papers in the general direction of the garbage can, not caring whether they made it or not.

With a nod of false satisfaction, Ariel propped her feet on the desk. She began to jot down a list of things to take with her, but the list turned into things she should have said to Scott.

"You stupid jerk, you love me. Admit it!"

No, he would just have retreated into his shell of logic.

"Even if you won't give me a child, make love to me."

That would have gotten his attention, at least. Better yet, say it not in words but in actions.

Her mind wandered through a fantasy in which she seduced Scott slowly, thoroughly and delightfully, thus earning his pledge of undying devotion. It wasn't a bad idea, either. They had talked too much and made love too little. Playing with the top button of her blouse, Ariel glanced out the window.

No, she decided, not after all that had happened. She lacked the nerve to set herself up for that huge a humiliation. She drew angry lines through her notes to Scott.

Without thinking, she grabbed a sheet of notebook paper and began a letter.

Dear Scott,
I love you. I think you love me. What in life is more important than that?

Ariel glanced out the window toward the cabins. Where here was life, there was hope. She had enough nerve for a letter. At least she wouldn't have to watch him laugh as he read it. She began pouring her heart onto paper. The first page was filled in minutes. She began another, then another.

"Whatcha doing, lass?"

Angus stood close to the desk, watching her curiously.

Ariel jumped and used her arms to cover the jumble of sheets on the desk. "Nothing. Nothing at all. Aren't you early?"

"Nope. You're late. Pretty involved in your writing, too, since you didn't hear me come in."

He picked up the garbage can and muttered about all the year-end garbage. "What about those papers?" He pointed his chin in the direction of the sheets Ariel was sorting into order. "Those go in the garbage, too?"

"No." Fifteen pages? How long had she been writing? She couldn't hand this to Scott. Well, she had to give it to him—she *had* to—but how could she bear his pitying expression when he felt the weight of this cry from her heart?

Angus lingered by the desk, sniffing the bottle of cologne the class had given her. He cocked his head to one side, unabashedly trying to read upside down.

"Love letter, eh?"

Ariel folded the sheets so he couldn't see.

"You've leaving tomorrow, aren't you, lass?"

"Yes." She pulled an envelope out from a drawer an
wrote Scott's name on it.

"Be back in the fall?"

Ariel paused with the envelope flap near her lips. Sinc
she wasn't expecting a child, she had no reason to move nea
better health care. "Yes."

The old man gave a gap-toothed grin. "The fishy ma
won't. From the chatter I hear over the radiophone, he'll b
lucky if they let him stay in the country, let alone at Black
fish Bay."

Ariel gave him an annoyed glance. She sealed the enve
lope.

"You're not very talkative today, lass."

"No."

The fat envelope weighed in Ariel's hands as heavily a
the entire world. The amount of willpower needed for he
to keep from staring toward the cabins was painful.

"If the fishy man's leaving," Angus said, "that must b
a goodbye letter."

Ariel's lungs seemed to stop working. She looked up fror
the letter to see Angus's sad gaze upon her. "Angus, you'r
never nosy. Why are you starting now?"

He jumped as if she'd poked him with a cattle prod. H
began gathering erasers from the ledge below the chalk
boards. Ariel thought he wouldn't answer, but he did. "
want what's best for you, lass."

Ariel drummed the envelope against her palm as sh
stared out the window. She knew she was taking a tremen
dous chance, but if she wanted to avoid Scott, it was he
only option. "Then take this to him."

Angus dropped the erasers in a flurry of chalk dust an
cussing. He stared at her.

"Please, Angus. I don't think I have the courage to giv
it to him." Ariel walked to the old man, looming over him
"Please. Just slip it under his door."

"It'd never fit."

"Then wedge it between the frame and the knob. Please."
Angus looked as though he wanted to run for his life.

"You said you wanted what's best for me," she reminded.

"Yeah, but you were doing so well on your own—"

"I love him, Angus."

"Love," he said with a weary sigh. "Are you sure this is
what's best for you?"

"Please, Angus."

He stared at her for a few seconds, then grabbed the envelope. "I told you once that I'd been engaged. I also told
you I came to my senses and skipped town."

"I remember."

"Well, I lied. She jilted me. I tracked her down and
begged her to marry me anyway, just like you're begging the
fishy man." Angus waved the letter in his fist. "She still
turned me down, and she *laughed* at me. Lass, don't do
this."

"I'm so sorry, Angus." Ariel swallowed past the lump
that made her voice a husky whisper. "But I don't have any
choice."

The old man stared at her for several seconds. With a
disgusted snort he stomped out of the classroom.

Ariel watched through the windows until he disappeared
into the trees, and then she still watched.

"I'll get it, Daddy."

Scott, sitting at his desk, looked up from the reports that
he'd been staring at without reading. "I didn't hear anything."

"I did." Still light with end-of-school bubbliness, Deb
skipped across the living room and opened the front door.

She screeched and retreated from the door.

Scott sprang to his feet, sending papers flying. He jerked
the door open and glared at the old man who stood there,
bent over as if to...well, as if to pick the lock.

"Can't you knock like a normal human being?"

Hiding something behind his back, Angus pulled himself
to his full height, somewhere around Scott's collarbone. "I
didn't knock."

Deb hid herself behind her father. "He scratched at the door," she announced indignantly, "like a cat."

Angus's eyes narrowed and he half turned as if to leave.

Scott hugged his daughter. "What do you want, Angus? I'm not in the mood for games." Ariel's departure loomed over his thoughts like storm clouds. Scott held Deb tighter to reassure her and waited impatiently for the old man to speak.

Angus cleared his throat, but the words still came out squeaky. "Ariel sent me."

"Is she hurt? Did she have an accident?"

Angus jumped back to the bottom step of the porch, making Scott realize that he'd taken an aggressive step forward.

"She . . . she gave me a message for you."

Scott's heart grew heavy. Any message brought by this relic couldn't be good. "Stay inside, Deb." He stepped onto the landing and closed the door. "What's the message?"

Angus's arm stirred. He glanced at Scott, then looked away.

Scott stepped forward, looming over Angus's face. He kept his hands off the other man with an effort. "Damn it, what did she say?"

Shielding himself as if to ward off blows, Angus backed away. "I only came here because I want what's best for her," he whined. "I don't see what she ever saw in you, you big bully."

"I'm sorry." Scott stuffed his hands in his pockets and forced calm into his voice. "Now, what's the message?"

"She said she doesn't want to see you again, ever. She said she's better off without you. She said she needs to rebuild her life on her own, and she doesn't want you to come say goodbye before she leaves. She said she hates you."

Angus skittered away. He stopped at the edge of the trees and looked at Scott defiantly. Turning, he threw something into the cold waters of Blackfish Bay, then hurried away.

* * *

When the floatplane angled into the mouth of the bay, its roar was magnified by echoes off the cliff behind Angus's float house. Ariel heard the sound, felt its trembling in her heart, but didn't turn to look. Instead, she remained facing the fractured glimpses of white visible through the trees, exactly as she'd stood for the past fifteen minutes.

She finally turned when the bush pilot tossed her a line to tie the plane to the dock. Her body felt so heavy that she was dully amazed she could climb into the plane. Resting her temple against the cool window, she stared at the trees. The roar of the engine scarcely registered on her consciousness. When the plane turned so she could no longer see any glimpses of white, Ariel squeezed her eyes shut. A tear slipped down her cheek.

He hadn't even said goodbye. After all they'd been to each other; after all they could have been to each other; after that soul-baring letter, Scott hadn't even said goodbye.

Her lips mouthed a goodbye, but she couldn't bring herself to say it aloud. Something inside her died.

In the cabin the roar of the plane was like a drill boring through Scott's soul. Deb shook, crying without sound. He tightened his grasp on her and buried his face in her hair.

Somehow he'd never imagined Ariel leaving. Strange. It had seemed as if all the time in the world stretched between them. Of course, the end had to come. All relationships ended.

Then why did this moment seem so unreal?

"She didn't even say goodbye," Deb whispered.

"I know, kiddo." He hugged her tighter. Why, dear God, did he fall in love with women who left without a word?

Scott froze as he replayed what he'd just thought. *Why did he fall in love*... After an eternity he jerked his head to look out the window, straining without success for a glimpse of the floatplane.

He rose and stared out the window. Though the engine still assaulted his ears, there was nothing to see. Without realizing what he was doing, he edged toward the door....

Scott jerked to a stop. Taking a deep breath, he shook off the annoying buzz of the plane.

"She's gone," Deb sobbed.

Without even a glance toward the window, Scott took his daughter on his lap. "Let's look at this logically," he said in a voice that was brittle and devoid of emotion.

All his emotions had just fled, too.

Chapter Fourteen

"Nice to have met you, Dr. Arnold."

"The same, MacKenzie." Thomas Arnold, whose grizzled beard and weathered skin belied his image as a professor, shook Scott's hand. He preceded Scott into the humid, echoing hall lined with folding chairs, most of them filled.

"Sharks," Arnold said with a snort, "hoping for a feeding frenzy, as if we can't be trusted to do right by the calf."

Scott looked around, but saw only ordinary people, many in the standard north-coast attire of jeans, work boots and plaid shirts, fanning themselves or chatting while they waited for the public meeting to begin. "They're here because they care."

"You're more generous than I, MacKenzie. Anyway, you think about my offer. If we can pull off this meeting, we'd love to have you on our team."

Scott, his mind on a floatplane that had left three days ago, merely nodded as Arnold headed briskly toward the speaker's table. Ariel, of course, wasn't here. And that seemed . . . well, strange. Not right.

Her words about this meeting rang in his ears like a curse. *They'll crucify you.* If they did, Arnold's plan to have the University of Victoria fund the rescue of B-18—Flopsy— would sink, along with Scott's career.

It wasn't much of a career anymore. Right about now, he wasn't sure he really cared.

Scott wandered through the crowd, cool and aloof. What had Ariel called him—an iceberg drifting alone as the tides wore him down? Yeah, that was him. An iceberg lost in a sweltering room.

Scott reached the speaker's table, where Deb sat beside Phil Majesky with her face even more solemn than usual. Another surreal aspect of this day was the realization that he trusted Phil with his daughter. The man had always been good with children, and he was trying hard to be friendly. He must know he'd won, and so he could be generous.

"We'll be starting soon," Phil said as he rubbed nervously at his mustache. "You go sit with your friends, Deb."

"Okay." She squeezed Scott's hand, then went to the front row where several families from Mowitch Island sat, including the Fearsons and all the Prescotts.

Phil, impeccably dressed in a conservative navy blue suit, watched her go. "You have everything, Scott, and you don't even know it. You're a fool."

"Careful, Phil. You probably won't be my boss for long, so I don't have to act polite and humble."

"You never were humble." Phil's laughter held an edge of self-deprecation. "Being humble is second nature to me, of course, because I have so much to be humble about. And look where humility has gotten me. You can go only so far in a bureaucracy on ability, you know."

Scott watched as the crowd sought seats. Despite everything, he still liked this man. Phil's wife had gotten custody of his children, and after that his ambition had hardened into ruthlessness. Scott wished he didn't know, didn't understand, what being alone could do to a person. Even Angus, who'd made a nuisance of himself by hanging around since Ariel left, kept seeking reassurance that Scott was all right.

He wasn't all right, damn it. But of course he wasn't about to admit it.

"Don't do it, Scott."

He turned back to Phil. "Don't do what?"

"Antagonize all these people just because you're sure you're right. I can see in your eyes that's what you're determined to do." Phil started to walk to the podium, then paused. "Bend. Compromise. Show them you're human and that you're on their side."

"You almost sound as though you don't want this crowd to eat me alive."

Phil met Scott's stare. "I should shut up and let you hang yourself, shouldn't I? But we were friends for a long time. I hate to see you so hell-bent on being stubborn and independent that you're willing to ruin your career."

Scott turned away without answering. Shades of Ariel. But then, everything reminded him of her.

He scarcely listened to Phil's opening remarks, nor paid much attention to the Save The Whales placards waving at the back of the packed hall. He wished that Ariel was beside him. Why wasn't she? He knew the reasons, but somehow they didn't add up to anything sufficient to keep them apart. Funny how he'd never looked at it that way before.

Or maybe the pressure was just distorting his outlook. He tried to recapture his perspective.

He was called to the podium to explain the capture proposal. Scattered boos greeted his introduction.

Scott stood and adjusted the microphone. "Ladies and gentlemen," he began.

Deb caught his eye. She was slouched in her chair, as if trying not to be noticed. Though her mouth quivered and her eyes were wide with apprehension, she gazed at him with love.

Her vulnerable trust made him pause. He loved her so much. He wanted to rush from the podium, take her in his arms and reassure her that everything would turn out right.

But would it? Was he even doing his best, both for her and for himself?

Scott opened his mouth, then closed it. His speech fled from his mind. The little of it that he remembered seemed irrelevant. *Unique research opportunity*... what was that compared with happiness? With love? It wasn't just his career he was ruining. It was his life.

Stubbornness was his prerogative, he supposed. But did he have the right to ruin Deb's life, too, by cutting her off from security and love?

Just so he wouldn't have to admit he loved a baby whale. *Or Ariel.*

Members of the crowd shuffled impatiently in their seats. Deb smiled at him bravely.

Her smile gave Scott courage. Ariel's smile would have given him even more courage. With the support of his two women he could take on the world. Without both of them he was... alone. Not an iceberg, scarcely even an ice cube.

People coughed and shifted impatiently in their chairs. Deb studied her hands. Phil looked at him with a mixture of anxiety and encouragement. And Ariel wasn't there to look at him at all.

He needed her. Didn't she know that without him having to say it? And didn't these people know he'd never hurt Flopsy?

The answer was painful but obvious.

Scott's mind went totally blank, yet strangely he didn't feel at a loss. "Ladies and gentlemen," he began again in a calm, clear voice.

Even as he opened his mouth and words formed, he had no idea what he was going to say.

The distant view through the motel window was of a snow-clad mountain rising over the sapphire gem of Dutch Lake. The closer view, dim and ghostly, was Ariel's reflection.

She touched her scalp, then her face. Her hair was rumbled and wild. Even in the reflection, dark circles were visible under her eyes.

It didn't matter, of course. Her appearance matched how she felt. Ariel turned from the window and sprawled on the bed.

She was in Clearwater, where she'd lived before moving to Blackfish Bay. Strange, she thought, how she'd left this town to escape a romance that had been all in her own mind, and had now returned to escape a romance that had been more real than anything else in her life.

Her friends, Chantelle and Grant, were meeting her for lunch in less than two hours. Ariel looked forward to their visit with ambivalence. She liked both of them. But two years ago she had helped Chantelle wrest a proposal from Grant. That memory was a reminder that she would have no proposal of her own, and their seven-month-old son was a reminder that she would have no baby of her own, either.

She probably should start getting dressed soon. These past few days it took forever to do even the simplest chores. Brushing her teeth was today's big accomplishment.

She had intended to spend a week in Victoria with her parents. It hadn't worked.

Scott's aura had hovered over Victoria. The thought of Oak Bay was like a magnet, drawing her toward the house where he used to live. How many times, she'd wondered while having tea with her mother, had Scott strolled the inner harbor? Viewed the Olympic Mountains across the windswept strait? Examined the totem poles in the provincial museum?

Ariel had fled Victoria after three restless days. Scott had never been in Clearwater, so she'd expected to escape memories. She'd been wrong. His aura permeated this tiny logging town, too.

Getting over him would be hard. No, not hard. Impossible.

Ariel felt worse the farther away from him she traveled. And yet she couldn't have stayed without some indication

that there was hope. Could she? She was too old, sh
thought with a weary sigh, to be lovesick and indecisive.

Ariel dragged herself through a shower, but the stingin
spray did little to revive her. She wrapped a towel around he
hair, then stood on the bath mat staring into space. He
terry-cloth robe would have to dry her. She lacked the ini
tiative to towel herself.

After closing the curtains, Ariel sank listlessly to the bed
At times like this she could almost understand Angus's nee
to shun the world. Understanding Angus was scary.

The newspaper she'd bought days ago but never read of
fered temporary escape. Her eyes skimmed words withou
comprehension, until she reached page six. The wor
MacKenzie grabbed her attention more effectively than th
sound of a gunshot.

She sat up straight. The article was a report on the publi
meeting. Fully alert now, Ariel began reading.

It was a short article, because the meeting had failed t
deliver the fireworks expected. Only two paragraphs men
tioned Scott.

Government marine biologist Scott MacKenzie, widely
criticized for his proposal, explained that the baby
whale whom he called "Flopsy" was dangerously
young to be on its own.

The capture proposal had been made out of concern
for the creature. He challenged protesters to devise a
better plan to save Flopsy, saying further that none of
them loved the young orca as much as he did.

Thomas Arnold of the University of Victoria then
detailed his plans....

Ariel spread the newspaper on the bed with a careful, al
most reverent touch, then went to her hands and knees t
reread the article. Scott had admitted loving Flopsy. It sai
so in black and white, for the whole world to witness.

Her heart began pounding, her pulse racing. A few day
ago he'd been no more able to admit his feelings about th

whale calf than about her. Now something had changed. She didn't know what or why, but something had changed.

Ariel put her fist to her mouth and bounded off the bed. There was still hope. She knew it.

Maybe she was searching desperately for an excuse to return to Scott, but that didn't matter. Neither did her so-called dignity. Her parents, she suddenly realized, had prized dignity more than the love behind her breakfasts in bed. She could learn from their mistakes. She wasn't doomed to follow their example.

She'd serve Scott breakfast in bed every day for the rest of his life, if that was what it took. It was never too late for love. She'd learn the truth about his feelings if she had to strangle the words out of him as she served his toast.

No, a better idea. She could seduce the words out of him.

A shout exploded from her. "Yes!" She did a sprightly dance that sent the hem of the robe swirling.

After one last spin, Ariel stripped off the robe and rummaged through her suitcase. She quickly slipped on her panties, then pulled a brush through her hair. After a few seconds, however, her hands stilled. She smiled at herself in the dresser mirror. For a few crazy seconds she felt she could see herself through Scott's eyes.

A warm, delicious feeling spread through her. At this point in their relationship, seduction was definitely a better idea than strangulation. After thirty or forty years of marriage she might want to strangle Scott, but she doubted it.

Quickly she finished brushing her hair and decided that a ponytail would have to suffice. There was so much to do, and she was so impatient....

She tried phoning Grant and Chantelle to tell them she couldn't make lunch, but there was no answer. Darn. If she left Clearwater soon—like, in fifteen minutes—she could be at the coast in time to catch an evening ferry to Victoria.

That was only the beginning of the journey, unfortunately. She had to drive over three hundred miles, take a long ferry ride, drop off her rental car in Victoria, take a bus to Kelsey Bay on the northern part of Vancouver Island and then charter a floatplane. It was a two-day trip.

No. It was a lifetime trip. Ariel began singing as she headed toward the closet.

The motel room door burst open.

Ariel squeaked. The door had been locked, she was certain. In a startled, mindless panic she grabbed the closest thing at hand to cover her breasts—the newspaper. The article about Scott touched her heart as she turned to the intruder.

"Scott?" She blinked, hoping she would still see him when she reopened her eyes.

She did.

He closed the door. His gaze traveled hungrily from her bare legs and thighs to the headline pressed between her breasts. "I see you've read about the public meeting."

She remembered to nod. The nod turned into a confused shake of her head. "What are you doing here?"

He flirtatiously raised his eyebrows as he advanced toward her. "Getting aroused, for one thing."

"But the door? And how did you find me? And where's Deb? I don't understand."

"Later." He touched the edge of the newspaper. "Are you going to be so rude as to read while I'm here?"

"No, but—"

"Then let's put this down." He pulled the newspaper from her fingers and tossed it aside.

His gaze swept over her, as light and palpable as a teasing caress. Ariel's nipples grew firm. Her abdomen grew warm and fiery. Scott edged closer, or maybe she did, till there was no emptiness between them. When she slipped her arms around his waist, Ariel's ache of longing was heightened by the desire she felt in his body.

"Later," she agreed.

As his hands roamed her smooth flesh, she pulled back to look at him. Yes, it was really Scott. She knew it was him, of course, from the evidence of her ears and eyes and skin. Mostly from her skin, which spiraled to the level of instant arousal that only Scott had ever produced. Yet it was hard to believe.

"Scott?" She buried her face in his chest, repeating his name over and over. His masculine smell pleased and delighted her more than the most expensive cologne.

"Scott." She wanted to whisper the words into his very flesh. Her hands fluttered with the buttons of his shirt. Wiry hair brushed her cheek as she nuzzled him and called his name.

He raised her chin with hands that were firm and demanding. When his lips met hers, Ariel's world seemed to spin. His tongue invaded her mouth, inviting her to an erotic dance. She united willingly, with a moan of joy, and sent her tongue twisting and pulsing against his. When they fell onto the bed, the kiss was interrupted but not ended. Ariel wanted the kiss to last forever.

No, she realized as his lips slid down her neck and chest, it wasn't just the kiss that she wanted to last forever.

She lifted his face so she could look into his eyes. They were sultry and full of desire. "Scott," she said, "what does this mean?"

Fingers replaced his lips on her breasts, teasing the nipples to hard readiness. "You really want to talk now?"

Desire, long postponed, was funneling into her from his touch. She didn't want to talk. Yet at the same time she wanted to know everything, and she wanted to know it now.

"Yes," she managed to say.

Even as she nodded, Scott was sitting up and removing his shirt and slacks. "You're sure you want to talk?"

Ariel's mouth felt too dry to talk. "Well..."

"Okay, we'll talk." His hands continuing removing the last of their clothes. "Nice weather we're having, isn't it?"

The heat of Scott's flesh pressed full length against her. "Uh, well, it's getting awfully hot."

"Summer's like that," Scott agreed as his hands explored the womanly delights of her body.

Ariel's voice came out as a languorous moan. "Getting hotter all the time."

After a few dazzling minutes Scott spoke again. "Ho enough for you yet?"

"Oh, yes." Impatiently she urged him on top of her.

"Do you think we'll have a storm?"

"Uh...well..." Clouds rolled and mushroomed inside her. She began to shake with rumbles of impending thunder. "As a matter of fact..."

He was staring intently into her eyes. His lips curled into a wide grin that was more joy than humor. Despite the ardor of his lovemaking, he managed to keep talking—a feat that was becoming increasingly difficult for Ariel.

"I think," he said in a voice that was growing more husky, "we'll have clear skies from here on."

Thunder was rumbling closer, sending Ariel's hips jerking. Lightning flashed, signaling the imminence of an electrifying downpour. "But for...how long?"

Scott's eyes closed. His voice slowed as his other movements grew faster. "For the rest of our lives."

Another lightning bolt struck, closer this time. Ariel felt herself being blown away by the gusts, being carried up to the heart of the clouds themselves. She wrapped her arms and legs around him and moved in rhythm with frantically swelling crashes of thunder and lightning, rain and storm, ecstasy and fulfillment, passion and...and love.

"Scott?"

"Yes?" His voice was rising.

"Shut up now."

"You say the..." He arched against her, straining and rigid. "Oh, God, Ariel...the sweetest...ahh...sweetest things."

As they lay in each other's arms, content but momentarily exhausted, the sun warmed Ariel's heart. When she closed her eyes, it was as if she could see a rainbow arching over the two of them like a benediction. She reached toward the rainbow. When she touched it, it didn't disappear. Its texture was smooth and warm, with firm muscles and prominent shoulder blades—the most wonderful feeling in the world. A smile of elemental satisfaction engulfed not just her face but her entire being.

They lay side by side for a long, glorious interlude. Ariel basked in Scott's nearness, gloried in running her fingertips along his arms and his back and his legs. She could tell that if they pressed against each other like this much longer, they'd make love again. Which was more important, making love or finding out why and how he was here?

Both were important. Very. She ran a hand through his hair, the way she'd seen him do so many times.

"Let's talk now," she said with some reluctance, "but if you say one word about the weather, I'll—"

"You'll what?"

"I'll..." Ariel lost her train of thought when Scott put his hands on her buttocks and pulled her so close that they touched everywhere. "I...won't ever make love to you again."

He had the grace not to laugh outright, but he did chuckle.

"Well, not for fifteen minutes or so. Maybe ten." She sighed and snuggled her cheek against his shoulder. "I love you, Scott." Her heart drummed in her chest as she waited for his reply.

"And I love you, too."

"You do?" Ariel sat up quickly, letting the sheet fall to her waist.

"Yes, I do. Now come back down here, woman."

Ariel went willingly into the sheltered harbor of his arms.

There was magic in this woman, Scott decided. He didn't care if magic was an unscientific concept. It was the only possible explanation for the incredible pleasure that radiated from her flesh to his. Even his toes, pressing her ankle, were transformed into an erogenous zone.

"Tell me everything, Scott. Why are you here?"

"Because of...I don't know, because of everything. Mostly Deb, I guess."

Some of Ariel's magic danced out of her in a laugh that felt as good on Scott's ears as her breasts did on his chest. "That little matchmaker."

"No, nothing like that. Not even anything she said. I'm not sure how to explain, but my love for her was the wedge that let my love for you squeeze in." He shrugged his shoulders. "Does that make any sense?"

"No, but don't worry," Ariel said with that gentle, caressing laugh that seemed meant just for him. "We'll work on your ability to talk the language of love."

"I'll be an eager pupil."

They paused for a lesson in the fine art of kissing. When they finally pulled apart, Ariel gazed into his eyes and again broke into her soft laugh.

Scott ran his fingertips through the hair at her temple. "Do I qualify as teacher's pet?"

"I don't know. Let's hear you bark."

He pretended to scowl at her. "Has anyone ever told you that you're silly?"

"Little Miss Dependable, silly?" She giggled. "God, it feels good not to have to act sensibly."

Scott felt her laughter and elation vibrating through him. Life with Ariel was going to be fun.

She composed her face. "Back to the facts, sir. You were telling me how you ended up here."

"Right. You read about the public meeting. Well, at the beginning I was still inflexible and stubborn. But when I stood up, I forgot my speech. I honestly didn't know what I was going to say until I opened my mouth."

"I read about what you said."

"You would have been proud of me," he said. "First I called Deb up to the front and put my arms around her while I spoke. Real mushy stuff, and it had absolutely nothing to do with science. And then, since I didn't know what else to say, I repeated almost verbatim what you had said about my reasons for trapping Flopsy. Every word was true, too. How did you learn to recognize my motives even better than I do?"

"Some of us," she said with a pleased shrug, "are more talented than others."

"Well, you're a genius." He ran his hand from her shoulder to her neck, and was rewarded by seeing her chest rise and fall more quickly. "A very sexy genius."

"Hurry, Scott."

"After the meeting a man from the University of Victoria offered me a job guarding Flopsy and then establishing a permanent university laboratory to study whales on the B.C. coast."

"Did you accept?"

He nodded. "It's time for a change from fisheries. The new job will mean some time in Victoria and some out in the field at Mowitch Island."

"That sounds great."

"It is. Until you get pregnant, at least. Then we'll probably want to—"

Ariel interrupted him by flinging her arms around his neck. Pregnant? Her heart beat with a rapid sense of gratification that seemed to promise that life and love had just begun. She laid a string of hard kisses along his cheek and temple. When she got to his ear, she whispered, "Finish your story. Very quickly."

"After the meeting I knew I had to find you. No one on the island knew where you'd be staying, so I asked Angus. He'd been acting guilty for days, and he started blubbering right away."

"Why?"

"First you have to promise not to be angry with him. He was very clear about that."

Ariel shook her head in loving confusion. "You're defending Angus? When you decide to change, you sure go all the way."

"I intend to, again, as soon as you promise."

"I promise," she blurted.

"You're an eager little thing," Scott said. "Anyway, Angus apologized for throwing your letter in the bay—"

"He did what?" Again Ariel bolted to a sitting position. Her indignation didn't overshadow the joy that still shone in her eyes. "That miserable, filthy slob! I'm going to tear both his hairs out, one by one."

"He wanted what's best for you, and by his definition that meant being alone. After he thought about it, though, he felt guilty."

She was too lovely, sitting like that with her face full of fire. Scott pulled her down to his lips, and felt her tension transform into passion. He drank greedily of her sweet tasting enchantment, filling his lungs and his heart with the heady potion that was Ariel Johnson.

She sighed lustily when the kiss ended. "I really want to hear what happened, Scott, but my mind's turning to more pressing matters." Her hand roamed down his body, making him twitch with pleasure. "The evidence proves," she purred, "that the same is true for you. Can you give me a condensed account so we can get on to, well, other things?"

"Not if you keep doing what you're doing," he warned.

"Sorry." Ariel rolled onto her back and laced her fingers over her stomach. The primness of the gesture was spoiled by the generous cleavage that peeked from the sheet.

Scott turned on his side and propped his head in his hand. "Angus gave me your parents' address in Victoria. Once he got going, he forgot all about being timid. He said that if I had the brains of a fishy, I'd have realized ages ago that you were the best woman in the whole world. He threatened to beat me up if I didn't go after you, since we seemed to need each other."

"The old coot," she said fondly.

"In Victoria I dropped Deb at my sister's before I asked your parents where you were. Your mother had tears in her eyes when I told her I wanted to marry you—"

Ariel poked him in the side. "You told my mother before you told me? You'll pay for that, MacKenzie."

"For the rest of my life," he agreed with a smile.

Ariel made a soft sound that was a mixture of contentment and desire as she settled her head on his chest once nore. The pounding of his heart was like a song to her spirit. She shifted so that she was lying on top of him.

"Anyway," Scott continued in a voice that was becoming low and raspy, "when I got to Clearwater, I contacted our friend Grant—"

"Oh, my God." Ariel jerked her head to look at the clock. "He and Chantelle will be knocking on the door any minute to take me to lunch. They'll catch us like this."

"They know."

Ariel glared at him for a moment. She wagged her hips, which did astounding things for Scott's heart rate. "They know we're about to do *this?*"

"Well, I suppose they might be able to guess, but all I told them was that I was going to marry you—"

She poked him in the ribs again. "Is there anyone beside me you *haven't* told?"

He rubbed his chin. "Let's see. Deb knows that I'm going to marry you, of course. Then there're your parents, Angus, my sister and her husband, my niece and nephew and Grant and Chantelle. But I didn't tell Phil."

"Oh. Well, as long as there's someone you didn't tell."

Scott pulled her tighter against the warmth of his body. "Chantelle is the one who convinced the motel clerk I was your husband so I could get the room key to surprise you. We have our privacy. You can relax."

She rocked her hips. "Easy for you to say."

"Not really," he said in a choked voice.

Ariel edged across him just the right distance and hovered so that his body was poised at the portal of fulfillment. "Are you done yet?"

"Almost."

"What now?" She moved her hips again, tantalizing both of them with the nearness of ecstasy.

"If you're too impatient to wait for my proposal of marriage, well—"

"Proposal?" A laugh of joy catapulted from her mouth. On an inspiration born of love, she lowered her hips slowly and carefully. Her body became a cauldron of moist, receptive passion. Breath hissed through her teeth as Scott filled her.

She gritted her teeth and forced herself to remain motionless despite an overwhelming urge to begin the rhythm of love. It was hard to stay like that, hard to prolong anticipation and delay passion. Suddenly she felt too weak to hold up her head. Her chin lolled against Scott's chest.

"Go ahead," she whispered. "Now you can propose."

"We'll never be able to tell our children how I proposed," he cautioned.

"MacKenzie!"

"Oh, all right. Will you marry me?"

A shudder of intense pleasure shot up Ariel's spine and then back down. The buzz of elation and desire spun dizzily through her abdomen before lodging, hot and vibrant and ready to start all over again, deep in the core of her femininity. It was many heartbeats before she could speak.

"I..." A saucy smile splashed across her face. "I'll think about it."

With a sudden deft movement that caught her by surprise, Scott rolled over and pinned her underneath him. "I'm not moving a muscle until you answer."

"What a bully," she said in a breathy whisper.

"I'm waiting."

Ariel tried to rotate her hips, but his weight trapped her. "If you're going to be like that, I guess I'll have to marry you."

"Say it again. With feeling."

Ariel draped her hands around his neck. Scott's eyes, so warm and masculine, promised everything she had ever dreamed.

"Yes," she murmured.

When he began thrusting into her, she closed her eyes and arched wildly against him. Fulfillment was close, startlingly close, and utterly overwhelming when it cascaded through her. Love filled Ariel's world with spasms of flashing blue and throbbing yellow and all the other colors of the rainbow.

Later, when they lay exhausted in each other's arms, Ariel finally spoke again. "Yes, Scott. Forever."

He twined his fingers through hers, linking the two of them in body as they were linked in spirit. "Forever."

Epilogue

Sound was muffled, vague, making her feel as if her senses were wrapped in seaweed. It was like that whenever she raised her head from the water. Yet sight was brighter and clearer—a teasing shred of salmon tossed out by the Creator to compensate those unfortunate creatures who spend their lives in the pitiless dry air.

She'd known this boat forever. Her first human-sighting had been this boat. In the year since her mother had died, the boat had been a friend, feeding and guarding her.

How could she be friends with something that wasn't alive, let alone part of the pod? She would have to ponder this during the dark season. If she was lucky, the others would help her. The thought might be deemed worthy to spread to other pods.

She squealed in excitement. She'd never had a thought pondered by others.

The girl, whom she called Dark Hair, appeared at the side of the boat. Probably the sound of her squeal drew it; humans could hear to some extent. Today its removable skin was gray and fuzzy. If only she could solve the riddle of why these creatures changed their skins.... Now, there was a thought that would spread to all the pods!

The girl held out a rubbing stick. With a quick thank-you, she let the stick rub her head. Dark Hair missed all the best spots, as usual. Things like that made it so hard to judge how intelligent humans were. They seemed to be the smartest of the dry creatures, however. Even Max agreed with that.

The two bigger humans, Fuzzy Top and Pretty One, were standing behind the girl. They held each other, as they usually did. They didn't wear the shiny, orcalike skin that meant they would come into the water to play. Though the boat sometimes held other humans, it was these two who were the objects of this year's most intriguing thought.

This spring the matriarch of the pod had shared a thought with all the orcas gathered at the rubbing stones. She claimed that the love that pulsed between these particular humans was loud enough to pierce the distance from here to the big island. Even a fish could tell they were in love. Beings capable of such a love might have the power to bridge the communication gap between species. If humans could love, then there was hope.

Max countered that though humans *might* feel love, he could never know for sure. Best to merely note that those two were always together, and held each other a lot.

Personally she agreed with the matriarch. Max, after all, was only a bull.

Dark Hair put down the rubbing stick. "Can you keep a secret?" It giggled. "Silly of me! You're not going to tell Tammy, are you? Well, I'm going to be a big sister." The girl leaned closer. "That's not a secret, of course. The secret is that the doctors think it might be twins!"

She wondered what Dark Hair had said. Communication had *almost* happened with the humans of this boat—though Max cautioned that these particular humans might merely be better trained than others, rather than smarter.

A warm sadness prompted her to slip under the water as she remembered how her mother had talked to the humans. In return, they had saved her life with their food after her mother had died. She'd loved her mother. And now she loved . . . these humans.

A decision had been building in her for a long time, but suddenly it came as clear and real as a breath after ten minutes in the depths. She knew now what she would devote herself to—in between fishing and thinking and talking and living a full life, of course.

She would study humans.

* * * * *

Silhouette

SPECIAL EDITION™

THE DONOVAN LEGACY
from Nora Roberts

Meet the Donovans—Morgana, Sebastian and Anastasia. They're an unusual threesome. Triple your fun with double cousins, the only children of triplet sisters and triplet brothers. Each one is unique. Each one is . . . special.

In September you will be *Captivated* by Morgana Donovan. In Special Edition #768, horror-film writer Nash Kirkland doesn't know what to do when he meets an actual witch!

Be *Entranced* in October by Sebastian Donovan in Special Edition #774. Private investigator Mary Ellen Sutherland doesn't believe in psychic phenomena. But she discovers Sebastian has strange powers . . . over her.

In November's Special Edition #780, you'll be *Charmed* by Anastasia Donovan, along with Boone Sawyer and his little girl. Anastasia was a healer, but for her it was Boone's touch that cast a spell.

Enjoy the magic of Nora Roberts. Don't miss *Captivated*, *Entranced* or *Charmed*. Only from Silhouette Special Edition. . . .

SENR-1

HE'S MORE THAN A MAN, HE'S ONE OF OUR

Fabulous Fathers

Dear Christina,

Stationed here in the Gulf, as part of the peacekeeping effort, I've learned that family and children are the most important things about life. I need a woman who wants a family as much as I do....

Love, Joe

Dear Joe,

How can I tell you this...?

Love, Christina

Dear Reader,
Read between the lines as Toni Collins's FABULOUS FATHER, Joe Parish, and Christina Holland fall in love through the mail in LETTERS FROM HOME. Coming this October from

Silhouette
R O M A N C E™

FFATHER2

**It's Opening Night in October—
and you're invited!
Take a look at romance with a
brand-new twist, as the stars
of tomorrow make their
debut today!
It's LOVE:
an age-old story—
now, with
*WORLD PREMIERE
APPEARANCES* by:**

Patricia Thayer—Silhouette Romance #895
JUST MAGGIE—Meet the Texas rancher who wins this pretty
teacher's heart...and lose your own heart, too!

Anne Marie Winston—Silhouette Desire #742
BEST KEPT SECRETS—Join old lovers reunited and see what
secret wonders have been hiding...beneath the flames!

Sierra Rydell—Silhouette Special Edition #772
ON MIDDLE GROUND—Drift toward Twilight, Alaska, with this
widowed mother and collide—heart first—into body heat
enough to melt the frozen tundra!

Kate Carlton—Silhouette Intimate Moments #454
KIDNAPPED!—Dare to look on as a timid wallflower blos-
soms and falls in fearless love—with her gruff, mysterious
kidnapper!

**Don't miss the classics of tomorrow—
premiering today—only from**

PREM

VOWS
A series celebrating marriage
by Sherryl Woods

To Love, Honor and Cherish—these were the words that three generations of Halloran men promised their women they'd live by. But these vows made in love are each challenged by the tests of time....

In October—Jason Halloran meets his match in *Love #769;*

In November—Kevin Halloran rediscovers love—with his wife—in *Honor #775;*

In December—Brandon Halloran rekindles an old flame in *Cherish #781.*

These three stirring tales are coming down the aisle toward you—only from Silhouette Special Edition!

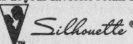

TAKE A WALK ON THE DARK SIDE OF LOVE

October is the shivery season, when chill winds blow and shadows walk the night. Come along with us into a haunting world where love and danger go hand in hand, where passions will thrill you and dangers will chill you. Come with us to

In this newest short story collection from Silhouette Books, three of your favorite authors tell tales just perfect for a spooky autumn night. Let Anne Stuart introduce you to "The Monster in the Closet," Helen R. Myers bewitch you with "Seawitch," and Heather Graham Pozzessere entice you with "Wilde Imaginings."

Silhouette Shadows™
Haunting a store near you this October.

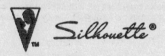